# TUG OF WAR

## A Novel by
## TRIX ROSEN

Cover photos by Trix Rosen (c) 2020

Cover design by Dana Bree, StoneBear Design

StoneBear Publishing LLC - 01/2021
Milford, PA 18337

**www.stonebearpublishing.com**

# Acknowledgements

I wish to extend *utang na loob (deep Tagalog)*— a debt of gratitude to:

Joanmarie Kalter for teaching me to write.

Gretta Goldenman for her editing.

Virgie Puyoc for her friendship and loyalty.

Ama Puyoc for teaching me Kalinga legends.

The Puyoc family for their kindness and hospitality.

Bea Jacinto for early inspiration.

Dana Bree for bringing my story to print.

# Table of Contents

About the Author . . . . . . . . . . . . . . . . . . . . . . . . . . . . . . . . . . . . vi

Chapter     1.    The Cordillera Mountains - The Philippines
                         - Oct. 1986 . . . . . . . . . . . . . . . . . . . . . . . . . . . .8

Chapter     2.    The Rebel Commander . . . . . . . . . . . . . . . . . . . 19

Chapter     3.    Signs from the Spirits. . . . . . . . . . . . . . . . . . . . .28

Chapter     4.    Broken Promise . . . . . . . . . . . . . . . . . . . . . . . . 37

Chapter     5.    Excuses and Shame . . . . . . . . . . . . . . . . . . . . .46

Chapter     6.    The Ambush . . . . . . . . . . . . . . . . . . . . . . . . . .54

Chapter     7.    Special Friends . . . . . . . . . . . . . . . . . . . . . . . . 61

Chapter     8.    Manila - December 1986 . . . . . . . . . . . . . . . . . 67

Chapter     9.    Whose Viewpoint Matters? . . . . . . . . . . . . . . . .76

Chapter     10.    Pinky and the Bus Trip to Bontoc. . . . . . . . . . . 81

Chapter     11.    The Cordillera . . . . . . . . . . . . . . . . . . . . . . . . .89

Chapter     12.    Gold and Greed in the Cordillera . . . . . . . . . . . 97

Chapter     13.    Pinky and Tony. . . . . . . . . . . . . . . . . . . . . . . . 110

Chapter     14.    Don Silvero . . . . . . . . . . . . . . . . . . . . . . . . . . 116

Chapter     15.    Café Bugos, Manila. . . . . . . . . . . . . . . . . . . . . 121

Chapter     16.    The General. . . . . . . . . . . . . . . . . . . . . . . . . .128

Chapter     17.    The Gray Cafe . . . . . . . . . . . . . . . . . . . . . . . . 133

Chapter     18.    The Cordillera . . . . . . . . . . . . . . . . . . . . . . . . 139

Chapter     19.    Point 7 in the 'Code of Behavior'. . . . . . . . . . . 149

Chapter     20.    New York. May 1987. . . . . . . . . . . . . . . . . . . . 154

Chapter     21.    Sisters - sharing laughter, wiping tears . . . . . 163

Chapter     22.    Washington, D.C. . . . . . . . . . . . . . . . . . . . . . . 174

Chapter     23.    The National Archives . . . . . . . . . . . . . . . . . . . 187

Chapter     24.    Florida . . . . . . . . . . . . . . . . . . . . . . . . . . . . . 193

Chapter     25.    August 31, 1987. Manila. . . . . . . . . . . . . . . . .201

Chapter     26.    The Funeral . . . . . . . . . . . . . . . . . . . . . . . . .208

Chapter     27.    Decisions . . . . . . . . . . . . . . . . . . . . . . . . . . . 213

Chapter   28.   The Traitor . . . . . . . . . . . . . . . . . . . . . . . . . . . . 218

Chapter   29.   The Impossible Choice. . . . . . . . . . . . . . . . . . .227

Chapter   30.   The Magnet to Men's Hearts  . . . . . . . . . . . . .234

Chapter   31.   Manila - Devastating News . . . . . . . . . . . . . . 241

Chapter   32.   The Cordillera. . . . . . . . . . . . . . . . . . . . . . . . .247

Chapter   33.   The Golden Buddha . . . . . . . . . . . . . . . . . . . .252

Chapter   34.   Revenge . . . . . . . . . . . . . . . . . . . . . . . . . . . . . 257

Chapter   35.   Yamashita's Treasure. . . . . . . . . . . . . . . . . . .262

Glossary of Tagalog & Kalinga Words and Phrases . . . . . . . . .270

There are a lot of words used in the traditional Tagalog and Kalinga dialects denoted by italics. Check the glossary for the full description.

# About the Author

Born in Brooklyn, New York, Trix Rosen is a NY/NJ based photographer. Her career has embraced the fields of fine art photography, photojournalism, portraiture, and historic architectural preservation. The scope of her fine art is driven by a desire to make a difference by addressing social justice issues that can transform local and global perspectives. Her spectrum of portfolios explores gender fluidity and identity within the LGBTQ community as well as documents endangered architecture.

Her original 1980's slide show MAITRESSE (https://trixrosen.com/maitresse/) is part of the Museum of Modern Art's exhibition, "CLUB 57: Film, Performance and Art in the East Village, 1978-1983 (https://trixrosen.com/club-57-film-performance-and-art-in-the-east-village-1978-1983/)," October 31, 2017- April 1, 2018, a major exhibition examining the scene-changing, interdisciplinary life of downtown New York's seminal and fabled post-punk alternative space in New York's East Village.

In the twenty years that Rosen has been photographing the French performance artist, Fred Koenig, she's produced images that survey gender fluid, queer identity and open up the possibility that we each hold a myriad of alternative selves within us. The images in *HE-SHE* showcases their daring bond of friendship and art. It depicts a vision of gender authenticity and empowers being true to yourself. *HE-SHE*, (http://www.blurb.com/b/7395116-he-she), celebrates the right to self-identify anywhere along the gender path.

Portraits of her female friends document the birth of the gay liberation in New York City and the emerging feminist movement. Rosen photographed women athletes working out in gyms and posing in her studio, and published the collection in STRONG & SEXY (https://trixrosen.com/strong-sexy/), THE NEW BODY BEAUTIFUL, (Delilah, 1982) one of the first books to chronicle the emerging wave of women bodybuilders.

After leaving her job photographing stories that were aired as photo-essays on WNBC-TV Live at Five and News4NY in New York City, Trix focused on assignments in the Philippines, where she lived and worked between 1984 and 2013. She produced A KALINGA JOURNEY THROUGH TIME, documenting her work in the northern indigenous Cordillera region and the transformation that the villages of the Kalinga people experienced.

Trix Rosen was the subject of a half-hour documentary about her life and photography, URBAN STORIES, Documentary Japan, Inc. (1997).

She helped to develop the INSIGHT OUT! Digital Storytelling Workshops to teach visual storytelling and empower her participants with the skills to document their lives. She taught this program in New York City, Jersey City, Thailand, Indonesia, and the Philippines. The project is based on her experience as an editor and international advisor to the award-winning InSIGHT OUT! Storytelling Project based in Bangkok, Thailand.

Trix Rosen's photography can be seen at https://trixrosen.com

# Chapter 1

## The Cordillera Mountains.
## The Philippines - October 1986

"Stay out of the Cordillera!" was one of the warning messages that traveled quickly through the mountains and down to Manila with Filipino gossip's lightning speed. The *tsismis* had spread as if by telepathy among the tightly-knit community of local and international journalists. Jesse Beckerman downplayed the threat and was characteristically blunt in vowing that not even a guerrilla commander was going to tell her what she could or couldn't do. "Stay out of the region," was his harsh admonition. "Travel through our 'red zone', and the rebel army will no longer protect you."

Undeterred, and with optimistic defiance, she had decided that it had to be a mistake. If *Ka* Noel appeared in front of her right now, she would assure him that she'd done nothing wrong. "I thought you knew that you could trust me," she'd firmly say, with an edge of righteous indignation. He'd see that this edict was based on a misunderstanding.

Jesse stroked her *anting-anting*, the lucky charm on her necklace, then slapped at the bug bites that were turning her back and arms into nasty red welts. For more than four hours, her companion, Tess Gadag, had been guiding the way up and down the narrow, twisty steep paths through the rice terraces, but there was still no sign of the rebel encampment.

"Hey... Tess. Slow down," she yelped, breathing heavily while forcing one foot then the other to move.

"There should be a road here," the Kalinga woman said when her companion finally caught up, "but after the stones were laid down, there was no money left for cement."

Jesse wiped the steady rain of sweat from her eyes and brushed some grit off her face. "What happened? The local officials steal the money?" She saw Tess's eyebrows arch upward. "C'mon Tess, *kurakot*... corruption, was the first word I learned in Manila. Lucky for me, the next was *takbo!*"

"*Takbo*. You must know the word for run when you're traveling with our friends in the countryside." Tess glanced towards the hundreds of rice terraces surrounding them on the mountain trail. Far below, the Chico River silently wound its way through the deep valleys and gorges of Kalinga, flowing from village to village as it had for generations. Two elderly barefoot women trotted swiftly down the rocks in single file past them, smoking blunt rolled tobacco cigars, balancing woven baskets filled with vegetables and tools on their heads. Tattoo lines, drawn in a cross-hatch pattern, covered their arms like tight sleeves on a thinly knit sweater.

Tess pursed her lips as if she were pointing at the women before they disappeared around the mountain curve. "*Talaga* (really). The stones were placed here to make traveling easier during the rainy season."

"Easier for you." Jesse sighed while shifting the heavy weight from shoulder to shoulder of her over-packed camera bag. Any misstep would mean a debilitating ten-foot fall into the mud-filled water of a lower terrace. Not a pretty picture, she thought, pushing aside the auburn curls that stuck to her forehead. Usually, a generous smile added sparkle to her angular face. Today, cramped muscles were knotting her shoulders. Her knees and butt were aching from jumping up and sliding down the hand-hewn rock steps defining the path. Unlike the tribal woman whose honey-toned complexion had turned a soft bronze, the freckled skin on her nose, cheeks, and shoulders was beet red and blistering. Impatiently, Jesse pulled her fingers through the tangled strands of hair that straggled down to her shoulders. When a large knot refused to unravel, she ripped out the matted clump and unloosed a barrage of profanities, first at herself and then at her photo agent.

"Damn. Damn. Damn and holy hell!" She explosively cursed, as if she was talking to an invisible partner. "Your relentless drives' gonna kill you yet, girl; you'll never make it to thirty-five." The words of the repetitive lecture from her close friends were pounding a spike into the side of her head.

She was always trying to prove her fearlessness, willing to follow any story at a moment's notice. Now here she was hiking up and down the mountains, despite the danger and ignoring death threats. All to prove that I can get the pictures Davidson wants, she told herself. "Damn Jonathan to hell," she mumbled, grimacing with pain. She understood that no matter what the difficulty, her agent expected that she would get him the photos.

But she knew it was her own dedication and sense of duty that drove her to tell the story of the violence in the war-torn Cordillera region. She was unwavering in her determination to depict the humanity of people who had no international voice. Her deepest passion was to shoot images that revealed both the hidden and tangible wounds of hatred, greed, and cruelty. And Davidson did say that it came across in her work. She'd also learned the importance of adding contextual images that showed some of the humor, beauty, joy, friendships, vernacular structures, and historical details that personified each place.

Lost in her thoughts, she tripped over a twisted root and looked up to see Tess swinging herself over a huge boulder obstructing the dirt path. Challenged by the younger woman's stamina and envious of her agility, she tried to control her wheezing. She grabbed the same branch, landed behind Tess with a thud, and took hold of her arm.

"Wait up," she said, pulling Tess to an abrupt stop. "Last time I was here, the rebels gave me a nom-de-guerre, so I believed that *Ka* Flame became a *kasama*, a friend of the underground."

Tess's dark eyes hardened like coal. "I'm sure you've heard the gossip, too," Jesse continued. "Making *tsismis* is a national pastime; everyone from here to Manila seems to know that I've been banned from the mountains."

She pulled Tess closer. "Listen. If the commander's angry because I missed our last meeting, I'll apologize. But Ka Noel needs to know that that I had another assignment." Her words speeded up and became more belligerent in tone. "And how could I let him know? The horizon isn't exactly dotted with phone lines to his camp." She reached into her pocket for her cigarettes and lit one. "By now, I've proved my dedication to your struggle. Last time we were together, mortars were pounding the nearby mountains. We were dodging constant threats of a military ambush at every damn turn in the road."

Tess turned and began walking faster. Jesse, staying as close as possible to her back, continued talking.

"Didn't I keep on shooting the story even when mudslides obliterated the roads? Grabbing onto branches was all that saved me from sliding down the collapsing hills. Those photos were featured in an American magazine, Tess. I thought Ka Noel would be pleased."

Her Kalinga guide showed no indication that the plea was persuasive. Tess stopping for a moment turned and narrowed her eyes while studying the outsider's face. "Let's go now," she brusquely replied.

*I'm in the middle of a war zone. My safety depends on her protection, and she's not telling me why I've pissed people off,* thought Jesse. "Am I crazy to have come back without *Ka* Noel's permission?" she mumbled, without expecting an answer.

In the rapidly diminishing light, even the shadows rustled with frightful noises. The high-pitched screams of a circling hawk seemed to mix with the squish of rubber shoes and crescendo inside her head. She scanned the bushes, imagining the obsidian eyes of the rebel commander, tracking all her movements. When Jesse thought she saw him, she lost her footing on some loose pebbles and started to slide down the path. Despite the avalanche of tiny stones that hit Tess, her sturdy body, sculpted by a lifetime of rugged mountain climbing, seemed rooted to the earth.

"I'm sorry," Jesse cried out, embarrassed by her clumsiness. "The last time I was here, the climb seemed so much easier."

"We've had so many typhoons this season. We're lucky if there's any path to follow."

"I must be crazy to be hiking the mountains during the rainy season," Jesse muttered under her breath while bending to scratch the rash prickling her ankles. She tossed back her shoulders with a sigh and turned to her companion. "When do you think we're gonna meet up with Ka Noel?"

Seeing Tess scowl at the mention of his name was enough to make her drop that question. "One thing's for sure, Tess. Hiking has been great for my legs. Look at these muscles! And I must have lost some weight." She spread her fingers on either side of her waist. "There are no temptations here. Only rice and…"

"Stop," Tess interrupted, "There's a mudslide over here." She pointed to what was left of the trail—a narrow ridge, not more than twelve inches wide, that abruptly ended in a four-foot-long gaping hole. "You have to jump across it." Before Jesse had a chance to protest, Tess stretched her arms to hug the boulders, inched herself over the muddy ground, then gracefully leaped to the other side.

The water was hundreds of feet below. Jesse raised her head skyward and was pelted with large drops of rainwater ricocheting off the mountain wall. She wanted nothing more than to fling herself to the ground and close her eyes. *Damn this daredevil nature hike and my meeting with Ka Noel*, she thought. *My stomach's churning. My legs are strained to their max. And my back feels like a rubber band before it snaps. I'm so worn out.* No, she quickly goaded herself. *Don't give in to the fear and pain. Focus and remember—you didn't give in to the fear in El Salvador. When the military demanded your film, you stuck it in your bra and handed them a blank roll. Still, I fucking hate heights*, she told herself before a crash of thunder shook the rocks with fierce vibrations.

*"See, you should've stayed at home, where you belong,"* the wind seemed to rage as if her mother's scalding taunts had been hurled across the ocean to hammer at her insecurities. Jesse flinched when the sky crackled with light. *Do you think you can strangle me with your fears? Nothing has changed my mind, mom. I'm doing*

*EXACTLY what I wanted to.* The next unholy crash was deafening. She flinched and instinctively touched her cheek, never forgetting the wallop that followed each childhood act of defiance.

"Damn..." she screeched across the void that separated them, "...how am I gonna cross this thing? It's straight down to the river! We're on the edge of a mountain, in the middle of a fucking storm, and all of a sudden, there's no path in front of me. I'm not a goddamn acrobat!"

Tess looked back at her severely. "What about our *kasamas*? What about *Ka* Noel? If you want to meet him tonight, you'll have to cross it."

"Okay...okay," she cried out, fixing her gaze on the water below. With the next peal of thunder, she clutched at the slippery mountain wall.

Tess grabbed Jesse's outstretched hand, easing it away from the rocks. "Move your right foot towards me," she commanded, raising her voice.

Jesse obediently raised her head. She took a hesitant step, then another. When one sneaker touched the edge, Tess yanked her across the precipice and into her arms. She held her tightly until she had stopped shaking and then pointed to the opposite ridge. A gauze-like fog was cloaking dozens of thatched huts that resting on the side of the cliff.

The fog stretched across the mountains, threw the view out-of-focus as if covered with a ghostly organdy shroud.

"Holy shit! Tanduhan looks like it took a breath 500 years ago and didn't exhale." She leaned on a rock and let the damp velvety air hugging the emerald hills wash over her. She inhaled deeply as if the pungent vegetation would become an elixir for her own longevity.

Tess smiled at the sight of her village. "I'll meet you by the river," she promised while kicking off her rubber flip-flops. "In this mud, you might find it easier to walk barefoot. And watch out for leeches." She laughed softly, whispering, "Only kidding."

"Thanks, but I'll keep my sneakers on," Jesse retorted as she watched Tess disappear down the path. To her surprise, leaping across the abyss had bolstered her flagging confidence. Her thoughts returned to Ka Noel. It was obvious. Despite the danger and his malice, the handsome revolutionary fascinated her.

She had observed him closely during the days and nights that followed their first meeting, eight weeks before. Tagging behind as he walked with his cadre, Jesse took pictures of the young revolutionaries as they treated medical conditions with acupuncture needles and held daily meetings with the tribal elders.

Partially hidden behind her camera, she would stare at Ka Noel for hours: how his face would become rigid during ideological discussions, how his sultry eyes would narrow slightly, how his lips, usually so full that they had an appearance of sensuousness, would tighten at the corners. Jesse attributed his severity, as well as the gauntness in his face, to years of sustained hardship.

When he did catch her staring, Ka Noel would peer directly into the camera lens and shift his mouth into an amicable, reassuring smile. She'd flash a grin and hold the camera steady against her face to cover the reddening flush on her cheeks.

"Namumula ka, your face is getting red," he told her, "like the color of your hair."

She'd learned enough Tagalog in Manila to enjoy the flirtation. She found the commander magnetic and admired Ka Noel's dedicated leadership in the struggle for human rights. He was often quoted as the charismatic spokesman for the outlawed New People's Army among international journalists.

*Damn my idealism*, Jesse chastised herself, thinking how a compelling story had once again overshadowed her concern for personal safety.

By the time she met Tess, the rain had abated. A line of mauve clouds hung suspended in front of a luminous copper-colored sky. Jesse pulled out her Leica and, using a nearby rock to steady the camera, shot several exposures as a beam of sunlight lasered across the Chico River. So intensely was she focused on the scenery that she never heard the rebel cadre's stealthy approach.

"*Kumusta ka na*, Tess."

She heard his voice, involuntarily shivered, and jerked her head around. Ka Noel emerged from the shadows, accompanied by two men dressed in black fatigues carrying M-16s on their shoulders. He wasn't smiling. She'd been imagining a verbal battle and had never considered that he might shun her. She reached into her bag for a cigarette and offered him a Marlboro.

Ka Noel took the pack and passed it around to his men. "Welcome to our side," was his only dour comment.

She stared at his dark olive skin and the slash of his prominent cheekbones. "I need to talk to you... privately." She hoped her voice didn't sound pleading and distractedly ran her tongue over her lips. Although they were both the same height, Ka Noel seemed taller than she'd remembered. The rebel commander stood preternaturally still, silently assessing Jesse's request, then abruptly turned his back to her.

"*Halika na*-let's go," he ordered, signaling the group to follow.

Tess and Noel walked quickly along the riverbank, conferring in Kalinga dialect. Jesse trailed behind them, followed by two guerrillas. Her heart skipped a beat when she saw him turn towards her, but he was only motioning to his men.

"Abel...take her pack, Sadek, her camera bag so we can walk faster," he barked his orders.

Jesse's veneer of confidence evaporated. Was Tess telling him he'd made a mistake? Why didn't he give her the chance to explain? She began wheezing and inhaled to open her constricted throat and get more air into her lungs. "Bastard," she hissed in a brittle voice that sounded distant as if it was unconnected to her body.

Did she hear something in the bushes? She jerked her head back to look. Jesse was sure that she heard something moving that was now parallel to them as they walked along the river bank. Her jumbled senses gave her mixed, confusing signals. Jesse looked at her watch. For almost six hours, she had been going up and down the mountains in the rain. She was tired, hungry, and her head was pounding with the beginning of a migraine. When the last vestiges of color dramatically stained the sky with crimson, she chided herself for her foolishness and for not taking the commander's threats seriously.

Spotting the bamboo bridge precariously suspended between the rocks in the cliff, she began to shudder. It had taken all her courage to cross the forbidding 100-foot-long span on her last walk with the rebels. Many of the bamboo slats were missing from the narrow footholds. Jesse imagined herself on the bridge as it swayed high above the river. She'd be grabbed from behind. She'd be pushed off. She'd be sucked down to her death. Her hysteria mounted. Accidents happen all the time in these mountains. Her heart pounded harder and faster.

"Why are we using that bridge? There are other routes into Tanduhan," she stammered, catching up to Noel.

"Are you afraid, Jesse?" he asked, addressing her for the first time. When he said her name, it sounded like the crack of a pistol. "You've crossed this bridge before."

"Afraid?" she instantly retorted. "You are joking, right? My flashlight's in my backpack, and I could get killed walking across in the dark." She shifted her eyes from the rope bridge to Noel's face and back to the bridge.

As seconds went by, Jesse knew she had to move. She hoped this was only a test that the guerrillas were known to share with their foreign visitors to heighten their sense of danger. Still, she couldn't be sure. His cold, unforgiving stare more than hinted at his smoldering displeasure.

"I'll follow you across," Jesse promised. And if the last guy makes a sudden turn, I'm going to hold on real tight. If I go over, they do too.

The commander went first, running the bridge's length with his rifle held tight to his chest. When Tess stepped onto the first slat, Sadek and Abel followed close on her heels. Jesse fell into step right behind them.

The bridge flapped back and forth with the weight of four figures, then roller-coasted sideways. Jesse's hands skimmed the ropes as she saw the glow of Sadek's flashlight on the wooden rungs ahead. *Keep to the center*, she told herself. The bridge almost tipped when she shifted her weight to grab at the ropes to steady her body. The twisted fibers of the hemp sliced into her clenched palms like hundreds of tiny knife blades. With the boom of a wave against the rocks below, Jesse dashed ahead. It was only after her feet touched solid ground that she inhaled. None of them had waited for her. Quivering from the rush of adrenaline, she ran after the figures now disappearing around a curve.

A quarter-moon was rising when she arrived at a small bamboo-walled hut on the outskirts of Tanduhan. Jesse followed the others inside, but could not sit, stand, or think. She wanted a drink of water and a change of clothes. The room was filling up with tribal people, guerrilla soldiers, and children talking in a mixture of Kalinga, Tagalog, and Ilocano. Jesse stood alone. "Here are your things," said Tess, producing her backpack.

"*Nasaan ang mapa*? Where is the map?" the commander demanded. "Or did you give it to your friends in the military?"

Jesse pulled out the chicklet-sized packet, taped shut, and damp from the sweat that had soaked through the pocket of her jeans. She defiantly slapped it into his palm. The crack hit his hand as hard as she could pound it.

"Take your damn map, Noel. Do you really believe I'd show the military where your contacts are located? I would never do that!" she exclaimed as if she needed to answer her own question.

He stood still. More than a minute passed. "No? *Talaga* Jesse. It was expected that you would arrive at the camp as we planned."

Noel carefully slit open the tape with his thumbnail. He spread open the square. She could see the hand-drawn route with friends' code names in each village and the x's that marked the roadblocks to avoid as she traveled to their secret base.

"Jesse, what should I believe? Do you think we are playing games here?" He waved the paper to punctuate each syllable. "You promised to return on a specific day. When word reached us that you weren't seen at any of the checkpoints, we worried the military had stopped you. Later, a constabulary unit accompanied by two choppers attacked our base. Ka Geordie was killed by the mortar strafing." He turned away to refold the drawing into a small square.

The enormity of the situation rendered Jesse speechless. Her whirling thoughts were consumed in a jumbled turmoil. *Ka Geordie... could they...did they ...a terrible mistake...not an informer...how could they believe... she would never tell the military the location of their hidden camp.*

"No, no! It was a coincidence." As her carefully rehearsed explanation faltered, she burst into a torrent of frenetic words. "I would never tell anyone... I would never tell the military how to find you. I know I missed our meeting. I had another assignment. I had to go to Mindanao. I didn't know how to get a message to you. That's why I didn't return. Of course, I wanted to... I wanted to help." She couldn't continue and looked into the commander's eyes, hoping he would encourage her to say what she meant. His stoic features now seemed chiseled out of granite.

Tess, standing next to Noel, was silently searching Jesse's face to discover a clue to her aberrant behavior.

"There are very serious charges against you," Noel said flatly. "Tomorrow, you can tell your story to the tribal elders. They will decide what should be done."

# Chapter 2

## The Rebel Commander

Jesse spread the mat Tess had given her onto the bamboo floor. In the last few hours, how much she had underestimated the severity of the situation had become increasingly clear. She lay down and repeated each detail of the day's events while obsessively berating herself for her conceit and shallowness. The pressure in her chest grew so heavy that her breath came in shallow gasps. *Tess should've warned me. Why didn't she? Tess knew the score. What did I expect? Why would they believe my sincerity?*

At thirty-two years old, Jesse Beckerman wanted her due—a prestigious overseas assignment that would give her the international acclaim others in her agency had already achieved. Ten months earlier, Filipinos had poured into the streets of Manila, demanding an end to the twenty-year reign of Ferdinand Marcos. Scores of foreign correspondents were descending on the capital city to cover the action. When Jesse heard that one of the other photographers at her agency was about to bag the assignment, she had stormed into Jonathan Davidson's office.

This time, she came armed with the knowledge that she had done her research; a well-placed contact had promised introductions to the military officers, government officials and wealthy families who controlled the political hierarchy in the Philippines. A second source had briefed her on the leaders of the National Democratic Front, the underground organizations and the locations of 'red zones' where rebel soldiers in the New People's Army were often sighted. Davidson had rewarded her diligence with a guarantee from *L'EXPRESS*.

"Today's your lucky day," he'd told her after agreeing to pay her airfare and split expenses—food, hotel, and film—against the twenty-five hundred dollars offered for a five-page spread about the upcoming elections. "It's going to be a helluva story. An award-winning assignment. If you're on top of it," he'd teased, "sure to make you a contender for one of those African assignments you've been begging me about."

She remembered how the blood creeping into her ears turned them red with the obvious heat of her discomfort.

"You're a bright woman with a strong-minded vision, he said as if one or two compliments would offset his continuing harangue. "You've got the balls to get yourself into a place, the detachment to shoot what's needed, and the tenacity to get yourself out. But it's your empathy," he said while pointing to his heart, "that engenders the trust and honesty you get in your pictures. And for the most part, you even remember to focus."

"I can always count on your support, Davidson. And your backhanded praise. I'm sure you'll be standing right by my side when I get my Pulitzer," she retorted before slamming his door.

When she hit the street, it was sleeting. There were no taxis in sight. Although her face was stinging, Jesse fantasized her black leather coat had become an impervious skin, and like a panther, she could weather the elements. Each step through the icy storm was a challenge, testing her strength for the trip ahead.

At home, she packed one bag and her copy of Amado Guerrero's book: "*Specific Characteristics of People's War in the Philippines*," an ideological bible of the outlawed Communist Party. Then she was out of New York in as long as it took to buy ten bricks of film and say a few good-byes.

Jesse joined hundreds of international journalists following the campaign for the presidency, and photographed the final hours of the Marcos's before they fled to Hawaii. She shot portraits of nuns placing wooden crosses with candles into barbed-wire barricades. She was at the front of the free-for-all battle between Cory's supporters and the Marcos Loyalists outside Malacañang, and photographed the storming of the fences as the palace fell, along with the jubilant crowds trashing the opulent symbols of the dictatorship. Giant framed portraits of Imelda and Ferdinand were thrown to the ground and set on fire. The garishly decorated rooms and Imelda's astounding collection of clothes, shoes, and even her bras, were exposed to Jesse's opportunistic scrutiny.

Her dramatic pictures of the siege of the palace became full page covers for *L'EXPRESS*, and the international edition of *NEWSWEEK*. Others were featured prominently in magazine stories. Her candid black and white shots from the streets and EDSA were syndicated in magazines and Sunday supplements.

Jesse was as pleased with her success as Davidson. She was thrilled when he offered to pay for her ticket to Thailand and assigned her two weeks to photograph the Karen refugee camps along the northern Thai-Burmese border.

After suffering the effects of a nasty bout of dysentery, she did not have the inclination to meet a wider circle of contacts or the stomach to travel long distances.

When she got back to the States, she prodded her agent about the follow-up stories she could do in the Philippine provinces. Eager to leave, she offered to pay her own plane fare but wanted a guarantee for the story. By August, she had garnered another assignment: covering the initial peace talks between Cory's government and the insurgents in the northern part of Luzon for *ASIA WEEK*.

It was well known that the New People's Army had been active throughout the islands since 1969 and had grown to more than 15,000 members during the Marcos regime. As part of its program of reconciliation, the Aquino government was offering amnesty to those rebels who would come down from the mountains and surrender their weapons.

Jesse was the only foreign correspondent assigned to cover the secret Cordillera peace-talks rumored to be happening in the mountainous northern indigenous tribal region. At one of these covert meetings, she had met Tess Gadag, the twenty-five-year-old emissary of the Kalinga Tribal Association, and accepted an invitation to visit Tanduhan, her village. It was an alluring proposal;

Tanduhan was reputed to be a rebel stronghold. When eight heavily armed guerrillas appeared one evening as they were eating dinner, Jesse was neither surprised nor frightened. After being introduced to the infamous commander, her eyes were glittering with excitement.

Ka Noel was one of the military's 'most wanted' outlaws. In his dozen years underground, the elusive soldier had written many communiqués to the press but had seldom been photographed. Ka Noel appeared younger than his forty years and at moments almost shy. Pulling out a pack of Marlboro's, she had offered him one and observed his expression as he rubbed his fingers back and forth across his lips.

"So, are you going to be swayed by Cory's proposal to surrender?" she had brazenly asked, delighted to be in a position to break the story. She was sure *THE TIMES, NEWSWEEK,* and other newspapers and magazines would be interested. Especially since Cory was planning to soon address the United Nations. The new President would like to assure the world about how peaceful the Philippines had become.

Jesse smiled while the minutes passed before Ka Noel began to talk. He started slowly, explaining that while they were willing to listen to President Aquino's plan for a settlement to the armed struggle, there were many issues that needed to be resolved before he'd come down from the mountains.

"Tell me, Jesse. Is it fair that the Igorots have become squatters on land where we have lived for generations? First, Marcos tells us we don't exist and sends surveyors with maps indicating there are no villages along the Chico River. Then his cronies in the logging companies are given laws so they can legally cut down our trees. Now Aquino wants us to believe her government's talk about a cease-fire while the military continues their counter-insurgency missions. I would like to tell Cory that we are not considering surrendering any weapons until the military withdraws from their armed camps in the Cordillera."

During that night the group sat cross-legged on the floor, drinking heavily sugared black coffee and quietly sharing their stories.

"When our *pangat* - tribal chief, Macli-ing Dulag, went down to

Manila to meet with Marcos, the military offered him money," said Tess. "What did they think? That we can fill our belly with paper? Macli-ing told them, 'I do not own the land. The land owns me. I belong to it, and when so required...'"

"...I will die for it," chorused Ka Abel and Ka Benji in unison.

"It is not only the trees they want to destroy," added Tess. "The government wants to build a dam on the Chico River. One-hundred-thousand people. Where would we go while they flood our rice terraces and burial grounds? What vengeance would the ancestors hovering about bring down upon the people if they were abandoned? Years ago, our Kalinga warriors would have gathered their shields and spears and set out on a head-hunting raid against our enemies."

"The spears of our ancestors will not be enough to defend us," Ka Noel angrily retorted, "and neither will the Church's doctrines. After I joined the seminary, my superiors asked me to ignore the terrible things that were happening. I was told to stop making trouble. What I see now is when you teach the people to stand up for their rights, you are branded a subversive."

"Or a communist," said Ka Abel. He told her how two of his brothers had been arrested for attending a meeting with organizers from the lowlands. Their bodies were discovered in a ditch by the road. Both boys had been beheaded, their torsos burned by acid and trussed with wire as if they were pigs. Ka Benji, the youngest rebel in the cadre, was nine years old when the military had come to his village, supposedly looking for his cousin.

"Soldiers surrounded my house with their rifles ready to shoot. The lieutenant yelled at my mother to come out, or he was going to open fire," Ka Benji matter-of-factly related. "When we went outside, he grabbed my younger brother and put the gun to his head. My mother yelled for them to leave us alone. 'Isn't it enough you murdered their father,'" she accusingly cried out. "It happened so fast. I saw him shoot my brother, and when I turned to take the baby from her arms, a bullet hit me in the back. They shot her twice in the chest, killing the baby too." He displayed the patchwork quilt of scars covering his back. "I lay very still under their bleeding bodies. They thought I was dead."

Jesse listened until morning. In El Salvador, she'd heard similar stories. That didn't lessen the horror of each new description of brutality. The inhumanity of Ka Sadek's experience in prison where he had been tortured with electric shocks to his genitals, left her outraged with the Marcos government. She was in tears when Ka Benji took her hand and asked, "Can you help?" with the hope that his personal testimony would reach an international audience.

The rebels stopped talking when the cigarettes turned their dialogue into raspy whispers. As the men drifted off to sleep, Jesse admired their poignant tenderness. The rugged guerrilla fighters held hands, familiarly rested their bodies against one another, and slept together under shared blankets.

In the morning, Ka Noel had given her permission to photograph the group. She looked for images that would humanize the young cadre while maintaining their dignity. In the foggy ochre light, she took her shots as they were drinking coffee while hugging M-16 rifles with fully loaded ammunition belts slung casually over their shoulders. She followed as they were helping villagers with the morning chores. Before they left Tanduhan, Ka Noel had taken her aside. "Would you like to meet the other commanders?" he had asked. "We have a meeting scheduled in two weeks."

"I'm already packed," she'd replied, watching as he painstakingly drew the map to their secret base of operations. The last time she had seen Ka Noel, he was waving good-bye. As the Fierra jeep pulled away to take her down the mountain, Jesse could see him leaping into the air, his fist clenched, a broad smile on his face.

"Say hello to Cory," he had yelled.

But when she returned to Manila, there was a message from Jonathan Davidson. He needed photographs of the striking sugar workers and their starving children on the island of Negros. Then she had to fly to Mindanao, team up with a German reporter, and meet Nur Misuari, the commander of the Muslim rebels for a magazine story. There was no way she could budge her agent on the deadline, no matter how hard she'd tried.

"You wanted assignments," Davidson had insisted during their phone conversation. "That's the job. And my advice for when you get back to the mountains," he'd added, "...concentrate on getting action shots. You've done the artsy portraits of men holding guns and babies, Jesse. Make your Cordillera essay more salable."

What did he want her to do? Arrange an ambush? Photograph the military and rebel firefight while perched in a tree?

"Bastard," she'd yelled before she hung up on him. "You know how far I'll go!"

By the time she returned from the south, rumors had begun filtering down to Manila: She was no longer welcomed in the Cordillera.

Jesse was astounded. Surely, she had established a rapport with the guerrillas and gained Ka Noel's confidence. What more proof of her support for their cause did she need to offer? He should have trusted that she had a good excuse. It wasn't as if she could easily get in touch with him and explain her delay.

Soon her expulsion from the 'red zone' had become a hotly discussed topic among members of the correspondents club. Every overheard comment and insinuation added another painful stroke to her deep-rooted insecurity. And she couldn't ignore the *tsismis* (gossip), especially the talk about whether or not she was having an affair with one of the rebels.

She'd heard stories from other female journalists about their sexual exploits. She did have fantasies about the handsome commander. He was very *guapo* (handsome), and like the classic story-book charismatic hero, had put his life on the line to fight for justice. At the end of the day, she knew how hard it was for her to leave the stories behind and walk away unhampered. She could not chance even one night's romantic passion. It might open up her heart so that she'd have no control over her emotions. Although it was a sizzling temptation, her detachment was the key to getting the work done. And that, she continued to remind herself, was her priority.

During the last days of September, Jesse gave in to a mounting depression. She smoked some locally grown pot, hoping the rush would recharge her inspiration. It only made her more high-strung and nervous. She did a shoot with some of the street kids she knew, but the hopelessness of their economic situation and the fact that Davidson expressed no interest in the images added to her gloom. She wondered whether anyone would care if she ever took another photograph. She couldn't sleep. When she did, suffocating thoughts of failure woke her every few hours.

To pass the nights, she'd visit the local clubs, consume beer, vodka, or Tanduay Rum with cola, while practicing conversational Taglish, her English mixed with Tagalog words and expressions. She could prove she was good at something, having quickly learned how to curse, then how to joke. And she had mastered enough Filipino phrases to debate the virtues and flaws of Cory's administration with friends.

One evening Rudy, the bartender, told her a story about an American reporter who had disappeared a few years back; he was on a trip to meet with the guerrillas in the mountains. "What was left of his body was found in a deep ravine months later," he said before adding, "No one knows what had really happened, but the *tsismis* is that the death was not accidental."

"Damn the threats and restrictions on my traveling," Jesse had blurted out, crashing her beer bottle down on the bar. "I'll go up there and explain why I missed the meeting. My friends will understand."

The next day she wrote a note to Tess Gadag, stating the date and time of her arrival. After dropping it off at the main post office with a prayer that it would be delivered, Jesse headed for a hole-in-the-wall bar where the local journalists shot pool. Optimistic that her convictions far outweighed her fears, she drank every offered beer and sunk ball after ball in the pockets, wiping away her opponents until there was no one left to challenge.

Now, she pulled out a cigarette and smoked it down to the filter. Why would Tess and Noel have any reason to believe her intensions; they knew so little about her political background, her sense of justice, and her commitment to opening people's eyes through her work. She wished she'd brought along clips from her El Salvador story to show them. Perhaps she was driven by idealism, she reasoned, but it was always a hope that her projects might help influence the course of events.

When she finally shut her eyes, Jesse pictured herself on a nearby ridge engaged in an animated discussion with Noel. Before drifting off to sleep, the scene had shifted dramatically. His soldiers were pointing guns at her back.

# Chapter 3

## Signs from the Spirits

"Let's go now," said Tess in a voice, frayed thin from weariness. "Night after night, we sit here. We wait. We watch the stars. We pray to the sky-world to show us a sign."

Agunay did another rhythmic brushstroke through Tess's thick straight hair. "When it is meant to be, *alam mo* (you know) we will see this sign."

"*Hindi* (No), Agunay. Sometimes, I wonder if we are foolish to believe in dreams like the old people."

"See what happens when you go off to college? You get mixed up. What we know is how the *dawak* (shaman) sees the future. It has always been that way. Your mother had the power to see these visions."

"*Talaga* (Really)," Tess interrupted, "and we wait patiently for her predictions to come true. Tonight, before my legs began to cramp, I was praying for the glowing sliver of moon to display some marks. *Apo* (God). Even a bruise would have meaning. But the spirits continue to tease us while *Kuraraw* (female ghost) plays her hide and seek game with a cloud. Why does the ghost refuse to sing after midnight? Why is the 'Queen of the Night,' so silent?" She looked into Agunay's eyes, so credulously accepting the myths of their childhood, and confessed, "I don't know what I believe."

Tess got up from sitting on the flat cement block covering her grandfather's grave. After one last glance towards the recalcitrant stars, she took hold of her friend's arm and walked back to her house. Inside, they squatted in front of the smoldering wood fire to get warm.

The kerosene lamp's flickering light cast a dull amber glow on the wood walls and bamboo floor. Across the room, Jesse chattered incoherently in her sleep, twisting from side to side while the shadow-ghosts mimicked her movements. Tess wished the woman had never appeared. Among Kalinga, the rules of behavior were clear—one belonged to the clan from birth to death and beyond—one was dependent on the family for protection, and responsibilities and faults were shared. All members were held accountable. Coming here alone, what did the American know of these things? With her golden passport, Jesse could travel in and out of the country like a welcomed guest.

Ka Noel had scoffed at the American woman's loyalty after Tess had shown him her note. "We are nothing more than a story," he'd insisted. "She has no family here. No ties to our place."

Tess whispered to Agunay, "Jesse would not dare to come to our village if she gave information to the military. Would the sister of Mary Da-way who lives in New York send her to us if she could not be trusted?"

"They could have made a mistake."

"What I know is that the American was destined to come back here." She watched Agunay's lids flicker with surprise, and the words withheld from even her closest friend poured out like a stream of confessions. "Before I went to Babalasang, before the peace talks, in my dream, I saw a woman with hair the color of corn silk on fire."

"Like her hair. Red as the flame trees in bloom," Agunay shuddered.

"There is more. Along the way, an *i-daw* (the revered bird that forecasts omens) flew by me, singing out pitpitpit... pitpitpit... pitpitpit. *Apo*, that tiny bird, that *i-daw*, is an omen that something important will happen. It was raining at the same time the sun was shining when the red-haired woman arrived with her cameras the following day. Agunay, can we ignore the signs of the ancestors?" she asked, and answered in the same breath, "no one would ever refuse to listen."

"You said it was foolish superstitions."

"That is why I did not say until I was sure." She half-covered her mouth and leaned so close that her hand touched Agunay's cheek. "Jesse wears a chain with an *anting-anting* (protective charm). When I reached my hand out to touch her charm, my fingers... they stung. They burned like they'd brushed over nettles!" Tess crossed herself like the Catholic priest had taught.

"She could be a witch."

"Ka Noel thinks she might be working for the Israelis. There can be other explanations. I was the one to ask Noel to meet her at the Ampwillan Pass. Testing her courage is one way to discover if there is truth to the omens. If it is not meant to be, she will soon give up and return to Manila."

Tess glanced over to watch how the sleeping woman rolled her body tight like a fist, and silently asked the spirits once more why they had pointed out the foreigner.

Before the soldiers had entered her village, Tess never questioned the Kalinga way of life. She pounded rice twice a day, gathered vegetables, and cared for the younger children exactly as the women had done for generations. She never ventured further than a neighboring barrio. When her grandfather died, Tess stayed by her mother's side and carefully observed the rituals. Mario Calam-ang's spirit remained near the corpse and, if not properly satisfied, would inflict illness or death on his relatives. When her brother, Ruben, developed a high fever, she took it as a sign that the anitos (spirits) were angry.

"Apo. Who is causing this sickness? What do you want from this boy?" the mandadawak (shaman) had chanted, invoking her invisible helpers, the arans (ghosts) who lived nearby in the rivers, mountains, and graves. The shaman placed antique beads on a porcelain plate, danced around and around, ringing the plate with a stick and chanting Calam-ang's name and the names of dead relatives from two generations back. A pig was sacrificed, and its liver examined; it was neither spotted nor marked. The dawak told her family to put tobacco and a hand-woven blanket near Calam-ang's grave so Ruben would not die.

But traditions and magic are not effective weapons against the ammunition of this government, thought Tess as she placed another log on the fire. She knew history had sped up for her people.

In this last quarter of the twentieth century, the entire force of the military had been hurled at the tribes. Bombs dropped from helicopters and low-flying planes. Mortars fired into villages. The natives were forcibly evacuated from their homes to places where the military could monitor their activities. Rice terraces were declared free-fire zones with strict curfews imposed to make farming difficult. Meanwhile, the soldiers waved their guns with impunity, stealing whatever rice, pigs, and chickens they could find.

Ruben had joined the spreading rebellion along with the boys from every Cordillera province. Putting aside their long legacy of tribal wars, the men signed peace pacts and pledged to fight their common enemy. Within months the Igorot cadre had earned a proud reputation as the best rebel soldiers in the New People's Army.

At first, Tess was angry that they wouldn't let her 'take to the hills.' It had been decided that she could be more effective staying above ground and organizing legally. After dark, she'd walk across the terraces to visit a neighbor's house, drink coffee and try to convince her friends to join the food buying cooperative she'd started. It wasn't long before the military retaliated.

Tess watched the small circle of light grow dim. "Remember how it was, Agunay, when my parents disappeared after marketing their rice in the lowlands? How we worried that the jeep had broken down. How we thought there had been a landslide. The Fierra could have fallen into a ravine. Everyone could've been killed."

"There were no accidents reported on the second day," continued Agunay, repeating the story word for word, as if each telling etched the incident deeper into their bones. "By and by, with no bodies found in revenge killings, we knew the whispers were true."

"It was certain that the military had them imprisoned. We went to the local garrison, but the Provincial Commander refused to investigate."

"We sat and waited more than two hours before he agreed to listen."

"Then he questioned us about Angelina, the catechist from Bontoc. How well did we know her, hinting that she disappeared after meeting with the communists?"

"*Apo*. We knew she had been 'salvaged.' Another victim of the military's execution," Tess added bitterly. "Her body was swollen and cut up so badly when it was found in the river that you could not even see her face. Then he taunted us, saying my brother, Ruben, should visit him, and together they would locate our parents."

Suddenly her stomach jolted. Tess doubled over, moaning from the stabbing pain.

"What is wrong?" Agunay asked anxiously.

Tess stared at the corner beam over the hearth until the cramping passed. She had not looked behind that bamboo curtain since childhood. "Let me be." She straightened up, and as if hearing a command, drifted over and pushed aside the covering. Reaching in and out quickly, she cradled the forty-year-old packet like it might disintegrate at any moment in her fingers. Squatting down, she carefully untied the leather strap and spread its contents onto the floor.

With Agunay staring wide-eyed by her side, Tess picked out the snapshot first and placed it on her lap. A small triangle had cracked off at the corner. The once shiny surface of the sepia-toned photo appeared to be rubbed, creating a dull halo around the smiling face of the young, dark-skinned woman. She was wearing a broad-shouldered dress and holding a straw hat with one white-gloved hand as if it would spring from her head if she let go.

Tess delicately touched the cursive inked inscription. She glanced to check that Jesse was still sleeping before reading it out to Agunay.

"*A smile for my Joseph. I am praying for your safe return. With all my love. Emily-lou. Florida, 1941.*"

Tears welled in her eyes. "The last time I touched this was the night my mother was released from prison. Do you remember, Agunay? Long streaks of gray hair overshadowed the black. New deep creases accordioned around her eyes and crisscrossed near her mouth. Her skin seemed as parched as her spirit."

"She had a fever and cough from pneumonia," whispered Agunay.

"And burns from the cigarettes they put out on her body."

"I remember how *Ina* (mother) would climb out the side window onto the rail above the pigs and whistle for the chickens."

"And the woman who returned... she had to struggle to raise her arm high enough to point out this hiding place." Straining her ears, Tess closed her eyes and could almost hear her mother chanting a favorite *salidummay* (a chanted oral history):

*I am Mary from the Bulano tribe.*

*My mother comes from Abra.*

*My father is Kalinga.*

*From one generation to the next, we thank our ancestors*

*for the mountains, the streams and the forests.*

*We thank the tree before cutting it down and the fish for letting us eat.*

*That is the way it has always been for Kalinga.*

*By and by the outsiders arrived.*

*They did not ask permission before unleashing fires that burned our villages.*

*They destroyed our fields. The arans yelled in the trees.*

*The Fire God disappeared from the sky.*

*Now the old ways are changing, and the land is red with death.*

Grim-faced, Tess glanced down at the aging photo. She fingered it and then touched her lips, expecting the sour taste of blood. Although her heart was racing, she carefully unfolded the yellowed sheet of paper and smoothed it flat with her palm. A graceful drawing of a cross-legged Buddha seated on a flowering rock, with one hand resting on a foot and one hand reaching downwards, filled the middle of the page. Simple lines indicated the arched eyebrows, downcast eyes, pointed nose, and smiling lips. Ink smudges made the soft folds of fabric barely visible. Six rows of protruding curls covered the statue's head, encircling it like a tight-fitting cap that dipped at the center of the forehead and rose upwards to a flame-like jewel.

Agunay broke the uneasy silence. While pointing at the drawing, she whispered, "Is that a Buddha? It is like the elders described in their stories. Before the Japanese surrendered, it was said that they buried a gold statue. The old people said it was nearby our place. But Tess, *bakit* (why)? Why keep this hidden... even from me?"

Tess hugged herself tightly before she spoke. "The night she returned, I promised *Ina* to keep her secret. I promised not even to tell *Ama* (father) about these things. She was so sick. I worried she might die. At first, I thought that being in prison had made her crazy. She was telling such strange stories about the war and remembering about the days when she and *Tito* (uncle) Nestor were children. How they found a soldier almost dead from his wounds and carried him to safety, to a cave by Patucan Ridge. *Ina* would go to where this American, Mr. Joseph, was hiding and bring him food and water. *Ina* told me about Mr. Joseph. She said that he would never forget her. She told me that he was giving her this packet as a remembrance gift for her kindness. Agunay, when I promised to keep the secret, I saw the light return to her eyes." In short visual bursts, she could see her mother singing, as if an apparition had appeared in the room. *Watch how the fire god will flame. How the rain god will feed the land. How the sun will glow white in the sky.*

Tess stared with wet eyes at the drawing. She touched the paper to her chest and wondered if sometimes the omens could lie. *Ina* had died a few days later, after returning from her imprisonment. Ruben was killed in a military ambush. It was never determined what had happened to *Ama*, although the village was certain he too had been 'salvaged.' She tried to choke back the long-buried grief. Her red-rimmed eyes were becoming painfully seared from the tears.

She was mourning not only the loss of her parents and brother, but also the way of life of her tribe. It was not for herself that she prayed but to quiet the weeping of her ancestors. There was no more time. Her people needed money to fight back. How else could they continue to protect their traditions and make the land safe for the children?

"I will never forget you," she repeated as the ghostly image disappeared back into the corner darkness. Tess wrapped the packet tightly and returned it to the hiding place.

"Enough, Agunay," she said to her friend. "We will talk more in the morning. Let's sleep now." She lay down on the bamboo floor between Agunay and Jesse and covered them with the blanket her mother had woven. Warily, she glanced at the *anting-anting* that dangled from the American woman's necklace.

"Wait for a sign," *Ina* had cautioned, "and keep a pure heart. Ask guidance from the spirits. I promise that the ancestors in the House of the Dwarfs will protect you."

After all that happened to her family, Tess had refused to believe such predictions. She'd vowed never again to look at the packet. The tattered drawing and photograph seemed nothing more than an empty dream, like the priest's Sunday sermon of salvation. Yet, like a dutiful child, she now silently invoked the names of her parents and their parents. *Apo. What should I do?* Within minutes her throat and head were as hot as if she had drunk a whole bottle of *Ginebra* (80 proof sugar-cane alcohol). She envisioned the rice fields burning. Above the flames floated Jesse's *anting-anting*. The magic charm had become a statue as big as a mountain.

I will not forget you, a man's voice murmured before she saw Emily-lou wave her hat. Then the photo began to char and crumble into white dust. In this dream-like vision, she could see the trees along a top ridge of Sleeping Beauty Mountain silhouetted against the sky.

Tess bolted upright. *Wait for a sign from the sky-world.* Jesse brought such a sign from the sky-world. I will never forget you, Mr. Joseph had pledged. *Utang na loob.* Blood debts run deep. No matter how many years had passed, the soldier's debt of gratitude would be paid.

Let Jesse believe she is here to take pictures, thought Tess. She reached over to Jesse and stroked the fiery charm, trusting with absolute certainty that the small Buddha *anting-anting* had cooled.

# Chapter 4

## Broken Promise

The cacophony of the back and forth crowing of distant and nearby roosters followed by the barking dogs and the squeals of the black-bristled pigs beneath the split bamboo floor had awakened Jesse from a fitful sleep. The smoky aroma of pine twigs and kindling filled the cold room as fresh roasted black coffee and a pot of rice simmered over the wood fire. It was still dark at four am in the morning. As the rays of dawn light filtered through the smoky air surrounding banana trees, the noises of children sweeping the ground and pumping water from the well announced that morning activities had begun.

Like most one-room octagonal houses in Kalinga villages, this one was constructed on thick wooden posts four feet off the ground. The pitched roof, once thatched with cogon grass, was now modernized with corrugated metal sheets. Walls made of rough hand-hewn boards and split-and-plaited bamboo had a brownish-black patina, scarred from years of exposure to sun, rain and soot. Two large rectangular openings served both as windows and side doorways, with crisscrossed woven mats that pulled down like shutters.

There was no furniture besides a large wooden storage trunk in the corner. A faded print of the Last Supper, a portrait of a beatific Jesus Christ, and an outdated calendar with a picture of the local Congressman's family were the only interior decorations hung on the walls.

Behind a small partition dividing the back quarter of the space, three large stones were placed on a cement-lined hearth. On top balanced a heavy aluminum pot filled with steaming rice. Tess squatted nearby, arms on either side of her knees, stirring the cooking rice with a wooden spoon. Straight black hair fell across her broad shoulders. She poured a cup of steaming coffee from a smaller pot and carried it over to the foreigner. While Jesse sipped the sugary hot liquid, Tess took hold of each leg and slowly rubbed the muscles from knee to ankle with her palms.

"Ow.... ahuh... yeah," moaned Jesse, before the gentle strokes pushed her past the slim control she had maintained over her emotions to guttural sobs and tears.

Tess was concerned that she had offended her. "It was courageous to come back by yourself." A half-smile now replaced yesterday's cool stare.

"It wasn't so much courage as naiveté," Jesse hesitantly answered, wiping her nose with the back of her hand. "As usual, I didn't know what I was getting into." She reached into her backpack for a handkerchief. "I am so, so very sorry about Ka Geordie, Tess." Before she had a chance to respond, she continued, "But now... after thinking it over, I'm surprised that you even agreed to meet me."

Tess raised her brows and sighed. Spirit visions and omens were a heavy load to keep to herself. "Despite Ka Noel's apprehension, I thought you should be given a chance to explain your situation."

"Tess, believe me. I knew nothing about the military attack, only *tsismis* that I missed a meeting. I came back to explain. I'd never give any information to the military or intentionally hurt you."

Tess stopped smiling. "It's not up to me," she responded coolly. "Why didn't you return as promised? After all, you gave your word."

Jesse shook her head. "I'm sorry. I really am. I couldn't turn down a paying assignment. I know you think all foreigners have a lot of money. You don't understand how hard it is for me to get by. I paid my own plane fare to get back here after the peace-talks ended. Now my agency wants me to shoot more 'action' images. Tell me. Do you think Ka Noel plans to retaliate?"

Tess blanched. "Let's eat," she said, "you must be hungry." She went to the fire and returned with a large plastic dish filled with steaming mountain rice and a smaller one with fried sayote leaves.

Jesse was used to eating with her hands and pushed a small amount of caked rice into her mouth, followed by the soft green vegetables. They remained silent until Jesse lit a cigarette and unconsciously touched the charm around her neck. Tess stared at the talisman and quickly crossed herself to ward off any evil spirits lurking nearby.

Jesse noticed her furtive gaze. "I've been collecting charms for years," she offered, rubbing the miniature Buddha with her thumb. "This one's my guardian angel, supposedly a guide across the river to enlightenment. I found it at the night market in Bangkok. The street-hawker was insistent that I buy it. He said the charm was an emanation of Amitabha, the Buddha of the Future."

She reached into her camera bag and displayed a pressed-in-plastic four-leaf clover, a tiny Mother and Child figure, and a six-sided star. "I'm superstitious... like you. I keep lucky charms near my cameras. For real protection," she said while reaching into her bag and pulling out a small can, "Mace! It's a spray that can blind someone temporarily. Before I left New York, my friend, Alex, made me promise to carry it. Considering the situations I find myself in, I need all the help I can get."

Tess's eyes opened wide in amazement. "*Apo.* Jesse, put those *anting-antings* away before you see Ka Noel."

Jesse's throat tightened. Hit by a sickening wave of nausea, she sharply sucked in her breath and willed the food to stay down. She tucked the amulets and mace back into her bag and reviewed the situation: perhaps the rebel leader had altered his unjustified opinion of her behavior. She had a solid case to present in her own defense. Once the facts were established, he would surely see she was not responsible for the tragedy.

While Tess cleared the floor of dishes, Jesse took a towel and toothbrush to the well in the center of the village. She pumped the handle up and down, helping a mother bath her baby with the cool stream of water. When it was Jesse's turn to wash, the woman worked the pump, and the little boy, slung across his mother's back, followed each of her movements with round eyes. Back at the house, she watched Gan-ao, who lived in the house behind Tess, hanging laundry on a line; her daughter, Vickie, sat in the doorway nursing her youngest.

A steady stream of villagers wanting to see the American came in and out throughout the morning. Rosie, the owner of the nearby *sari-sari* store (convenience store), brought her cigarettes. Iss-oc, a ninety-year-old grandmother, grabbed Jesse's hand, shaking it hard. Her thick gray hair was twisted in a knot on top of her head and entwined with agate beads. The skeleton of a snake and a wood pipe were stuck into the braided bun. Iss-oc's earlobes were stretched downwards by circular gold earrings that were equal in value to the price of a caribou.

Jesse pulled out some photographs from her backpack. Iss-oc sat back on her heels and glanced at her portrait. With a toothless laugh, she lit her pipe with a stick from the fire. She repeatedly jabbed at her portrait while speaking rapidly in the Kalinga dialect.

Later, Agunay, Rosie, Isabel, and Cecilia took turns picking music tapes for Jesse's cassette recorder. Though the women were sympathetic to the rebels, feeding them rice and beans when they passed through the village, they never mentioned Ka Noel's accusations. As Tess passed around cups filled with hot coffee, the group surrounded Jesse on the floor.

"How do you find the conditions here, like not having an outhouse?" Cecilia asked.

Jesse burst out laughing. "Carrying a stick to beat away the pigs when I go into the bushes is a totally unique experience."

Rosie grinned and smoothed back the straight bangs that covered her eyebrows. Like Tess, Cecilia and Agunay, she was in her mid-twenties, with lustrous black hair bluntly cut in a traditional style that rimmed her face and covered her ears. Rosie stood up and improvised some dance steps to the reggae beat of a Bob Marley tape. "What's it like in your place?" she asked. "Is it much different than here?"

Jesse pulled a cigarette out of her pocket and lit it, taking a long drag. She hated talking about herself, and it always amazed her that sharing personal stories seemed to be a daily ritual in each village she visited. These talks could last for hours. Sometimes the gathering might be small, like this one, or as many as fifty people would ask questions. Attribute it to the lack of electricity, she had often thought. No radios. No tvs. No diversions. Her standard response was a political and economic analysis of the conservative policies of the Reagan administration. But at this moment, she welcomed the diversion, grasped at the warmth and familiarity offered by the group, and answered more intimately.

"In New York, the streets are pulsating twenty-four-hours a day with a nervous, almost electrical energy. It's not like anywhere else in the world. It can be extremely creative or, if you are not on guard at all times, dangerous. There is no military roaming around like here, but lots of people besides the police have guns. And sometimes they get crazy. You know when they say in Manila that someone 'ran amuck' with a bolo, slicing up his neighbors? It's the same in New York."

"What about your family? How do you protect your parents and the small children from these crazy people?" Rosie asked.

"I don't live with my family. I moved away when I was seventeen," admitted Jesse.

"Away from your family?" questioned Rosie. 'How could you eat?"

"It's not like here." She went over to the window and tossed out her cigarette; two women wearing tee-shirts tucked into their hand-woven *tapis* (wrap-around skirt) walked side by side with baskets of laundry on their heads. They were laughing, absorbed in their private stories. As the women moved out of sight, she heard the voices of children. Was it the sound of the kids in the distance or the shared jokes of the two women who had just passed that reminded her of Jan? She was caught by a wave of melancholy, missing her sister and the familiarity of home.

"I live with my friend, Alex," Jesse continued.

"Is Alex your *mahal*?" Rosie asked.

"He does love a boyish body, but no, he's not my sweetheart. He's gay. You know... *bakla*. He's the ideal combination of male and female. He'd make a great father if I ever wanted to have a kid."

When she saw Tess pull her eyebrows up, Jesse added, "C'mon! Some things are universal. I'm sure there are a few men here that are bakla and have children. What about your sister's little boy, Tess? She calls him Rexanna instead of Rex because he likes to wear skirts and hang around the girls. And how about Cesar, the healer? Remember the night he dressed as a woman, and you asked me if I thought it was strange. I told you that I know a few men who look better in a dress than me." She took a breath, watching Tess's spontaneous smile signal her agreement.

"Alex and I have shared ten years' worth of life, loves, and apartments. He is a man who truly appreciates an intelligent woman. Doesn't mean our friendship isn't difficult, but he can make me laugh and doesn't flatter me with lies. I've also seen him be a real tough guy in a barroom brawl," she added. Knowing that this conversation was getting a bit risqué, she spoke faster. "Try to imagine a really *guapo* guy with a mane of streaked blonde hair to his waist. He is tossin' it from side to side as he flirts with a group of sailors in a bar. Next thing he's trading punches with the Fifth Fleet."

Jesse's mock one-two punch into the air sent the women into giggles.

"More stories," said Rosie as she clapped her hands.

"I've shared apartments with a succession of roommates and once with a boyfriend, but it's hard to maintain a romance—I get an assignment and just get up and go. Alex understands me, but most guys can't accept it."

The few times Jesse had tried to get close to someone, it hadn't worked out. Her last lover accused her of using her work as an excuse to leave him rather than commit to their relationship. The one before that implied that she was gay since she hung out with Alex and his friends, and wasn't interested in enjoying his advances. Even her mother would criticize the 'emptiness' in her life. "Pictures won't keep your bed warm," Jesse had heard her say so often that she now accepted the inevitability of sleeping alone. Still, there were times when she missed the warmth of a body lying next to hers.

Agunay waited until she caught Jesse's eye. "Why do you travel to such a remote place with no comforts?" she asked.

"Alex understands," said Jesse while reaching into her pack for his wrinkled letter.

She stumbled over the first words she read out loud, "*I admire... your generosity... especially when describing the sheer determination of the rebels and their belief that the land is worth dying for. I can only say, dear girl, that you've always had a soft spot for the underdog. Hopefully, your adventurous spirit won't land you in a headhunter's stewpot. Knowing you, you'd be telling jokes while the water's boiling and soon drinking rum and cokes with the village toughs, probably get engaged to the head chief's # 1 son, who's drop-dead handsome with rippling muscles just begging to be stroked, and wind up taking lots of award-winning pictures of the whole tribe. I worry about ambushes and torture, as well as ordinary dangers like scorpions and snakes, but I can picture you crawling through the mud to get your shots. I'm proud of you for sticking with a powerful story.*"

Jesse looked up and smiled at Tess. "I let him tease me because he understands how hard I've worked to take pictures that make a difference. That means everything to me." She recalled Nick Ut's searing photograph from the Vietnam War of a naked Cambodian girl running down the road after being napalmed, her arms outspread as if she had been crucified and related how the horror of war's effect on kids had undeniably shaped her destiny.

"In the '70s in America, the National Guard opened fire on students during an anti-war demonstration. A photo was published of a girl screaming in anguish, kneeling over the body of a murdered student. I could hear that cry of despair, as if the image was yelling... screaming at me." Jesse shook her head and exhaled deeply. The words flew faster as her fervor increased. "College students all over the country went out on strike. The photo had become a catalyst for action, and action was all that mattered." Jesse turned to face the women; her jaw clenched tight. "I had to do something, so I recorded what was happening around me. Even then, I understood the power of photography; that one single image could have the emotional force to move people. After all, what better way for an activist to speak?"

She looked at Tess, her eyes shining with a brilliance that seemed almost incandescent. They remained silently locked in each other's glance.

"Your *Ina*... did she help you?" Tess asked as she shifted her gaze to the charm on Jesse's necklace.

Jesse blinked and tried to shut out the image of her mother's care-worn expression. She answered "No," in a scarcely audible voice. "She believed in the American dream. Mom would've been happy if I had helped out at home, dated local boys, married, and given her grandchildren. But I just couldn't. So, I left." She pulled another cigarette from the pack. Dredging up these memories caused a nervous ache in her stomach. "I took a couple of semesters of photography courses at a city college and carried my camera everywhere there were social actions—demonstrations in Washington, hunger strikes, poor people's marches. At night," she continued, "I hung around some of the local dance clubs, taking pictures of musicians and portraits of the people who gravitated around the bars. I sold a few to the local papers. After one magazine published a black and white essay about teenage runaways living on the streets of Manhattan, my photos came to the attention of the Dispatch Agency. They got me more assignments. And here I am," she concluded, exhausted from the recitation of personal history. It was uncomfortable talking in this much detail about herself.

Jesse moved away from the beam of morning light coming through the opening—the brightness hurt her eyes—and turned to Rosie. "Tell me... what about you? Didn't you go to college?"

"I was one of the few girls in the village able to go away to school, but returned as soon as my teaching course was completed. I grew frightened and missed my friends and wanted to be with my own people. No one else understood me."

Tess began to gather the empty coffee cups. She stopped in front of Jesse. "I wanted to go on with my studies. Saint Williams College in Tabuk is only five hours away, but when the militarization started, it could have been across the ocean." She turned her head, looked out at the mountains, and said in a tight voice, "I've paid a high price because of this war. After my parents and Ruben were killed, I dedicated myself to helping the people in Tanduhan. Three years ago, a man asked me to marry him, but I refused. Marriage is giving only to one person. I had to do something more."

Jesse stared down at her tightly clenched hands. She had never looked back after leaving her family. Unlike these women, nothing binding held her here or anywhere else. She was an outsider and could always leave. Or could she? Jesse anxiously chewed on a frayed thumbnail.

How soon would she be face to face with Ka Noel and the elders, she wondered. It was impossible to sit still any longer.

"Come on," Jesse said and grabbed Tess's arm, "Let's go for a walk around the village."

# Chapter 5

## Excuses and Shame

"Americano. Americano," screamed Katya, Luis, Marie, Angelita, and Tomas in unison as they jumped directly in front of Jesse's camera lens. "Picture me, picture me," they chorused. Jesse dropped to her knees to photograph their smiling faces. It had taken a while to overlook the thread-bare tee-shirts; she had stopped hearing the deep coughs and seeing the runny noses.

Tess led Jesse through the village. Built in 1915, Tanduhan was nestled deep within the hand-carved rice terraces of the Cordillera. There were still a few of the original traditional houses like the one that Tess lived in, built on levels of packed dirt and surrounded by rocks that had been carried up from the Chico River. These historic structures were now dwarfed and sandwiched between the newer, concrete and wood two-story homes that were being constructed with additional multiple rooms. What remained of Kalinga's significant vernacular architecture seemed to be rapidly disappearing, noted Jesse. Elders squatted in small groups smoking tobacco, some sitting on the rocks and boulders that also marked the property lines.

They walked to a plateau of rice fields above the village. Looking through the coconut palms, they could just make out the women down below washing dishes at the water pump. For as far as she could see to the north and south was a curving pattern of emerald, jade, and silver-green; the rice and vegetables about to be harvested. To the west snaked the Chico River and the provincial road along which she had traveled. To the east lay Sleeping Beauty Mountain.

"For centuries, a harmony has existed between my people and the land," said Tess as they walked back to her village. "For the Kalinga, the land is our life." She squatted and picked up a handful of dirt, letting it run slowly through her fingers. "My ancestors carved the terraces with their hands. The bones and blood of everyone who breathed and died here are mixed in this soil."

Smoky rays of morning light wafted through the coconut and banana trees, and a fragrant breeze of burning cedar, fresh coffee, and spongy vegetation flowed over Jesse's skin and through her hair, like soft fingers caressing and calming her spirit.

They passed some elders going to work in the fields. Old men wearing G-strings with geometric designs tattooed on their chests and deformed, flattened toes splayed wide to grasp the rocks echoed a landscape filled with primordial traditions. Children and bare-breasted women washed in the river, while others walked back to the village balancing freshly scrubbed pots on their heads.

When Agunay saw them approach, she stopped sweeping the leaves that had fallen from the large narra tree in front of her house.

Jesse shot a few frames of film before walking over. "I have a black and white photograph of your mother laughing. Probably at something silly I did. She'd just finished chopping wood and she's carrying the bundle in her outstretched hands. The crosshatching tattooed on her arms follows perfectly along the contours of her muscles. And the design on her chest is like wearing an engraved necklace. What is the Kalinga word for beautiful?" she asked and then remembered, "*mamagkit?*"

"I don't think muscles look *mamagkit*," Agunay replied, pinching her own well-defined arms. "And no one here wants to get tattoos anymore. Not since the men stopped taking heads during tribal wars."

"Tattoos are a symbol of individual expression in America. They used to be considered a mark of rebellion, but now they've become an acceptable part of our pop culture. Call it suffering for style."

"Would you tattoo your arms like my mother?" asked Agunay.

"I wouldn't do a linear pattern up and down my whole arm. I'd keep my first one simple," Jesse admitted, "like a narrow band of leaves around my bicep. What do you think?"

Agunay rubbed her bare arms. "It would hurt too much."

Jesse thought about the numbers that had been unwillingly etched into her father's wrist and self-consciously rubbed her forearm.

"Let's go to my place and eat. I'm hungry," said Agunay as she picked up the empty pot.

Tess playfully poked at Agunay's stomach. "You're always hungry."

Before Agunay led the way up the bamboo ladder, she turned to Jesse. "It is our custom to feed anyone, neighbor or stranger, who happens to be in the village at mealtime."

"Is it true that if I eat in your house, your family must protect me, like I'm a sister?" asked Jesse, while placing her sneakers next to the flip-flops beside the door.

"This is a serious responsibility," Tess replied as she followed them inside. "If you left our place and someone killed you on the road, the entire tribe would be obligated to find your murderer and avenge your death with the same loyalty as if you were a member of our family."

"I appreciate how you watch each other's back. It must make you secure to know that someone will always be there to pick you up if you fall."

"But you must be very careful, Jesse, to never share the food of someone who is your enemy," added Agunay. "It is dangerous. Your belly will swell very big from the poison, and your body will turn blue."

"Blue?" Jesse repeated, shaking her head. She was still amazed by the superstitions heard around the village.

While Agunay and Tess prepared the rice, she slipped outside to relieve herself in the bushes. On the way back to the hut, she stopped to gaze across the mountains.

"It's time for the meeting," a soft voice said from behind her.

Jesse turned to face Abel. She looked directly into his dark almond-shaped eyes. "Do you think the commander believes me?" she asked, but Abel's youthful face did not betray his thoughts.

"*Hindi ko alam*—I don't know," Abel answered, without changing his expression, "but I think that he will listen."

She saw Tess anxiously watching her from the window opening and pointed to the rebel soldier. "Toss out my backpack," she called.

Abel led the way to the house of the village chief, *Ama Pu-yao*. The pangat's youngest daughter was squatting outside the door, and her eyes followed every move the foreigner made. Jesse counted the flip-flops and sneakers paired on the bamboo floor. "I did nothing wrong," she repeated one more time.

Jesse stepped through the low doorway and paused while her vision adjusted to the dim light filtering into the room. Then her eyes moved quickly, taking in everything. Three soldiers, Pu-yao, and nine elders sat in a circle on the floor. Along the wooden wall, she could see the shapes of long spears leaning next to machine guns and Ka Noel's profile against the blue sky, framed by the open window. She broke into a cold sweat. *Damn it, girl. Get a grip*, she told herself.

The men were conversing in Kalinga as she eased her way to the darkest corner and sat down. She watched Noel rubbing his hands across his mouth, half hiding his face.

She'd photographed that gesture the first time they were alone. He had been leaning casually against a reed fence, smoking a cigarette when she tried to nail him down with her questions. "Do you ever have doubts about your life as a revolutionary?" she'd asked.

While he was thinking, she photographed him—the hand covering his mouth, his eyes glistening slightly as he stared downwards. When he finally spoke, he looked directly into her eyes and candidly admitted that he'd been one of the first to make contact with the outlawed underground organizations.

"I was returning to the seminary when the military stopped me. They beat me on my head and ears until I was almost deaf. They hit me in the stomach and legs with sticks. Can you believe that no one ever hit me before? Never. Not even my parents," he confessed to her.

Jesse, who'd stopped counting the times she'd been whipped with her Dad's belt, was stirred by Ka Noel's childhood innocence and continued photographing as he spoke.

"I was put in solitary," he told her. "I have no idea how long I was there or how many times the guards tied me upside down and lowered me, headfirst into water. They gave me electric shock until I passed out. Later, I was put with other political detainees in an overcrowded cell. The toilets overflowed onto the floors where we slept, along with cockroaches as big as the rats. At night, each of us would describe our day and tell how we were tortured or just speak about our despair. If one of the boys was taken from the cell and did not return, I cried with worry until my stomach burned. It was only the thoughts of my friends and my family that kept me strong. Before they released me, I was warned to stay clear of the situation. I couldn't remain silent while my friends were prisoners. I vowed to continue fighting," he said. raising his fist, "until all Filipinos had their freedom. After this, the government called me an enemy of the state and put a P200,000 (*about $12,000*) price on my head."

Following him closely through the lens, she shot a portrait as he snapped his fingers. "Just like that, my life changed," he said. "They wanted me dead. Capture meant certain death. Or I could join the guerrillas. I had no desire to become a hero or martyr, but what was my choice?"

"In the long run, no one wins in war," she argued. "Show me how violence has made things better for the people."

"I didn't start this war," he replied, searching her face so intently that she felt impaled by his eyes. "If someone were to grab you on your streets, in your city... without any warning, if he attacked you. Would you fight back, Jesse?"

"Sure, I'd protect myself. But how can you deal with the guilt of killing?"

"Guilt?" he had answered, without a trace of remorse. "Better to look in your Bible where it says 'an eye for an eye.'"

"Jesse," Ka Noel called out loudly, bringing her focus into the present. "Explain to the elders why you've come back."

She shifted her stiffening legs, glanced at Pu-yao, then slowly towards the old men squatting across the room.

"Here," she said in a clear voice while reaching into her backpack, "are prints from the essay I was working on." She pulled out some black-and-white photos and placed the stack on the floor. When no one touched the pile, Jesse handed a few to Noel and passed around the others.

"That one's from the peace talks. From those 'secret' meetings you had with the military, "she said to him. "The next one I shot when we walked from village to village with your cadre." She didn't take her eyes off the guerrilla leader while her words were translated into Kalinga.

"I sent them to my agency for publication... just like we talked about. And I was getting ready for the trip to come up here again when Davidson, my agent, called with another assignment." Jesse reached for her cigarettes and lit one. "I had to photograph the sugar farmers for a German magazine, then interview Nur Misuari and the Muslim rebels." Her words started to flow faster. She checked them, although her voice sounded strained.

"I didn't know what to do. I had memorized the map you drew, but there is no way to get a quick message to you. Of course, I worried that you might not understand my absence." As her carefully rehearsed explanation faltered, she burst into a torrent of frenetic words. "But I never thought the ramifications would be this serious, Ka Noel. I'm so sorry. It was a coincidence. I had nothing to do with the attack. I would never tell the military how to find you. I didn't understand what had happened. How could I know that the military had strafed the camp?"

She leaned back stiffly and studied their faces for the slightest show of understanding. The silence was making her even more nervous. With sweating palms, she picked up her coffee and stared into the dark liquid.

Pu-yao whispered something to the rebel commander. "They want to understand your intentions. Journalists from all over the world contact our people. Some of those reporters believe in our struggle. Some of them make exorbitant promises—offer money and weapons."

He pointed to the photos in his lap. "You promised us help. You told me that your pictures would show what our situation was like." He gestured to Ka Sadek, who handed Jesse a ripped-out page from a magazine.

"It was purely coincidental, Ka Noel, that one of my photos of the rebels was published the same week the military operation occurred near your camp. There are no identifying landmarks to indicate a specific location in any of these pictures. You've gotta believe me. I would never betray you." She could hear Puy-ao talking to the elders and repeatedly heard her name as he glanced in her direction.

"You know I have no control over what the editors choose to publish," she added. "They pick the shots and write the captions. They decide whether to put portraits of the military next to ones of the rebels."

"By this time, we thought you would understand," replied the commander. "You have spent enough time in our place. You eat with us. You sleep in our huts."

"It's not fair to blame me for what I can't control." Jesse snapped with a grim-faced expression. There was an uneasy silence. "What about the innocent people who get caught in the cross-fire?"

"People here stand up for what they believe. There are no innocent people," he answered, concluding the discussion.

*Ama Pu-yao* cradled his antique spear in his arm. "Tribal loyalties are everything in our place. You must take sides," he told Jesse before following the others out the door.

Immersed in furious self-condemnation, she was oblivious to the exodus of the men. Had she mistakenly betrayed their trust to satisfy her personal ambitions? She glanced at the portraits on the bamboo floor. The tribal faces seemed to be taunting her.

Tears streamed down her face. Her bravado hadn't made a damn bit of difference. The pictures that once meant everything were nothing but worthless scraps of paper. Jesse began to rip them in half. How could she have imagined that her images would have the potential impact to change anything, let alone stop the military abuse.

Why did she think she had the power to make outsiders care about the survival of the tribes? Curses mingled with sobs as she repeatedly called herself "*a fuck-up and a failure.*" And worse still, she was filled with shame for taking pictures while people were suffering real tragedies. What about her accountability? Compelled by an insidious command that only she could hear, she began tearing her prints into shreds. *Perhaps you deserve to die,* she repeated over and over like a spiritually-driven mantra until her voice was hoarse and barely a dryly worn whisper.

# Chapter 6

## The Ambush

The wind whipped through the guyabano and mango trees, spraying gravel against the galvanized iron roof. Jesse awoke moments before Tess shook her and whispered, "Come quickly."

The luminous dial on her watch read 4:30. She pulled on her pants, sweatshirt, and groping her way to the door, climbed down the ladder. The moon had disappeared, leaving the dark night sky sparkling with an abundance of stars. She could hear people talking in muffled voices and tried hard to distinguish their identities.

"They want you to leave the village," said Tess, pointing toward two dark figures with M-16's. She instructed Agunay to bring Jesse's backpack and camera bag, then gripped Jesse's hand, holding her back from joining the group.

"Why? What's happening?" asked Jesse.

"Just go... don't ask questions."

When Abel took hold of one arm, she let him lead her towards the outskirts of the village. Exhaustion and defeat were all her mind could comprehend; yesterday's passionate defense now seemed as vacuous as her pictures.

The sky began to lighten as they walked. The only noise was the crunch of flip-flops on the stones, a slight whistle of the wind through the trees and the river current, racing past Tanduhan. In the prison of her isolation, Jesse glided effortlessly downwards; her body detached; her mind distracted.

The swaying bridge no longer seemed menacing, and she easily followed Abel and Sadek across. Noel waited on the far side—an M-16 slung across his shoulder, cartridge belts crisscrossed around his chest, one hand resting on the juncture where the bridge's knotted rope met the rock stanchion.

They started up the mountain trail. Mist filled shadows appeared lavender on Patucan Ridge as the rising sun dusted the canyon.

Suddenly, flashes of light and the piercing staccato of machine -gun fire ripped through the trees, tearing branches like spears in her direction. Abel roughly pushed Jesse down behind the bushes. He put his fingers to his lips and signaled her to silence. Noel gestured for the men to spread out. Another round of bullets whistled through the air. The gunfire was in front of her, blasting the rock on her left, sounding like a high-pitched jackhammer tearing up an asphalt street.

Jesse instinctively pulled a camera out of her bag, hoping she would pick the Leica body loaded with high-speed film. Let it be this one, she thought.

Abel crouched beside her, methodically firing his M-16 at the unseen enemy. While Jesse lay on her stomach and shot upwards with a wide-angle lens, spent hot cartridges flew out of his rifle, smashing the ground beside her. It was hard to focus; a thick gray smoke hung in the air after each burst. Oh no. *No. Oh God, what if I die here?* she asked herself. She willed the thought aside.

Incredibly, Jesse felt more aware of each extraordinary detail as the moments passed. She could see Sadek behind a bush to her right and reached into her bag for a longer lens. Jesse trained her telephoto on him. *Click. Advance the shutter. Click.* She talked herself through the process. *Okay, okay. Take a deep breath. That's right, girl. Hold your arm tightly to your hip. Don't shake. Focus carefully. This is important. Shoot. Focus.* Every second stretched out like a hundred. *Rewind. Not too quickly. Put it safely inside the bag. Okay done. That's good. Now put in another roll. Excellent.* She was in her own world, concentrating solely on taking the pictures.

When Sadek got hit, she kept shooting as his body jerked and fell backwards. A scream choked in her throat. She was shaking, and unconscious of the danger, inched into a kneeling position to get a clearer view. Whether it was her tears or her sweat flooding her eyes, it became hard to focus clearly.

"Get down," Abel yelled and threw himself in front while harshly pushing her to the ground. A hail of bullets clipped the top of the shrubs where her head had just been, leaving acrid smoke that burned her eyes and throat and turned her nostrils black. Jesse dropped her camera to the ground. Her body vibrated with each successive round of fire.

"Go," Abel yelled as he pointed to a bush ten yards away. Jesse stared at him as he looked directly into her eyes. "Keep your head down; I'll cover you."

Jesse slid behind the green branches a minute before the fusillade stopped. It was light now, and she followed Abel's lead, crawling on her belly to where Sadek was hit. A dark red stain bled through his shirt. Sadek was sucking in his breath with a rasp.

"I don't know first aid," Jesse said weakly as she ripped open his tattered, bloody jacket. Abel pulled off his own shirt and held it tightly against the wounded man's shoulder.

Then he looked at Jesse and muttered, "Not too bad," as he pushed the compress harder.

"Abel, what the hell's going on?"

Abel turned the bloody shirt around and pressed a cleaner piece firmly against Ka Sadek's wound.

"Last night we got a report that an army battalion was on its way towards Sagada to reinforce their PC unit," he said. "We thought they might plan to attack Tanduhan. Noel wanted you safely hidden at the camp." He peered into the foliage to see if any military still lingered nearby. "This must have been a smaller, advance group." His eyes continued to scan the area. "We had better take you back to the village. I can meet up with Noel later."

Abel helped Sadek stand. "Jesse, hold his rifle and this cartridge belt," he ordered.

The smell of gunpowder lingered in the tangled hair she pushed away from her forehead, strands matted with sweat and dirt mixed with the blood that had smeared on her hands. The skin on her arms and legs tingled like it had been smacked.

They cautiously made their way to the village. Jesse realized that her hearing had become exceptionally acute. It was as if the attack had shocked and altered her consciousness like a hallucinatory drug, separating each sound into distinctive notes. She felt light-headed, almost giddy, until she looked at her filthy shirt and pants covered with blood from Sadek's wound. She could taste the gunpowder on her tongue. *"Damn Davidson to hell. I've got the ambush pictures. He's gonna be thrilled."*

****

"It was a ten-minute firefight," said Abel, describing the details of the ambush to the villagers. Jesse still wore Sadek's cartridge belt and gripped his M-16. Her face was streaked with mud, her hair darkened from the dirt mixed with blood. Tess squatted down next to Sadek and began to bandage his shoulder.

Rosie took Jesse's arm, helped her up, and led her over to the water pump. "You look like one of us now," she said softly.

Jesse's hands clutched the weapon so tightly that she couldn't let go.

"Why don't you put down the rifle," Rosie told her while she was wiping the black soot off Jesse's nose with a wet cloth before they walked back to the crowd gathering around Abel and Sadek.

Abel was squatting, rocking back on his heels. "The military knows that we've stayed in your village. They might be deployed to look for us here." He stared up at Tess and *Ama Pu-yao*. With the help of two of the village boys, Sadek stood up. The two guerrilla soldiers headed for the back of the village and the path that led through the terraces.

"Beni, you go with Roberto to the Constabulary at Sagada and file a complaint of harassment," said Tess, taking charge of the group gathered outside her house.

"I want to go with them," volunteered Jesse. "They might be treated with more respect if a foreign journalist is present as a witness. Let me clean up quickly."

No. You must be here when they return with the military. Tess nodded her agreement. "Agunay, you go with her to the river. Then take Jesse to the schoolhouse and hide her on the second floor."

She turned to Jesse. "There is nothing to steal up there so they won't look, and you'll have a good view of the village from that height."

Jesse protested. She wanted to photograph the army as they entered.

"No more heroics today. It might be worse for us if they realize that you're here." She shooed away the chickens and pigs from the front of her house.

Still trembling, Jesse followed Agunay down to the river. She couldn't get the ambush out of her mind. Noel and his cadre could have died protecting her.

Jesse stripped off her dirty clothes and dove naked into the cold mountain water. As she swam, the powerful currents of the Chico River pulled her further from the shore. She turned on her back, floating between the cliffs until a raw energy that seemed to bounce off the ancient canyon walls surged through her body.

Through the schoolhouse's second-floor window, Jesse could see the military jeep arriving across the river in Poblacion and counted fifteen men from the 54th Infantry Battalion crossing the bridge, one at a time. Captain Raymond Hernandez went straight to Pu-yao's hut and demanded to see the *barangay* (village) captain. While some of the soldiers searched their houses, the villagers were ordered to assemble near the school. Hernandez made his way to the front of the group after his men surrounded the clan.

"There was an ambush on the Bontoc-Sagada road just before dawn," he barked loudly enough to gain each of the villager's attention. Then he reached into his pocket, pulling out a soft brown object.

"An ear from one of your rebel heroes." He held out the clump of flesh in his hand and raised it above his head, as if it were a trophy. "This is how we kill the communists," he threatened while pacing back and forth. "We chop them into small pieces and feed them to the dogs."

Agunay and Cecilia stood hand-in-hand. Tess was impassive, her eyes narrow and hard.

"We know there are rebel sympathizers in this village," Hernandez continued, "and even NPA." He grabbed Danny, Cecilia's 16-year-old brother, and twisted the boy's arm behind his back. The captain forced Danny down to his knees while pulling out his revolver and aiming it at the boy's head.

"No," Cecilia cried out. Three of the soldiers raised their M-16s as Pu-yao stepped forward. They took aim at the tribal chief. Two others set their sights on the boy.

"Tell your rebel friends to surrender, or we'll shell this area until every hiding place is destroyed. We will demolish your houses and ruin your fields. I can promise you the militarization will intensify," said the Captain. He moved towards Cecilia and, with a harsh laugh, stroked her face with the back of his hand.

"I'm gonna get that slimy bastard," Jesse muttered from the loft. She had snapped only four photos of the intimidation scene, afraid that each click of the shutter sounded like rocks exploding in a tin can. Before each frame, she'd held her breath, steadied her nervous hands on the telephoto lens, and prayed that the Captain's face would stay in focus.

Two armed soldiers guarded the villagers while Hernandez and his men entered the nearby huts. Jesse used her camera like binoculars and watched as one soldier caught a squawking chicken and put it under his arm. A boom in the distance shattered the silence. It made her skin crawl to see the Captain grin. Jesse turned her camera on Tess and caught the fury in her eyes, already editing how the image would look enlarged on a double-page magazine spread.

After the last of the military departed, Jesse came down from her perch. Families had returned to their homes to see what had been taken. Two children had spotted the bloody carcass of a caribou, blown apart by a hand grenade. She saw Gan-ao wailing next to Tess and pointing to her house.

"Her two long strands of amber and beads, worth more than twenty thousand pesos, were taken by the soldiers," Tess furiously told her.

Jesse stood mutely nearby, watching Tess comfort the older woman. She knew some antique stones came from the 16th century when Chinese traders had bartered with the Igorots, using the colored glass beads and amber for exchange. Their value was not just in money but represented a gift passed from woman to woman in Gan-ao's family.

Her camera hung like an impotent weapon around her neck. Instinctively she put it to her eye. No, she told herself, and reached instead for Gan-ao's hand. Later there would be time to photograph the ghosts.

# Chapter 7

## Special Friends

"Jonathan Davidson would lecture me to remain neutral. Be an objective witness. Just shoot the pictures. So would most of the journalists I know," said Jesse, jabbering nonstop about her ethics, personal beliefs, and sympathies to Beni and Roberto as they walked along the road. "But I can't keep sticking my cameras in people's faces without feeling part of their suffering. No one was killed this time, but where should I draw the line? One death? Two murders? The village hamletted or razed to the ground? No! Some lines are clearly drawn. I know there is a right and wrong, and I've got to take a side."

When they reached the Provincial Constabulary headquarters later in the afternoon, she demanded to see Colonel Feliciano. Jesse had previously interviewed the Colonel for a story about the Armed Forces of the Philippines.

Feliciano had expressed his support for the President's initiatives towards peace in the region under his control. The success of Aquino's plan was contingent upon the Armed Forces' ability to "win the hearts and minds" of the people. After the legendary military abuses that were suffered by the Filipinos during the Marcos dictatorship, it was necessary for the infantry to keep a low profile.

Jesse tried to remain seated on the hard wooden bench outside his office and wait for the Colonel to finish eating his *merienda* (snack). Unable to contain her impatience any longer, she burst into his office.

Colonel Feliciano stopped spreading the thick coco jam on his second helping of *pan de sal* (bread rolls) when he saw Jesse striding across the room.

"Colonel Feliciano..." she said and stuck her hand out to be shaken, "this morning, your men were sent into the village of Tanduhan. They harassed the civilians, using the excuse that they were looking for NPA."

She paused and noticed that the metal chair Feliciano sat on seemed dwarfed by the bulk of his stomach pressed against the desk. Although he was glaring at her, Jesse continued her speech in a confident voice. "Colonel, I've been staying in that place for the last two days and would have seen the rebels if they were there!"

The Colonel slowly wiped his mouth with a piece of cloth. His thick head of hair was turning gray, adding some measure of character to a soft, florid face. His smile seemed to be pasted on tightly. He motioned for Roberto and Beni to take a seat on the bench along the wall and pointed to the chair next to his desk for Jesse.

"Miss Beckerman. We know that Nicasio Juachon, or Ka Noel as he calls himself, has a cousin in Tanduhan. In fact, he uses the village as a base when he's in the area. We know that his unit was on the Bontoc-Sagada road last night. They attacked one of my units. Now don't insult me by saying you didn't see your rebel friends."

Jesse's expression didn't change.

"Do you realize that by lying, you are in complicity with them?"

Jesse stared at him contemptuously. "There were no rebels in that village. You'd better come up with proof, or I'll make sure that my story and photos wind up on an editor's desk at one of the big Sunday magazines. "HUMAN RIGHTS ABUSES IN THE CORDILLERA" will be the headline. With President Aquino's scheduled trip to address the United Nations coming up, I don't think she'd be too pleased."

Jesse turned her back on him and started walking slowly towards the door. "I remember a feature story last year about a certain General in Central America who was accused of human rights abuses. Made the cover of the *New York Times Magazine*."

She turned to Beni and Roberto. "Let's go. I think the Colonel wants to finish his snack," she said, not looking back for fear she might have pushed him too far.

As soon as they were a distance away from the military headquarters, Jesse gagged, put her head down, and threw up on the side of the road. Beni kneeled beside her.

"Don't worry," she said, "I'm queasy. I think that bastard believed me."

A salmon-colored sky framed the mountains in the west as they climbed the path towards Tanduhan. Danny had returned from the prison in Sagada, and a celebration was in progress when they entered the village. Ceramic jars of *basi*, the native wine, were brought out. Kerosene lamps illuminated the large area of the basketball court.

"Take off your jeans and put this on," Tess ordered when Jesse entered her hut. "My mother embroidered this tapis," she explained while draping and fastening the waist of the hand-woven skirt with a belt. Through the window, Jesse could see the large pots being set up over makeshift fires. She spied some teenagers chopping logs across the way, grabbed Tess, and climbed up the ladder to join them. They were joking when she heard a loud thud and saw the family dog being carried towards the burning logs.

"Isn't that Germane?" she asked Tess with a shudder.

"He was old and going to die soon. Why wait? Is it better that we throw out the carcass than use it for food, now, when we need it?" When she saw the disapproval in Jesse's expression, Tess added, "I nursed Germane when he was a puppy. I washed his wounds in alcohol and took care of him when he was sick. But he was ready to die," she said firmly. "You cannot be sentimental when people are hungry."

Jesse had eaten dog meat before, but as the smell of the burning fur reached her nostrils, she vowed this would be one meal she'd skip. She followed Tess to where *Ama Pu-yao* stood inside a circle of people. He was pouring drops of basi onto the ground and chanting the opening prayer. Tess took Jesse's hand and translated the Kalinga words:

*"We implore the guidance of the sky-world and invoke the anitos to witness.*

*The people of the Cordillera, from time immemorial, have lived in peace on their land.*

*The lands have given them sustenance and life, sheltered their*

*ancestors in deep slumbering, and provided them settlements where*

*community life flourishes. We must respect the land and make it productive.*

*It is our legacy from generation to generation; a continuity of our line and race."*

Roberto poured more wine into the glass, moved to the center of the circle ,and began chanting his *salidummay*:

*"Brothers and sisters of Kaigorotan.*

*Loved by Kaboniyan since long ago.*

*In the time of our ancestors the Spaniards came.*

*They saw the wealth of the land.*

*They used the book. The Bible and Christianity.*

*The spear and the headaxe were used by our fathers.*

*The Spaniards fled but others arrived to take our lands.*

*The Japanese came in '41. The Kalinga used their guns*

*and spears. Yamashita surrendered.*

*Later, the Americans and the government*

*decreed the mountains as public lands.*

*They prepared papers and contracts.*

*We were to rent our own land.*

*Kaigorotan. Pay for the forests, mines and rivers.*

*Pay for our land. How can one own the land?*

*The land is a gift.*

*Kaigorotan. Let us honor our ancestors.*

*By the flow of time in our homeland."*

*"Kaigorotan," chorused the crowd in unison.*

Abel, Roberto, and Danny picked up brass gongs and formed a circle. The boys leaned forward at the waist, hopping gracefully from foot to foot while striking wooden sticks against the gongs. The teenage girls, with arms spread shoulder height as if they were birds soaring through the sky, kicked their feet in a similar rhythm along an inner circle, gesturing and calling for Jesse and Tess to join them.

"Look. A Japanese souvenir from the war," said Tess, pointing out the human jawbone handle attached to Abel's gong.

"Jesse, come dance with us," yelled Danny.

Gan-ao handed Jesse a shawl and gently pushed her into the center of the widening circle. One of the elders, wearing a G-string and black rubber rain boots, moved into the center and danced little steps closer and closer to her as if he were flirting.

Jesse had watched the courtship dance before and draped the scarf over her shoulders. Just as they were about to meet, the man put out his hand, and just as she was about to grasp his hand, she danced away. She enjoyed the playful flirtation of the *sagsagni* (courtship dance) and, at the end, took one of the old man's hands, shaking it wildly.

She heard clapping, laughter. and felt a surge of affection from the chanting group. She felt safe and protected. There was no other place she would rather be than here. When she caught Noel watching her, she got chills on her neck. Her chest seemed unnaturally tight as she walked self-consciously towards the trees on the outskirts of the clearing. She didn't have to turn around to know he was following. When she stopped, his rapid breathing was right behind her, and she felt the top of her hair brushed lightly by his arms.

*"Para hindi ka makalimot.* So that you will not forget us," Noel whispered as he placed a necklace of braided rattan around her throat.

Jesse knew the handmade necklace was a symbolic present that the rebels gave to special friends. She turned, placed her hands on his shoulders, and kissed him gently. His body tensed at the contact. She kissed him again and acknowledged his smile as he took her hands to his mouth and brushed the knuckles with his lips. More than ten minutes passed before they returned to the crowd.

"Jesse, you're blooming," Tess said when she saw her face and noticed the braided necklace, hanging gracefully above the *anting-anting*. She glanced at Noel and back to Jesse. Mamagkit! Now you are beautiful," she said with a grin. "Come. Let's dance."

Jesse's body answered the percussive rhythms. No club in New York had ever seemed this wild or passionate. No drug had ever made her feel so graceful. The air seemed to envelop her in a magnetic energy. She could feel her heart dancing. The music pulsed from the earth to her feet with a joy that lifted her off the ground. Inspired, she improvised her steps and movement around the commander, twisting and flinging her arms like sheltering wings. They barely touched, but within their self-designed cosmos, she appeared like a fireball that was flooding her moon with light.

# Chapter 8

## Manila - December 1986

Jesse stared out the window of the air-conditioned bus. Graffiti painted on rusting metal walls and recycled cardboard used to make roofs were a glaring indication that they had entered metro-Manila. Squalid huts lined the avenues near the bus depot, a constant reminder of the widespread poverty in the capital city. On crowded streets, women fanned the flames of charcoal fires while Jesse imagined the whisper of wind through the pine trees.

It was a quick jeepney ride to the Associated Press Building, then into the elevator and down the hallways where clicking wire-copy machines and computer terminals heralded 20th-century technology. Jesse smiled at the staff and some freelancers she knew but didn't stop to talk when she picked up her messages. After shipping her film to New York, she hailed a taxi to Pinky Santos's house.

Six uniformed and heavily armed soldiers stood at attention guarding the front gate of the Santos house. It was a far cry from the rebel outposts in the mountains. When Pinky Santos had invited Jesse to stay at her home in Manila, she didn't realize that Pinky, like most unmarried Filipinos, still lived with her parents.

Call it fate or a lucky coincidence that Jesse had photographed a demonstration outside the Philippine Consulate in New York at the same time Pinky Santos was an official hostess for a handicrafts exhibition inside. After using the embassy's bathroom, Jesse had stopped to see the show. After Pinky introduced herself, Jesse had casually remarked that she'd like to visit the Philippines. That was all Pinky needed to hear before making a dinner-date in Chinatown.

Over a typical Filipino meal of barbecued spare ribs, noodles, and fried fish at a fancy restaurant, they talked about Corazon Aquino: The widow of the slain opposition leader, Benigno Aquino, had recently declared her candidacy for President.

Pinky referred to Corazon Aquino as *Tita* Cory. She also mentioned that her father was a General in the Filipino Armed Forces. Before they left the restaurant, Pinky had extended an invitation for Jesse to stay in Manila along with the promise of introductions to prominent friends and relatives.

The Santos house was one of many newly constructed mansions in the Corinthian Gardens, a private subdivision along Ortigas Avenue. Because of its proximity to Camp Aguinaldo and Camp Crame, the Corinthian Gardens complex was a favored site among officers of the Armed Forces of the Philippines. Those were the ones who had made enough money during the Marcos years to build massive homes fashioned expressly to upstage the older, elegant estates in the Makati district.

The taxi stopped at the guard booth and then was waved into the compound.

Jesus, the houseboy, opened the door and escorted Jesse into the garden, brightly lit with Christmas lanterns. On the table near the pool, she saw enough food to feed an entire Kalinga village. At the center of the buffet sat a roast pig with an apple in its mouth. Uniformed waiters circulated among the fancy dressed men and women offering cocktails and hors d'oeuvres.

"Jesse, it's about time! Where have you been? We were expecting you for the Christmas party last week," Pinky Santos trilled, rushing over to greet her and air-blowing kisses on both cheeks.

Pinky Santos was perfectly groomed—not a hair was out of place, and her make-up remained flawless, even in the muggy ninety-degree heat of Manila.

"I didn't have time to change. My clothes are dusty," Jesse stammered while looking at Pinky's satin sheath.

If Pinky was disturbed by Jesse's appearance, she didn't show it. She led Jesse to a group of her elegantly dressed friends—Doris Maranan, Marina Corpus, and Boy Ticzon—who were standing by the pool.

"Hey guys, look who's here! Jesse's just returned from the Cordillera," she told the group, "and I bet she saw her handsome rebel friends."

Doris looked with disdain at Jesse's jeans. "Do you think she's a communist?" she whispered to Marina.

Marina shook her head skeptically, "Oh no, I bet she's with the CIA," putting her hand over her mouth, "so be careful what you say in front of her."

Boy, who was heir to one of Manila's wealthiest family fortunes, was mystified why anyone would willingly endure hardships. "Kumusta? (How are you?) So how are the boys in the mountains?"

Jesse stared at Pinky's wealthy and obviously pampered friends and knew she could never tell them about the gunfire shattering the mist or Abel saving her life or the lie she told the Colonel to prove her loyalty. She certainly couldn't share her shameful feelings about the impotence of her work.

Jesse couldn't stop worrying about her deception, although she made a brave attempt to smile and listen to their gossip until Pinky pulled her towards the table where a tall, gray-haired man with an acne-scarred face stood deep in discussion with his friends.

"Dad, look. I'm so happy Jesse's here," she told him.

The General took hold of Jesse's extended hand. "*Hija* (daughter), what have you been up to?" He put an arm around her shoulder and turned her towards the man he had been talking to. "Don Silvero, this is Jesse Beckerman. She's a photographer for a famous American magazine and has been with the rebels up north. From what we hear, she's turning native. Living with the headhunters. *Alam mo*, she's seen more of the countryside than I have! Jesse, Don Silvero is a director on the board of Oro Consolidated Mines." Turning to Don Silvero, he laughed and said, "*Kaibigan niya ang mga kaaway mo*— your enemies are her friends."

"Can I see any of your photos in newspapers, Miss Beckerman?" asked Don Silvero with a patronizing tone.

"My photos from the peace negotiations were widely distributed. *The New York Times* reprinted a shot of Cory cementing the truce with the rebels."

The General nodded, but Don Silvero did not seem impressed. Though shorter than the General by six inches, his tightly compacted body, and ramrod straight posture contributed to the overall impression that he was a much larger man. Add to this imposing figure a loud baritone voice, and Jesse immediately got a handle on why Don Silvero Batungbakal was the center of attention in the room.

"Aren't you afraid? A young lady like you, going there with all those men? They could do anything to you," he intimated with a leering glance towards her breasts.

Jesse curbed her irritation and straightened her back. "I appreciate your concern, Don Silvero, but I've never had a problem in your country because I'm a woman. *Di ba* (right)? Look at your President. The Filipinos elected Cory Aquino to be the leader of her country. We haven't had a female President in the USA. It's true Cory comes from a wealthy political family, but I think her status indicates a measure of respect for women. And the fact that she's the wife of a martyred hero gives her some understanding of the dissidents."

"*Hija*, this may be true," the General responded, "but the NPA are criminals, and a pretty girl should understand the dangers of mixing herself up with these kinds of men. Just this afternoon, we received a report of a skirmish between our forces and the rebels near Sagada. Our military handled the situation," he smugly added, leaning closer to Jesse.

She wondered whether the General was hinting about the encounter she had witnessed. His words had shot like darts through his tightened lips. What if he was trying to trap her? She had better casually change the conversation. Later she could check out the information.

She chose her words carefully. "You know, Don Silvero, I traveled through many villages in the Cordillera. Everywhere I go, I heard a similar plea—the people want to be left alone to tend their fields. Besides..."

"How will they progress without our help?" Don Silvero interrupted. "Everything is so backward up there. And you journalists are not helping us. You think you understand the situation, Jesse, but you come from an industrialized country. You imagine all this bullshit about traditions is exotic."

As he droned on, Jesse wondered if Don Silvero really believed his elite assumptions. What if she could show him the value of the indigenous culture and traditions to Philippine history. Would that rock his world-view?

"And where do you think the United States would be if your ancestors had worried about the feelings of the American Indians?"

"*Tito*, leave Jesse alone. She must be starving and you're talking politics again."

Jesse was grateful for Pinky's interruption. She didn't have the energy or focus for a discussion contrasting the history of the Native Americans with the problems of the indigenous people of the Philippines.

Pinky led her over to the spread of food, and she spooned some *kare-kare, adobo*, and *pancit* (noodles) on her plate. Jesse had been very hungry when she arrived, but meeting the General and Don Silvero got her worrying about her friends in the north. She only picked at the Filipino dishes.

"I've heard that the Igorots still live in trees," said Marina as she made room for Pinky and Jesse at the table. "I've seen them in those funny costumes, dancing for the tourists in the park in Baguio."

"You know Baguio City was once an Igorot village," Jesse remarked, "before it became the favorite summer vacation resort for your families."

"We have a place right outside town," said Doris. "It's so hot in Manila during the summer months, so I stay in our house there. Jesse, do the Igorots really eat dogs?"

"What about headhunting?" questioned Boy, "Is it still being practiced?"

"Tell us more about the guerrillas," Marina interrupted.

Jesse didn't trust herself to sound objective and knew she had to be cautious, not only in her words but also in her tone of voice. By now Pinky's friends had probably guessed she was sympathetic to the rebel cause, but they had no clue as to the extent of her contacts. "Nothing much to tell," she said to cover her dilemma, and to change the topic added, "...I heard an interesting story about the origin of gold in the Cordillera." She glanced into the eyes of each of Pinky's friends to ensure their attention.

"There was an elder from the eastern mountains named Kabigat, who sent his adopted son, Bangan, to the west to look for his real father. The old man was frail when he found him, so Bangan carried him on his back towards home. Not far from the village, Otat died, and Bangan buried him on top of a hill. When he awoke the third day, he saw a tree with ochre leaves sprouting from his father's grave. The tree grew bigger and bigger until it bore huge oranges. Discovering they were made of gold, Bangan put as many as he could carry into his backpack and returned home to show Kabigat. The elder instructed Bangan that the oranges were a sign, and that he must take care of his father's grave so that the fields would prosper and be filled with golden grains of rice."

Jesse looked at Marina and added, "Many years passed. The story passed down from generation to generation was that Otat's body had turned to gold. And when the tree fell to the ground, its branches became the gold mines in the Cordillera."

Boy turned to Jesse and said, "So the miners are excavating Otat's body?"

"Yes. That's why some tribal people in Kalinga believe that only small amounts of gold should be taken from the ground," replied Jesse, "because the land will lose its strength. I suppose you could also see it as a rape of the Cordillera."

"*Ay naku* (oh no), you feminists. You turn every situation into the men's fault. How can you believe all those tales!" Boy remarked derisively.

"But gold stories are in the news again," added Doris. "*Talaga*. I just read a story about some American military guy in Manila. He's searching for the gold that was buried by the Japanese after the war."

Cutting her off, Boy interrupted curtly, "That's a lot of bullshit. So Jesse...how much longer do you think you'll be staying?"

"I don't know. I didn't intend to be here for this long, but you know Filipino hospitality. It makes it so hard to leave. Besides, I've heard so many rumors of a coup."

Pinky began to fidget and constantly looked at her watch.

"Pinky, what's eating you?" Marina asked. "I bet it's Tony Carandang, right? Stop worrying about him. He'll probably come late, as usual."

Pinky was embarrassed but made an effort to hide her concern. "I don't care anymore," she sighed.

Jesse watched her closely. Pinky was more affected by her boyfriend's absence than she showed. Among the tightly knit group, it was difficult to keep track of who was going out with whom. Although she had heard stories about Tony's philandering, she never repeated these to Pinky.

"Be back in a flash," she mumbled, trying to keep her thoughts about her recent experiences and the kiss from Noel in check.

She changed into her only pair of clean slacks and a pressed white shirt and returned to the party to look for Don Silvero. Her agency had requested photos of businessmen to accompany a magazine story on the Philippine economy. She weighed the possibilities. Not only would Don Silvero be a perfect subject, she realized, but she'd also have an opportunity to ask questions about mining in the Cordillera.

"Excuse me, sir," Jesse said, taking close hold of Don Silvero's arm. "I appreciate your earlier concern for my welfare."

"We Filipinos are known for our hospitality," he replied dryly. "Look at history, Miss Beckerman. We welcomed the presence of the

United States as our 'big brother.' And it was your government that gave us our independence."

Jesse didn't flinch at his barb or his formality. Instead, she turned and stared directly into his eyes. "You have an amazing country."

"It is indeed, Miss Beckerman. Perhaps you would understand the real problems if you spent more time talking to the business people who are trying to get the Philippines back on its feet."

"Don Silvero, thank you for the offer. I'd like you to help me set the record straight. I've got a story to do about the developing economic situation under Cory, and you could be the perfect subject for a feature story in the *New York Times*. Can I call your office next week to set up the appointment? I'd really look forward to our meeting," she said, noting carefully how eager he was to agree.

Later that night, exhausted from the intensity of the past week, Jesse welcomed the solitude of Pinky's guestroom. Two hours passed. She was still awake. She went into the bathroom and turned the gold-trimmed faucet handle as far as it would go. The popping sound of air came out of the pipes.

"Despite all their money, they still can't make the water flow in Manila," she muttered. Jesse opened a water-filled multi-gallon plastic pail nearby, dipped the floating *tabo* (dipper) into the cool water, and poured the cup over her head. When she returned to the bed, her mind wandered back to her dance with Ka Noel.

Jesse had no idea that at that moment, in the study downstairs, she was the focus of an intense conversation between Don Silvero and General Santos.

"Where did Pinky meet this American?" asked Silvero.

"Last Year. On her trip to New York. You know how my daughter thinks; that imported goods are more desirable than homemade."

"Have you investigated the woman's affiliations? How did she get involved with these people up north?"

Santos tried to reassure him. "Primo, from what I know, Jesse Beckerman's just another idealistic foreigner who doesn't understand what's going on in this country. Don't worry so much. I have my men watching her."

"You'll have to watch her more closely. I wouldn't be surprised if these bastards are using her. You know how they are. They love to hide behind the skirts of foreign journalists! She might cause us trouble."

"Primo, don't worry. I'll do something about it."

# Chapter 9

## Whose Viewpoint Matters?

Jesse had already gone through more than a dozen daily papers by the time Pinky came down for a late breakfast. The revelation about a military ambush in the Cordillera had her worried. She knew which particular papers to look at for alternative viewpoints. A single event could be reported ten different ways depending on who financially backed the paper. *THE MANILA TIMES* was the government's forum, and *MALAYA* was the paper of the left. *TEMPO* had the sensational stories and all the gossip about the movie stars that Filipinos loved to read.

Jesse scanned the headlines: MARCOS BENT ON COMING BACK. RAMOS CALLS ANTI-REBEL PLAN INEFFECTIVE. URBAN TERROR: NPAS PLANNING TO ATTACK METRO MANILA. She looked at the pictures, noting the credits of her photojournalist friends. By the time Pinky walked into the dining room, she had still not found any mention of an ambush.

Pinky called out to the maid. "Ansay, did anyone call?"

"No, ma'am."

"Shit," Pinky muttered.

"What's the matter?"

"Nothing. Tony never made it to the party. So, what are you doing today?"

"I have to run a few errands and call my agency. When I sent my film last night from the AP office, there was a note from my boss. Davidson wants me to shoot more photos of the Muslims in Mindanao."

"*Alam ko*, you just want to meet again with that handsome Muslim commander, Nur Misuari. I should write a sexy story about you and your rebels. *Ay naku!*"

"Pinky, all you think about is spicy romance," Jesse said, laughing. "I hope I haven't blown the assignment by staying in the mountains." She wished she could tell Pinky about the ambush. Describe the smell of gunfire and how time stopped when she saw Sadek get shot. She was used to being alone with her thoughts but suddenly desired a friend who she could open up to and share the complexity of feelings that had touched her soul. But it was out of the question. It would never be possible to discuss Noel the way Pinky talked about Tony. Instead, she inhaled and exhaled deeply and then flashed a smile. Jesse had long ago mastered the ability to shut down her emotions when necessary.

"Pinky. I need to set up some meetings with businessmen. What about Don Silvero? Tell me about him," she asked, maneuvering the conversation to another subject.

"*Tito* Silvero is President of the Oro Consolidated Mines in Baguio. Aside from being Dad's 'blackjack' partner, he does business with the military. I think he's having some trouble in the mines, and Dad's people help him. *Naku* (No) Jesse. I don't think he likes that you spend time with the rebels."

"Don Silvero did make that perfectly clear while we were chatting. But even you have friends who've joined the underground. What was the name of that former beauty queen...she was your classmate at UP?" She saw a shadow cross Pinky's face.

"C'mon Pinky. How can I ignore the insurgency or the problems in the countryside? When I'm doing a story about the farmers, and they're telling me how they lost their land during the Marcos years, I do understand their problems. How little money they make working for the *hacienderos* (plantation owners). How much money they need to feed their families. How the rebels have helped them in the struggle against repression. Cory's got a difficult job in the next few years. She has to bring the opposition to the table as well as steer the economy around. I'm interested in hearing any solutions."

"You're always so serious, Jesse."

Jesse took a bite of her buttered *pan de sal*. She looked at Pinky and then made an exaggerated gesture, fluttering her eyelashes. "Maybe Don Silvero would look forward to getting me alone in his office," she dramatically postured, accompanied by a teasing laugh.

"Oh, these men are all alike... young and old. But Jesse, don't play with *Tito* Silvero. You know how close-knit families are in the Philippines. My Dad wouldn't like it. Okay?"

"I'm joking. Don't worry. I'm only interested in his story as a successful businessman." Jesse glanced back at the newspapers on the table. "Besides, he's not my type. Listen to this Pinky," she said, reading the large headline: "SINGLAUB'S LOCAL OPERATIONS BARED—CONTRA ADVISOR MEETING OFFICIALS."

"So what? *Naku*, Jesse..."

"Don't you know who General John K. Singlaub is?" Jesse asked, speaking rapidly while waving the newspaper and her hands. "He's got a reputation for being rabidly anti-Communist. He's also admitted that he funded and gave arms to the Contras."

Pinky looked blankly at Jesse.

"Contras...Nicaragua?" Jesse repeated. Although the names didn't seem to affect Pinky's expression, she continued, "Singlaub funded the Contras after our Congress vetoed military aid to them."

"So, what has that to do with *Tito* Silvero?"

"I don't know. Let's see. I'll read it out loud. 'Singlaub is bidding for a sizable block of shares in a local mining firm, which has an extensive inventory of mining claims in the Cordillera.' It also says he's been in northern Luzon hunting for the fabled Yamashita treasure."

Jesse turned the pages, looking for the continuation of the article. "'Singlaub's traveling around the Philippines meeting with senior Government officials, businessmen, and politicians.' This treasure sounds like a pretty hokey cover to use while traveling into rebel-held areas in the north, Pinky."

"I don't know," she replied as she spooned some fried rice onto her plate.

"Look. Singlaub promotes counter-insurgency, maybe even sells arms, while telling the press that he's really looking for this treasure."

Pinky heard the word 'treasure' and put down her spoon. She turned to Jesse and raised her eyebrows as an expression of interest. "I heard *tsismis* about Yamashita's treasure when I was in school. There was a story about a Golden Buddha that was found by some guy in Baguio. Of course, it turned out to be a fake. If there really was gold hidden during the war, Jesse, by now Marcos found everything and has it hidden outside the country."

Jesse stood up from the table and slid the paper over to Pinky. "I'm going to the University library to do some research about mining and dig up some old clips about the war, Yamashita and the Golden Buddha. Maybe it'll give me a new angle when I talk to Don Silvero."

"Hoy, Jesse, don't tell me you believe all that crap?"

"I don't know. The only gold story I heard concerned mythical golden oranges. I don't know that I believe it and..."

"When are you going back up to the Cordillera?" Pinky interrupted her.

"Sometime in January, I think."

Impulsively, Pinky asked, "Can I come with you? I want to get away for a while. Maybe the time apart from Tony would show him what it's like to be without me!"

Jesse laughed. "Are you kidding? Your father would never let you go!"

"Who said Dad would know?" Pinky winked at Jesse. "No one will know. I'll tell him I'm visiting a friend in Baguio, and I won't tell anyone else." Pinky was getting excited. "*Sige na* (go ahead). I'll disappear for a few days without telling Tony. If he thinks I'll sit around waiting for him, he's got another thing coming."

Jesse remained apprehensive. After her last trip with Tess, she knew how difficult the traveling could be. "Do you really think this is a good idea? The bus ride and hike are very rough. There are no comforts."

"Sige na, Jesse. I really wanna go."

"Seriously Pinky. This is dangerous."

"I don't care. I just want to get away from Tony."

"What's the Tagalog word for playboy...*palikero*? Do you ever trust a man completely?" Jesse asked.

"I thought Tony would be different. In the end, they're all alike. I'm sick and tired of always having to be the one to wait. Let him wonder where I am! Let him worry," Pinky retorted. "Jesse, will I be safe there?"

"C'mon Pinky. No one can guarantee that. There are always risks. Last night your Dad mentioned military maneuvers in that region."

Pinky stared at her unblinking. "I don't care. Let Tony worry about me."

Jesse thought it over. She knew that most Filipinos from the Manila area were scared of going deep into the Cordillera, but Noel and Tess had told her how important 'exposure' trips could be. A visit to an indigenous village, sleeping on the bamboo floor inside a traditional nipa hut, and a walk through the rice terraces could help educate lowlanders about the ancestral history and current situation of the tribal people. She also knew that the guerrillas were extremely careful about showing themselves when 'guests' were in the area. Maybe this would be a good time for Pinky's 'exposure' trip.

"All right," she decided. "I'll take you. Anyway, it's about time that you get a firsthand look at the rice terraces. You've seen some of my photos. The mountain views are awesome. Just incredibly beautiful. You'll see Pinky... once we go a few hours north of Baguio, the Cordillera will take your mind off Tony."

# Chapter 10

## Pinky and The Bus Trip to Bontoc

Manila Airport was crowded with a melee of foreigners - missionaries, young adventurers, and tourists travelling to other islands, as well as Filipinos, either greeting or saying goodbye to their loved ones going home to the provinces. Pinky and Jesse were taking the afternoon flight to Baguio City the day before their scheduled trip to the Cordillera. Pinky had arranged for her driver to pick them up and escort them to the Santos's summer home in the mountains.

The next morning at six a.m., they made their way through the already crowded Dangwa bus station near the central market in Baguio. As she led the way to the ticket booth, Jesse was thinking how the sweet scent of ripe mangos and bananas permeated the cool mountain air, overshadowing the lingering ammonia odor of urine that flavored every bus terminal from New York to the Philippines.

"Go on and sit down in the first seat," she urged her friend as she handed over her backpack before purchasing tickets for their Kalinga destination. She laughed to herself that she, a foreigner, knew more than Pinky how to use Filipino buses and jeepneys to plan their route and final destination.

"One thing's for sure," she teased Pinky when she returned, "you won't disappear in a crowd with your fuchsia jeans and tee-shirt."

Climbing in and out of the old buses were people carrying packages and large cardboard boxes along with sacks of rice, baskets of vegetables, and squawking baby chickens.

"Did you see the tires?" joked Jesse. "Not at all like your Mercedes."

Pinky looked down at the seat, pulled out an embroidered linen handkerchief, and wiped off the dusty, frayed cushion. The euphoria of running away had dampened when she saw the run-down condition of the bus and the lower-class passengers.

The bus chugged its way up the hill, passing through La Trinidad, a small town on the outskirts of Baguio. Jesse smiled, relaxed, and settled in for the nine-hour journey. After the rotting garbage stench and open sewage in Manila, she happily sucked in the forest air as if to purify her nose, mouth, and lungs.

There was only one route from Baguio directly to Kalinga—the Halsema Highway—a narrow, one-lane dirt road. Buses coming from the other direction had to pull up tightly against the mountain to let their vehicle pass.

Pinky was reluctant to sit back and enjoy the ride. Everything made her edgy. She hated the smelly bus jammed with farmers and peasants returning home from the city. And the driver stopped every thirty minutes for the men to relieve themselves on the side of the road.

"What about me?" she asked Jesse the fourth time the bus jerked to a halt to let the men out.

"Let's look for a bush." When Pinky didn't move, Jesse added, "It's either a bush now, or wait two hours for a rest stop, Pinky. And then the bathroom's just a cubicle with a hole in the floor."

Women and children had surrounded the bus, selling chips, nuts, candies, vegetables, snacks, and fruit. After returning to their seats, Jesse reached out the windows and bought two cabbages for Tess and rice cakes wrapped in banana leaves along with a string of passion fruit for the trip.

Pinky made a face. "There's no way I'm eating that stuff," she said, pulling out a foil-wrapped bar of chocolate.

"*Balut, balut* (roadside food - duck egg with embryo)," vendors shouted at the bus when it reached the next barrio. After the men got out, a girl made her way through the crowded aisle with the balut eggs in a basket. Jesse bought one and offered Pinky a taste, holding it in front of her nose. "One of your national treasures," she said.

Pinky pushed the egg away with disgust. "Those baby ducks have already begun to develop."

"The first time I ate balut, Pinky, it made me queasy, I almost vomited. Now when I sip the liquid, it tastes like chicken soup. *Masarap* (delicious)." Jesse cracked the top half of the shell and drank the juice, then opened the accompanying packet of salt and sprinkled it on the egg.

Pinky stared miserably ahead. "How could you eat that unhatched bird and call it delicious? Can you see its beak? Does it have feathers?" She was not interested in food. She was occupied in replaying the events of the past weeks; the times Tony had stood her up.

He hadn't come to her father's party. The bastard hadn't even called. Pinky closed her eyes and imagined how much he was going to miss her when he realized she had disappeared. She'd show him. After all, she was used to having her way.

When everybody else was careful with expressing their thoughts, Pinky could always say what she wanted; her father was head of an Armed Forces unit. Growing up within this powerful family had also given her the ease and assurance that her position could be used to acquire anything.

When she was a child, and her father was just beginning to climb up the military ladder, the Santos family lived in a small bungalow at the camp. Her playmates were the children of the other military officers. As her father gained prominence because of his connections with Don Silvero, their lives changed drastically. The family moved to the house at Corinthian Gardens, and Pinky was sent to an exclusive school for the daughters of the wealthy. It was a calculated plan by her ambitious mother to ensure that Pinky would eventually marry into a well-known, wealthy family and legitimize their entrance into the upper-class society.

To her parents' consternation, Pinky did not turn out to be the wholesome girl prominent families would want for their son. When she first fell in love at 17, it was with Lieutenant Ramos, her father's assistant. The affair had been going on for six months before General Santos banished the soldier to Mindanao. Pinky quickly forgot about him in a one-month tour of European capitals.

When she returned from the trip, Pinky's head was filled with the romance of the paintings, and sculptures she had seen in Europe. She enrolled at the university and had an affair with her married, fifty-year-old painting teacher. After graduating, Pinky began to hang out in art galleries and fell in love with an up-and-coming performance artist. He also was a married man, and their affair, which lasted three years, was considered scandalous.

Her mother retreated into the spiritual world, avoided even her mahjong sessions, and spent her days in her private chapel next to her bedroom, saying novenas to various saints. Always, her plea was for Pinky to find someone to settle down with. "Oh God, just anyone who will keep her from mischief and scandal!" she prayed.

After Tony came into Pinky's life, her mother began to play mahjongg again and devoted only Wednesdays for her novena. Her dearest wish was for Tony Carandang to marry her daughter.

Pinky had met Tony at a party at the Polo Club. She had just broken up with the artist and decided that anything was better than sulking at home—even a boring reception for Senator Gonzales. She wore a strapless pink, raw silk gown from Pitoy Moreno's fall collection. It was short enough to reveal her slim legs and tight enough to leave no one guessing what was underneath. She had brushed her waist-length black hair until it had a lustrous shine, and tied it back with a simple gold clip.

A friend of her father's had stopped them in the hall as she walked in on her Dad's arm.

"General, your daughter is quite beautiful. *Saan ba nagmana 'yan*—where did she get her good looks?" Turning to Pinky, the white-haired man asked, "Why aren't you married yet? *Aba*, we have to find you a husband."

Although Pinky secretly envied her friends who were starting their families, she smiled coyly and replied, "*Tito*, I like being single. I don't need a boyfriend."

"*Aba, sayang nama. And ganda mo pa naman*. It's a pity because you are so pretty, the older man repeated in English before walking off with her father.

For more than an hour, she had flirted with the old men while their wives eyed her suspiciously. Just as she was getting ready to leave, Marina Corpus appeared, hanging on the arm of a distinguished-looking young man in a *barong Tagalog*, the traditional Filipino white dress shirt.

"Pinky, I want you to meet Tony Carandang. He's just back from the States. This is Pinky Santos, the only daughter of General Santos."

Pinky glanced at the man beside Marina. He was tall for a Filipino, almost six feet, and very dark. She felt a jolt in her stomach after staring into his deep brown eyes.

Marina was rattling on, "Tony has just been appointed Vice-President for Operations." And in a lowered tone, whispered to Pinky, "He's available. If I wasn't married, I'd go for him myself."

Tony's charm was immediately apparent. "I noticed you the minute I walked in the door," he said, "and asked Marina to introduce me."

"See. He already has a terrible crush on you," said Marina triumphantly.

Pinky laughed coyly, feeling secretly pleased with his flirting. "*Talaga*. You guys are all *boleros*—liars."

"I'll leave the two of you together. I have to go say hello to Doña Choleng. Tony, take care of her," said Marina as she disappeared into the party.

Pinky smiled. She was enjoying herself. "I'm surprised we haven't met before. You must have been in the U.S. for some time."

"I went to school there. Now I work for Don Silvero. And what are you doing at this boring party?"

"Mom hates these things, so I volunteered to go with Dad," she answered.

Tony looked around the room and said, "I've made my appearance. Let's go somewhere for a drink, or do you have to go home with your father, like a good little girl?"

"Are you kidding? Dad's probably starting a game of poker and getting drunk with his compadres. I'd love to go for a drink. In fact, I know a great place. Let me just tell Dad. I'll meet you at the door."

The crowd at the Gray Cafe was boisterous. The bar was managed by Gladys Katigbak, although it was rumored that the owner was a consul from the American Embassy. The regulars knew each other by face and name. Pinky waved to Gladys and headed for a table at the center. She saw some startled expressions as they passed among the casually dressed patrons; Tony looked out of place in his formal barong.

Conversation was almost impossible. Three video monitors simultaneously showed Peter Gabriel's hit, "Big Time." New wave music blasted from the speakers, and a few people were dancing in the small space between the stools and tables. Tony had moved closer to Pinky to hear her speak. Their knees touched, and before long, his hand was high on her thigh. Pinky flirted with him openly and playfully touched his hands and hair.

That evening when they returned to her home, Pinky marched Tony past the guards stationed at her gate.

"They're used to late-night visitors," she said. "My Dad plays poker all evening."

"Mr. Carandang has a meeting later tonight with the General," Pinky said to Jesus, who opened the front door. She knew that Jesus would not believe her, but it was best to show respectability.

"I think that you're the one used to having the late-night visitors," said Tony and pulled Pinky close to him, kissing her softly on her mouth.

"Let's go to my room," she said, leading him inside, then closed the door, turned on one soft pink light, and collapsed on her bed, giggling.

"Oh, don't look so serious. I'd love to have my own apartment, but you know how it is... girls must live with their folks until they marry."

Tony sauntered over to the bed, unbuttoned his shirt, and tossed it to the chair with the ease of a man who knows from experience that the lady would be his for the taking.

Pinky was leaning against the overstuffed batik pillows with half-closed eyes. She liked to be surprised by the moves of the men she was with. Tony had potential; he might make the perfect husband. Even her domineering father would approve. Not that she needed his approval. She had always defied him in the past.

She immediately liked the way Tony kissed her neck, not just in one place, but starting at the little space between her collarbone, under her chin, and pushing aside her hair, licked around her ear. When she rolled over onto her stomach, he unzipped her dress, putting one hand underneath her to pull it down to her waist. As Pinky slightly arched her back in response, his hand moved up her belly toward her chest and slipped inside her bra, making small circles with his fingers. His tongue moved up and down her back until she gave a small gasp. He slid his other hand under her stomach and down between her legs.

She could feel her nipples hardening, the moisture wetting her underpants, and his fingers deftly stimulating her excitement. When she couldn't stand it any longer, she rolled over onto her back, letting him slide her panties off. He ran his lips and tongue down the taut line of her inner thighs to her knees. Pinky opened her eyes to watch him undo his pants and smiled at the sight of Tony's lean body, towering above her. He stood still for a moment, knowing that she was admiring his physique. Her body continued to throb; as if the contact of his mouth and hands had electrified her bones. Tony lowered himself onto her body and entered in one swift movement.

She gasped as he thrust harder and pushed her legs so far apart that she thought they would be ripped from her hips. Pinky clawed at his back with one hand and used her razor-sharp nails to scratch a cut across his abdomen. Tony came so suddenly that his final scream was smothered against her chest.

After they made love one more time in her queen-sized bed, Pinky had started planning her wedding.

Now, she opened her eyes and looked at Jesse; she had to pee again. "Hey, is this bus gonna stop again or what?"

"Soon, Pinky. Very soon." Jesse replied.

Pinky closed her eyes and squeezed her knees together. Lately, Tony had begun to stay very late at his office. Then last week, she had noticed an item in *The Manila Register*. Chichi Gonzales, who had long been rumored to be Tony's childhood sweetheart, was visiting from Hong Kong.

The bus suddenly lurched to a stop. "Shit," Pinky said under her breath, "if that bastard was with her last night, I'm gonna kill him. He can't do this to me. I could ruin him!""

# Chapter 11

## The Cordillera

The driver shoved the stick into neutral and let the bus roll downhill to its final destination. Bontoc was as far north as most tourists would travel without a native guide. The less explored regions of Mountain Province, Abra, and Kalinga lay ahead for adventurous foreign backpackers. Lowland Filipinos rarely ventured into the heartland of the Cordillera. Before the vehicle crunched to a stop, the locals were climbing out. Men were heaving 50-pound sacks of rice, and women balanced baskets filled with bok choy and cabbages on their heads.

"This place is like a set from a Hollywood western," Jesse said to Pinky as they got off the bus. "The outpost where civilization ends and lawlessness begins. I could imagine the tumbleweeds rolling and a shootout between two cowboys along the dirt road."

"Don't talk about gunfights, okay?" She didn't share Jesse's fascination with frontier life and grimly wiped a layer of fine orange dust from her face.

Once the passengers had scattered out of sight, the weather-beaten storefronts on the town's one block seemed abandoned—shuttered against the dry wind that ripped through the surrounding valley. A black Fierra jeep, decoratively painted with red lizards across the doors, stood like a well-placed prop next to the ancient gas pump, rusting under the noontime sun.

Not far down the dusty road, between the bakery and a boarded-up building, was the cafe. Inside, the single electric bulb cast a dim light on the musty room. Jesse ordered two beers before she sat down next to Pinky at the wooden booth.

"This place gives me the creeps," Pinky admitted. She was sitting under a mounted dog's head. The glassy eyes stared directly at the crucifix on the opposite wall. "I'm thirsty, I'm tired, and I'm becoming depressed."

An old man with a weathered face and rough hands gave them both a sullen look before he placed down the bottles.

"*Naku.* How much longer do we have to wait, Jesse?"

"About a half hour before the Fierra leaves for Tanduhan. Come on, Pinky. Grab your beer. I want to show you Masferré's studio across the street."

A stooped-over, barefoot Igorot with hair wrapped in snake bones approached the two girls. She was wearing a Manila Hilton tee-shirt neatly tucked into her tapis. Opening a callused fist, she pointed with the other hand to a copy of the traditional gold hoop earrings.

"There's hardly any original traditional jewelry left here," Jesse said to Pinky as she pulled out three pesos for the toothless woman before pocketing the brass replica. "A German art collector in Baguio showed me a detailed map he had made of the Cordillera. He was methodically sending runners out to all the villages with small amounts of cash to buy any antique earrings and beads and whatever traditional crafts that the Igorots still possessed. His intention was to sell the items to museums across Europe."

"He was clever to take advantage of the situation," Pinky replied as Jesse steered her into Eduardo Masferré's historic studio-card shop. "*Talaga.* If he doesn't collect it, someone else will take the stuff."

Tacked to the studio's wall was a series of black and white photographs taken during the '40s and '50s in Cordillera barrios and villages. Jesse pointed to a print of a smiling bare-breasted Kalinga girl with five clay pots stacked high on her head, standing in front of a cogon-thatched hut. Chickens were pecking at the ground nearby.

"Tanduhan hasn't changed much since that photo was taken. That could very well be Cecilia right now, except Cecilia carries aluminum pots on her head."

After buying a few hand-printed postcards, they walked over to the jeep, climbed into the back, and placed themselves between two old men. Pinky put a hand against her outer thigh and used her fingers as a wedge between herself and the Igorot's worn-out pants. The young driver turned on his tape cassette and blasted a Kenny Rodgers song.

"I've been to a bar in Samuki, the barrio across the river," Jesse yelled over the music. "Every night, the Bontoc performers sing American country-western ballads. They seem to love those sentimental lyrics."

The air became thinner as the Fierra climbed higher up the road. Jesse pointed out the young rice shoots that had grown level with the terrace walls and how the terraces appeared to be carved into a mosaic of emerald carpets, like a huge curving jigsaw puzzle.

Pinky's interest in the terrain soon waned, and she pulled out her Walkman, put her headphones on, and closed her eyes.

Three hours later, they were dropped off at the outpost, a corrugated metal shack that marked the path down the mountain towards Tanduhan. At separate times, the hut had sheltered both the military soldiers and the rebels. With the song "Hotel California," still echoing in the distance, the jeep disappeared around a bend in the mountain road.

Jesse pointed east, across the river. "That's Patucan Ridge over there. It's called Sleeping Beauty Mountain by the Kalinga." She turned and pointed to the volcano in the west. "According to legends, the mountain and volcano were created during the great flood. Tess told me the story," she said as she helped Pinky put on her backpack. "I'll tell it as we walk." She started down the rock steps that led to the river.

"I'm right behind you," said Pinky, following close to her heels.

"A long time ago, there was a beautiful woman named Ta-u-ngay. Many men wanted to marry her. One day Suku-uk, a very handsome man from a distant tribe, arrived at her place, and they fell in love. As they prepared for their marriage, the sky became dark, accompanied by the crash of thunder, sharp tongues of lightning, and finally, heavy rain. In a few days, the place was covered in water, and the people had to run for their lives. The couple split up; Suku-uk went to the west and Ta-u-ngay to the east. When the rains subsided, Suku-uk was the only one alive among his companions. He waited for the floodwaters to go down and built a campfire, hoping that if other people were alive, they would see his smoke."

Jesse looked behind, saw Pinky's tense expression, and stopped walking. "Are you okay?" she asked.

Pinky leaned against a large boulder. "*Naku*. I'm not really interested in the story."

"I'm trying to take your mind off the hike, Pinky, so listen. When the water began to ebb, Suku-uk gathered wood to keep a fire constantly burning. That way, he could always find his way back. One day, as Suku-uk journeyed in search of his lover, a big cloud covered him, and he couldn't see the smoke from his fire. He became lost and never saw the face of the lady that was formed on the mountain ridge. This was where Ta-u-ngay had died. Kaboniyan, their God, had created the mountaintop in her image. The Kalinga named it 'Sleeping Beauty' as a remembrance of their love. Where Suku-uk built his campfire, Kaboniyan created smoke coming from underground. The Kalinga say that the slumbering east keeps on snoring, and the lively west continues to burn its volcanic smoke," Jesse concluded.

"*Naku*. Sometimes I think Tony and I are doomed lovers too."

"Give it a rest, Pinky. What do you think of the trip so far?"

"I'm just glad to be off that stinking bus and jeep."

"You surprise me. I thought there would be fear written all over your face."

"My face is so dirty you can't see the expression. Anyway, I'm too tired to be frightened."

"Pinky, look up. Do you see the profile of Ta-u-ngay?"

Pinky stared into the distance and started to smile at last. "*Naku*, it does look like a woman lying down. Amazing!"

"And check out the waterfall over there. Isn't it beautiful?" She pointed to a gushing stream of water pouring through the leafy vegetation on the mountain wall. "The light looks like diamonds dancing through the streams of water."

Suddenly, they were surprised by the giggles of childish laughter as Katya and Marie rushed up the path towards them. "Americano, Americano, picture, picture," they chimed in chorus. Katya grinned proudly and pointed to her new necklace.

"Good work," Jesse complimented the eight-year-old. "I brought a bag of tiny white, red and green plastic beads for the kids on my last visit," she told Pinky.

The girls led the way along a curving stone path between multi-leveled terraces. They walked past plots of gabi, bush beans, and *kamoteng kahoy* (cassava).

"You're very lucky that these kids are our guides. They're taking the quickest and easiest route into Tanduhan," said Jesse. She stopped to photograph a bushy weed growing by the side of the path. "I'm sure this is *borbortak*," she called out to Pinky. "Tess has been pointing out plant remedies. This bush is full of the natural iodine that women here need to take. You'll see how many of them have goiters in their necks."

After jumping over a waist-high reed fence, the group rested against the terrace's stone walls. Pinky reached down to pet a scrawny shorthaired mongrel that had rubbed against her legs.

"Watch out," Jesse admonished, "that dog might be cooked for our next meal." Pinky immediately pulled her hand off the pup's head. Jesse laughed. "Oh, that one's okay to pet; it's a female. Only the male pups are eaten. The girls are kept for breeding."

Tess was not in her house when they arrived, but Jesse knew they would be welcomed. When Iss-oc stopped by to grasp the foreigner's hands, Jesse introduced the grandmother to Pinky.

"This is my *lola* (grandmother) in the village. She reached into her backpack and gave Iss-oc the dried fish she had brought from the market in Baguio. Then Jesse acted out washing her face and arms. "*Manamos?*" she asked Iss-oc.

"Manamos," said Iss-oc, repeating the Kalinga word for washing.

The elder grinned at the girls as they took off their clothes and wrapped themselves in cotton batik *malongs*.

The waterfall was a ten-minute walk from the center of the village. Easing their bodies into the pool at the base of the falls, they settled in the waist-deep water until it was up to their necks. Katya and Marie jumped on and off the nearby rocks while Jesse serenely gazed at the verdant mountains. She closed her eyes and leaned back into the flow of water pouring down the rock. It was as if a magician's wand had conjured up a vision of paradise—children's laughter, flowing pools of crystal-clear water glittering in the afternoon light amidst brilliant pink bougainvillea, red hibiscus flowers, banana trees, and coconut palms.

"Someone's watching us over there!" yelled Pinky sharply. She dunked her head under the water to wash off the foamy shampoo.

"It's just the children," replied Jesse. When the bushes to the right of the falls rustled, she hoped it was children and not the older boys spying on their naked swim. "Most of the older women don't wear shirts; they're relaxed about their bodies."

"Yeah. But here I'm not," Pinky said warily. "*Naku*, I think it's time to go." She pulled herself out of the water and onto the rocks to dry off and brush her hair.

As they walked back, Jesse stopped near an empty hut. She pointed out the flat stone grave marker and the many bullet holes in the scarred wooden door. "That's where the tribal chief, Macli-ing Dulag, was murdered by soldiers six years ago. Killing their pangat was one of the major incidents that set the tribes against the government."

Two young women sat on the ground beside the stone; one had a baby asleep in a sling on her back and picked lice out of the woman's hair seated in front of her.

"Will the people know that my father is a General?" Pinky asked with a sudden fearfulness in her voice.

"Tess knows that I stay at your house in Manila. I think she might be curious about your family."

"Why didn't you tell me that before?"

Jesse put her hand on her hips and squinted at Pinky. She understood Pinky's insecurity, and remembered her own reaction after being grilled about American foreign policy by farmers in the provinces. The U.S. government had backed Marcos during his martial law years and trained Filipino military personnel in counter-insurgency strategies. Strategic hamletting, a program developed by the Americans in Vietnam, had been adapted in the provinces. Thousands of peasants from Mindanao to the Cordillera had been driven away from their homes and resettled in refugee camps. The rationale was to deprive the NPA of its mass base, but some people thought it was also used in areas where the government had development interests. Strategic hamlets had been set up in Abra where the Tinggians opposed the government's pulp and paper processing venture, run by the Cellophil Resources Corporation.

Perhaps more compassionate decisions would be made if elected officials had to answer directly to the people whose lives were drastically affected by their policies, Jesse thought. She hoped that if Pinky developed an insight into the problems confronting the tribes, she might relay these observations to her father.

Jesse measured out her words with care. "There are some serious issues at stake, Pinky. You should listen to what the people here are saying about their situation."

"But my father is serving the best interests of the people."

"Really? You explain that if you're asked," Jesse snapped, "but first look around you. These forests have been home to the Igorots for thousands of years. Now the mountains have been stripped naked by the lumber companies, and the mud running down them dams the rivers. The rising waters flood their ancestors' burial grounds, and they say that the spirits cry out from their graves. If that's not enough, the people are forced off their land by government decrees or military offensives. Don't you think they have the right to defend themselves?"

"Jesse, stop! People will call you a communist!"

"They can call me anything they like. I thought if you saw the way it really is, you would... damn it, Pinky. This is your country, and this place is your heritage too."

Jesse abruptly stopped preaching when she saw how the words had stung her friend. While she was attending demonstrations in the early 70s, Pinky and her friends were protected within convent walls where acts of social conscience were equated with giving canned goods to the poor each Christmas. Pinky's comfortable world was eons away from this place. So was her sense of culpability.

"Sometimes I get carried away by my passion," Jesse apologized while taking hold of her arm. "C'mon. One of these days, I'm sure you'll find your own way of helping out the people here. Maybe you should send some books for the kids to read. Meanwhile, you're here to meet my friends. Try to relax and enjoy the scenery."

# Chapter 12

## Gold and Greed in the Cordillera

"I don't know how you sleep comfortably on this bamboo floor. Why didn't you tell me there wouldn't be pillows? I always use two soft ones at home," Pinky whined to Jesse after breakfast the next morning.

"Maybe we should've lugged in a feather bed for the Princess as well," Jesse teased. "C'mon Pinky. My body always aches after the first night, but you'll get used to it," she promised. "I'm going on a hike with Tess, and it might be too strenuous for you this morning. You should stay here and rest." Jesse grabbed her camera bag and tape recorder. "Try to get some more sleep, and later, when you're not so grouchy, Rosie, Agunay, or some of the teenage girls can escort you around the village."

She didn't tell Pinky that Tess had offered to introduce her to 'a special person' if she'd come alone. Although her curiosity was piqued as they walked away from the village, she took her cue from Tess's silence and didn't ask any questions about their rendezvous.

They had been hiking for more than forty minutes when she heard the sound of a high-pitched flute. Jesse cocked her head, straining to hear the short, hollow notes, then followed her companion towards the music. A teenage girl was seated in a clearing, pressing a two-foot-long piece of bamboo to her nostril. Jesse crouched down to photograph the musician's hands as she rhythmically fingered the holes in her instrument. The resonant sounds seem to linger in the leaves and bushes as Jesse headed after Tess, who had disappeared into a nearby hut.

Inside, a woman was sitting on the floor in the corner, twisting the dials of a radio transmitter. This has to be a guerrilla outpost, was Jesse's first thought.

When the woman turned around to greet them, Jesse was surprised to see by her loose pants and large stomach that she was going to have a baby. "Ka Norma," said Tess, "is a commander with our underground forces."

Jesse had met a few females in the rebel forces, but Norma, with her long braids, child-like face, and white cotton apron bordered in a design of tiny pink roses, seemed hardly the image of an amazon warrior.

"The guerrilla existence is hard enough—hiding and moving every night from place to place," she said after introductions. "You're what... about eight or nine months pregnant, Norma? Isn't your life difficult?"

Norma patted her stomach and leaned back against the wall. "For seven years now, I've had no other choice," she said shyly.

Jesse set her tape recorder on the floor between them and adjusted the microphone. "When did you join the underground, the NPA?"

Norma glanced at Tess for encouragement as she tentatively began to speak. "In 1976, I was a nursing student. That's when I fell in love with Victor." She put one hand over her face to hide the blush. "We had ordinary dreams—to get married, buy a small house, and have a family. The first baby came the next year.

Meanwhile, the military started arresting people; one of our friends was taken to jail. Another was beaten with sticks so hard on his head that he lost his vision. Another was tortured; they pulled out the nails from his fingers. I heard about it later. I heard that they used electric shocks."

"To his genitals," Tess added in a bitter tone.

"All this was going on and can you imagine, I still didn't want to see how dangerous the situation had become. Victor wanted to protect me. He never told me he was meeting with people in the movement. When the military came to our home looking for him, I was the one who was surprised." Self-consciously Norma untied one of her braids and then redid it.

"You had no idea?" asked Jesse.

"He never told me. Victor narrowly escaped; he jumped out the back window of our house and went into hiding. I heard from friends that he had gone underground. I missed him so much. Later, it was arranged for me to go into the guerrilla zone."

Norma reached over to a book, pulled out a faded black and white photo, and handed it to Jesse. In the picture, she was dressed in camouflage fatigues with her hair in pigtails. Cradled in her arms was an M-16 rifle. Standing next to her was a good-looking man with an M-16 in his arms.

"I joined my husband. There were times when I cried because the training was so hard—carrying packs, arms, and boots up and down the mountains."

Jesse looked at Tess. "I know what you mean. But what about your baby?"

"This is the most difficult part... the intense loneliness; the long periods of separation from my children. They live with my parents. It's too dangerous to keep them with us."

"You had another child?"

"In 1984. A girl." She picked up a faded photo and touched it to her chest. "Victor didn't see our boy for six years. Eight months ago, I visited with my children for a week. Our nine-year-old knows his father only from photos," she said softly.

Jesse pulled out her camera and shot Norma looking down at the picture.

"I was captured once and escaped. I've been shot by the military," Norma said while pushing up her sleeves and showing Jesse the long scars that ran down the length of both arms. "Many of my friends were killed in ambushes." Norma pointed to the M-16 nearby. "Guns have become my second husband." She rolled up one trouser leg. "See, here is where the military cut me with their knives." She stood up and walked over to the large window.

Jesse followed with her camera and photographed Norma's bulky profile, shadowed against the wooden frame as she stared out at the distant mountains. "Norma, how do you deal with the guilt of killing someone?"

Norma shook her head. "Picking up a gun doesn't necessarily make you tough." She turned to face Jesse. "To shoot... the enemy cannot be seen as human. You have to turn off all your feelings. I've asked God so many times... why? Why me?" She patted her enlarged belly. "I'm a mother, and it's terrible not to be with my children. I love them. I want to see them grow up. I want them to be strong and have a future. I don't want them to feel this fear that I live with every day." A thin river of tears flowed down Norma's cheeks. She brushed them away with her hand. "I don't want to die."

Tess gestured that it was time to leave. As soon as they were outside, Jesse cursed loudly. "Goddamn, Tess. So many of your people tell me these brutal stories in such a matter-of-fact way. Life here is just not fair."

Tess stood silent, lost in her own thoughts as the sun began its descent like a fireball behind the mountains.

"Perhaps there is something you can do for us," she said a few moments later. "Your friend, Pinky... her father is in business with the director of Oro Mines. Don Silvero has let it be known that he'd like to have a meeting with one of the rebel leaders."

"You must be kidding. Don Silvero?"

"He says that he wants to discuss Aquino's plan to resolve the economic problems. And then there is the issue of autonomy for our indigenous people. Can you meet with this man, Don Silvero, and give us your analysis of his intentions? It would be helpful."

Jesse looked at her with astonishment. She was surprised by the request. It didn't seem likely that Don Silvero would hike into these mountains. Was this another test of her loyalty? Did Tess already know she was meeting with Don Silvero next week? She never figured she'd be used as a go-between. But if she could help out, why not?

"I'll see what I can find out," she promised Tess.

****

Later that afternoon, Pinky and Jesse watched Tess through the window as she pounded rice, sifting the grain by throwing it up in the air and catching it on a bamboo tray. The chickens pecked the ground to catch the chaff.

"I can't believe how poor the people are here," Pinky remarked. "And the kids... I don't think they've ever seen a dentist. Maybe I'll send them some toothpaste when I get home, although most of the older people don't have any teeth. I didn't want Agunay or Rosie to see how upset I was by the dirty children with their infected cuts and scabs. They could use a little soap as well. What do you think?"

"First of all, Pinky, the problem is, even if they could afford to see a dentist once, there's no money for follow up visits. It's easier just to yank the tooth when it hurts. Sure, you could send toothpaste, but why don't you organize some dentists and doctors in Manila to come up here and volunteer their services."

"It's time soon to eat," interrupted Tess as she walked inside with the cleaned rice and poured it into the pot to cook. She took some wood kindling branches from the floor and lit the fire, blowing into it to get the flames smoking. Jesse went next door to Rosie's *sari-sari* store to buy a few cans of sardines to add to the dinner. Tess passed around a basin filled with water so they could wash their hands before placing the food on the floor and sitting down cross-legged beside Pinky.

"There are some guys in this village that are very *guapo*, that's for sure," Pinky said between bites of rice, sardines in tomato sauce, and sautéed watercress. "Rosie introduced me to a few young men on our walk today. I think she wants to marry me off. I'm going to make my boyfriend jealous when I tell him that everything native is good," she boasted to Tess.

"Will you tell your father that as well?" Tess remarked as she got up from the floor to clear away the plates.

Pinky glanced at Jesse for support.

"I'm sure she'll have some stories to tell the General," Jesse commented curtly and looked hard at Tess. "Now, what about tonight?" she said in a softer tone. "Why don't I get some rum and coke, and we can visit with your friends?"

Pinky handed her an empty dish. "I love to party."

As they walked through the village in the darkness, the lights from small red fires dotted the path, and shrill sounds of cicadas pierced the night air. Tess stopped to talk to a few women squatting around a burning log, holding babies on their laps or tightly to their breasts. One woman spoke rapidly in Kalinga, touched her own nose, and pointed to Jesse while the others laughed.

"They want to know how, with a nose that big, you can kiss a man," Tess said. Jesse responded by pushing her nose up in the air with her thumb, bringing on more peals of laughter.

After they arrived at Isabel's hut, Tess repeated the story while Pinky poured the rum into cups. The women giggled every time the word 'nose' was mentioned.

"My nose is considered small if you judge it by American standards," Jesse protested.

Gan-ao and Iss-oc joined the party. The older women sat on the floor, smoking hand-rolled cigars of homegrown tobacco. Iss-oc pulled out her tobacco pouch and rolled one for Jesse. She handed her a burning stick from the cooking fire to light it.

Isabel translated as Iss-oc teased Jesse and described how funny she looked slipping and sliding down the village paths. "Iss-oc says that the women hold their hearts when they see you coming up the stone steps."

While Pinky refilled the drinks with a convent-bred poise, pouring rum into her own glass without the cola, Jesse stood up and acted out her tightrope walk along the narrow paths between the terraces. As a finale, she dramatically fell to the floor. After the laughing stopped, she turned to Gan-ao and said, "Tell us a story about what Tanduhan was like when you were a child."

Gan-ao looked only at Tess as she spoke, and paused every few sentences for her to translate.

"When I was young, Tanduhan was a much smaller village," repeated Tess. "There were many tribal wars. It was not much different except then, heads were taken when peace-pacts were broken between the tribes." Gan-ao pointed to the crosshatched drawings on her arms.

"Tattoos were a sign of great prestige to the warriors. During one of the tribal wars, her father took the head of his enemy from Tulgao and Gan-ao got her markings," Tess said and added, "The last time a head was taken when the Japanese came here."

Jesse's eyes widened. "Did the Japanese army stay in Tanduhan? What happened during their occupation?"

"Gan-ao is ashamed to use her English," said Tess, "but like many of the elders, she can understand more than she'll speak. She learned it during the war. There were schools in all the provinces run by the Catholic, Episcopal, and Evangelical missionaries. My father said their American teachers punished the boys if they spoke to each other in Kalinga. He still remembers..."

Gan-ao interrupted Tess and pointed repeatedly at Jesse.

"She is complaining that the U.S. Army still owes her money," said Tess. "When the American camp was surrounded by Japanese soldiers, the Kalinga women and children carried food, water, and supplies to the soldiers through the mountain paths. Gan-ao was paid one and a half pesos for as many as three trips a day."

Jos-we, Gan-ao's husband, entered the house while his wife was speaking and poured himself a glass of rum. He was dressed in a G-string and ripped gray woolen sweater that sagged so deeply from the V-neck that it barely covered the ink-blue crisscross tattoos on his chest. He gestured widely towards Jesse with his clay pipe while talking rapidly in Kalinga to Tess.

"Jos-we wants to tell you a story about the war," explained Tess. "He was about twelve years old when he volunteered to be a runner, carrying messages hidden in poles and bamboo pots from village to village. He guided the foreign soldiers and *hukbalahaps*, the Filipino guerrillas, through the mountains. After the Japanese occupied Lubuagan, my mother, *Tito* Nestor - my mother's brother, and Jos-we brought food to an American soldier who was hiding near the village. Jos-we can tell you in English."

"Were there many soldiers hiding in this area?" asked Jesse.

"Many soldiers passed through these mountains," the old man answered. "There was Colonel Moses, the commander of all the guerrilla units in the north and Mister Joseph. Mister Joseph had skin the color of charcoal and hair like the Agays on his head and face." Jos-we rubbed the still smooth skin on his own chin and looked to Tess to continue the story as if it were her own.

"When Mister Joseph arrived in Tanduhan, he asked for recruits to join the 11th Infantry and collaborate with the American and Filipino forces. The Japanese army had already occupied Bontoc, and Jos-we and Nestor joined as scouts. The Kalinga guerrillas were armed with Springfield's, shotguns, and bolos. They won their first encounter with the enemy, but the Japanese used another route, attacking the region from Abra, and occupied Lubuagan, Tabuk, and Balbalan. Later, one of the Kalinga boys arrived back in the village; he was nearly dead from hunger. He had been captured by the Japanese and escaped as they marched through the Bataan peninsula."

Jos-we interrupted Tess, "My friend... he saw the horrors of the Japanese invasion. He reported how the captured Filipinos and Americans were not given food or water and how they were beaten and murdered along the way. He saw women and children killed if they tried to drink water from the streams. He saw them stabbed with the bayonet if they stepped out of line. Along the way, he saw hundreds of bodies of men, women, and children." Jos-we gestured with a cut mark towards his neck. "He told us if we did not give the Japanese soldiers everything they demanded—our rice, pigs, and chickens—we would be killed. All night the warriors made themselves ready for fighting. We beat gongs, and when the sun appeared, we vowed to find the enemy, cut off their heads, and display them so everyone could see."

Jos-we took a long gulp of his rum. "For many months, Mr.

Joseph, Nestor and I would crisscross the northern provinces of Bontoc, Ifugao, and Kalinga, but sometimes Mister Joseph would go alone. After one of these secret missions, we found him on the road. He was almost dead. Nestor carried him to a cave to hide him from the Japanese. For more than five days, we heard the American planes drop their bombs. During the day, we could not go in or out of the village or on the road. It never stopped raining. Many people in the village were sick with malaria." Jos-we continued in a softer voice.

"In many places, the roads were covered with rocks and dirt. It was dangerous to go to the fields. Finally, we had to eat, and when the men went to work the *kiangan,* the vegetable field, across the ridge," he said, pointing north, "the Japanese soldiers surrounded them and took my *Tito* away. I went with Nestor to their camp to look for him. There was mud this deep," Jos-we said, pointing to his knees. "Because of the rain, many of their soldiers were sick with malaria. When we saw them packing up their supplies, we ran back to tell Mr. Joseph.

"After three months of hiding, his cave had become more a prison cell than a shelter," he continued. "Mr. Joseph was crouched in the darkness when we squatted down beside him and spread the pine chips for warmth. Then I heard shots and told the American to listen to the Japanese guns and described to him what was happening.

"I looked out from behind a slit in the cave wall and watched my family being force-marched into the jungle. They were walking in single file along the terraces; the smallest children in blankets were slung tightly across their backs. The retreating Japanese were armed with bayonets and rifles and set the pace, stopping only to set fire to the rice fields surrounding the village.

"Mr. Joseph wanted to know more about what we saw outside. But could we explain to our friend how the God of Wind carried the frightening wail of the spirits who lived in the burning trees? That the twins, *Kilat* and *Kidor,* were offended. That the poison clouds hurt their eyes, and *Kilat,* the God of Lightning, streaked the sky with light while *Kidor,* the God of Thunder, shouted with anger."

"So, what did you tell him?" asked Jesse impatiently.

He looked at Pinky and held out his empty glass. Pinky moved around the room, adding a little rum to each glass.

"The Japanese troops were running this and that way like crazy men putting supplies in jeeps. And there was something more. Something... *nakakagulat*."

"Something strange," translated Tess.

"*Apo!* It was not so big," Jos-we used his spread-out hands like a ruler to indicate the size, "still two men had to carry it. They tried to load it on the jeep, but they fell in the mud. Then the blanket opened, and I saw a statue... a golden statue."

Jos-we stopped talking, drank his rum, and gestured for Pinky to pour more into his cup. As Pinky refilled it, she looked at Jesse and shook her head, rolling her eyes in disbelief.

"Mr. Joseph told us about the gold and jewels the Japanese had stolen from the treasuries and temples of the occupied countries. His radio had tracked the Japanese army as they swept victoriously across East Asia and reported General Yamashita's arrival in the Philippines with the treasure."

"You believe he really brought his loot here?" asked Jesse, her attention sharply focused.

"Even my father told stories about this General Yamashita," added Tess. "He said that the Japanese were carrying a fortune with them. Beyond what we could ever imagine. His men took every last thing they could carry from those places they captured."

"Mr. Joseph said they took many gold statues with them," interrupted Jos-we, glancing at Jesse before he continued.

"When the General got to Manila, the tide of the war turned against him. Before all this treasure could be shipped off to Japan, the Americans started bombing Manila Bay." He paused to spit on the ground. "We heard stories that the Japanese attacked one of their own ships carrying gold bars across to Tokyo. To sink it and find the gold later."

"My mother told me that she heard that once Yamashita knew

General MacArthur had taken control of Leyte, that he was heading for Luzon," said Tess speaking faster as her voice rose with story's excitement. "And after the Americans took back the Philippines, the Americans were going to invade Japan. Yamashita had a plan to delay the attack."

"And he had to move fast," added Jos-we, "the American bombings were cutting off his supplies. Cutting off his food and his ammunition. By the end of December, this 'Tiger of Malay' took his troops out of Manila and headed north carrying..."

"... the gold," said Jesse, completing his sentence.

"They made their base camp in Baguio City," continued Jos-we. "By and by, Yamashita's troops were starving. He headed them towards the rice fields of the Cagayen valley. Yamashita thought the steep mountains in Ifugao would protect his men from the American bombs."

"But the Ghosts got them," Tess added.

Jesse was puzzled. "What do you mean?"

"The spirits in the sky-world were angry," Tess replied. "People from the Kiangan area say that Mt. Napulauan is a forbidden region. They would not dare to explore it. They would not dare to travel to the summit."

"I don't think General Yamashita cared about your superstitions," said Jesse.

"Mister Joseph, he believed our stories," Jos-we said.

"Nestor had carried him out of the jungle. My mother sent the *hilot* (healer) to fix his broken bones and put medicinal leaves on the wounds. Mister Joseph knew that the Japanese killed anyone caught aiding the American army. He told *Ina* that he owed us his life. *Utang na loo*b, a debt of gratitude," Tess said vehemently. "We cared for him like our kin, and here, blood debts run very deep. Mister Joseph said he would never forget us and what we did to save his life."

Jos-we drained his glass and leaned back on his elbows. "Before he left, Nestor vowed to him that our Ghosts would get their revenge."

Pinky was stretched out on the floor with her eyes closed. Jesse looked at Jos-we and thought about the statue he and Nestor had seen.

She could almost taste the story that was building in her mind: GOLD AND GREED IN THE CORDILLERA. After Pinky's reference to the Golden Buddha, she had xeroxed dozens of clips about General Tomoyuki Yamashita's arrival in Manila, his march through the mountains, and his surrender. More detective work could provide a sensational and more saleable angle to her essay. It seemed logical; Marcos had often admitted that part of his wealth came from finding a portion of Yamashita's gold. Maybe his land-grabbing decrees were not simply about securing the natural resources of the Cordillera Mountains. What if he wanted to remove the tribal people from the treasure spots? One gold Buddha had already been found near Baguio in '72, and Jos-we's story confirmed that there was another seen near Tanduhan at the end of the war.

If Singlaub's story was true, and he was here looking for the treasure... perhaps another portion of the loot was about to be dug up. How much treasure was stolen during the war and what would it be worth in today's market? Millions of dollars? A billion dollars? Her excitement kept growing; it could even be Pulitzer material. Jesse considered the research she wanted to do. They had better leave Tanduhan in the morning. She pointed to Pinky and said, "I think it's time to take sleeping beauty to bed."

****

When a light rapping on the door roused Tess, she opened the wooden latch letting three teenagers slip into the house. The boys squatted in front of Jesse and Pinky's mosquito netting.

"Americano. *Fafae*," they repeated in unison.

Jesse awoke to see three sets of dark almond eyes staring at her as Tess and the boys traded comment for comment.

"What do they want?" whispered Jesse, wrapping herself tightly into her blanket.

"To visit with you. They were drinking at a *palanos*, an engagement party in a nearby barrio, and heard about an American woman staying here. I told them that you're old enough to be their mother. I told them to go across to the house where the teenage girls are staying to be entertained."

"What did you mean 'entertained'?" asked Jesse after the boys finished their cigarettes and slipped out the door.

"When boys and girls are interested in each other, they go outside and entertain each other."

"Those boys are maybe sixteen?" said Jesse laughing.

"Fourteen... fifteen," Tess replied.

"I'm flattered they think I'm attractive. Right now, I feel more like a tired elder sister than someone's idea of a hot babe."

Tess crawled under the netting, chuckling. "Go to sleep. And sweet dreams, Jesse."

# Chapter 13

## Pinky and Tony

The luncheon crowd at the Gloria Maris started to arrive. Tony Carandang hated this place, especially at noon when the wealthy society matrons met for lunch to talk about their clothes, their travels, their men, and of course, other women. He knew that Pinky liked to come here to show him off. It was another job he had to perform; those were the rules of the game until they were married, and he controlled the family finances.

Even when Tony was young, he understood it was in his best interest to serve the rich ladies properly. When they came to his parent's store, he knew his place—to slip shoes delicately onto their carefully manicured feet, to call them Ma'am, and to remember the nicknames of each of their daughters. Tony promised himself that, one day, he would be part of their world.

While boys his age spent the afternoons playing *piko* (hopscotch), *tumbang preso* (hit the can), or *teks* (card game) in the streets of Marikina, Tony continued to work in the family shoe store. While his friends drank beer and joked their way through high school, he graduated valedictorian and received a scholarship to the University of the Philippines.

Ironically, it was the advent of martial law that provided him with introductions to the Philippine elite—only wealthy student activists like Titoy Poblador would talk to him. Why the son of a sugar baron from Negros would risk losing his wealth and position for the sake of a few peasants was unfathomable, but Titoy's friendship was a building block in the construction of Tony's plans.

"*Pare* (friend), your family is powerful. You can do more from the top," Tony told him one day as they ate rice and beans in the school cafeteria.

"Easier said than done, Tony. My *Tito* Ramon started out idealistic. He gave a small piece of his land in Negroes to the peasants who worked for him. The local military burned his house to retaliate. They said his hacienda was a breeding ground for the communists. *Tito* Ramon was on his way to make a formal complaint when he disappeared. When his body was found showing he'd been tortured, the PC said the rebels did it. Later, our family found out the truth that it was the military. *Talaga.* You can't fight the current when you're smack in the middle of it."

"Easy for you to say that," Tony had argued. "You grew up having everything you wanted. You have all the options."

"Pare. Options made possible by the blood of the masses are not for me," Titoy proclaimed, using the popular leftist lingo.

In spite of their difference in outlook, Tony stuck close to Titoy, copying his walk, his clothes, and even becoming immersed in the nationalist ideals his friend espoused. Like Titoy, he was a regular speaker at teach-ins and discussion groups. He wanted to be part of Titoy's world, even as he condemned it in his speeches.

Titoy often brought Tony home with him. On one of these visits, he was introduced to Chichi Gonzales, a family friend of the Pobladors.

"*Ang ganda,*" Tony had told Titoy, "she's beautiful!"

"Pare, no way. You don't want to get involved with that family."

Despite Titoy's radical proclamations about class oppression, he still believes I'm not good enough, thought Tony. Still, determined to marry into the upper echelons, he set out to charm Chichi and the Gonzales family. It took one visit to her parent's compound for Tony to understand the truth about entitlement– that he could remain Chichi's lover, but he would never become the son-in-law to an old-money family. Undaunted, he continued to hunt for the woman he would marry and slowly went through Chichi's circle of wealthy friends, taking care to leave each one well-satisfied with promises of future liaisons. When he met Pinky, the daughter of General Santos, he knew he'd found his match. The General had moved up the social ladder himself.

Tony glanced at his watch again. Pinky was late as usual. Although he was used to her tantrums, he had not seen her for five days and wondered if he had gone too far.

He had to be clever and play his cards exactly right. He was expecting another promotion from his boss, Don Silvero, when he married into the Santos family. Pinky was thirty years old and wanted to have children as soon as possible. Her pregnancy would make the family happy as well as keep her from meddling in his affairs.

Tony watched Pinky's haughty entrance. As he stood to kiss away the pout her lips had formed, she turned her face so rapidly that his lips merely brushed her hair. A whiff of Chanel filled his nostrils.

"It's so hot! I was held up in traffic at Veto Cruz and had to turn off the air-con because my car was heating up," Pinky said, sitting down. She snapped her fingers for a waiter. "Give me a Piña Colada," she told him and without so much as a glance at the man who handed her a menu, turned to Tony with a sour expression. "Well, how's my Don Juan?"

"I've missed you, Pinky. I don't want you to do that again. It's not funny. When I called, Ansay said that you'd gone to Baguio. I almost had your father's men start a search."

"And what about our New Year's party? Don't you think I deserved a call?" She emphasized the words 'our' and 'I.'

"Pinky, we talked this over last night," he said, trying to placate her. "Don Silvero knew I had to stay in Cebu for a meeting. I thought he would tell you."

"Who has meetings on holidays? Hey Tony, you'd better watch it. Your excuses are getting too ridiculous."

Tony curbed his irritation although he knew he had lied to her about his whereabouts that night. "Let's not talk about this anymore. You know I've missed you. Let's go to Pension and get away from this heat."

Pinky kicked Tony playfully under the table and pretended she was still annoyed. Tony took her hand up towards his lips and kissed it.

"So, which friend did you see in Baguio? If you were with another man, I'd kill him, and then, I'll take care of you!"

Pinky knew her plan had worked. "A small confession, Tony. I really went to the Cordillera with Jesse Beckerman."

"What?" he said, slamming his hand down on the table so hard that Pinky jumped. "You fool. I can't believe you did anything that stupid," he growled. "Didn't you consider your father's position? That's a rebel-held area. You could have been kidnapped. They could have taken you hostage! Could you imagine what he would have to do to get you out of there?"

"Tony, calm down. I never saw any rebels. Hey... look at me, I'm a big girl. The mountains may be beautiful, but *ay naku*, I hated all the food except for native rice. Sardines in tomato sauce for breakfast and dinner. It's not like being with Filipinos, you know, like us."

Tony tried to regain his composure. He knew the General would have held him accountable if anything had happened to her. "What did you do at night when it was dark, without me there?"

"Wouldn't you like to know," Pinky teased? "We drank basi and rum and cola while the natives told stories. Some of the older ones spoke in Kalinga, but Jesse's friends translated. You should hear their tales about gold statues and buried treasure. They seem so out of touch with the rest of the world."

The words about gold caught his immediate attention. Tony now listened attentively to Pinky's chattering. "But what stories? Tell me." He lightly ran his fingers up and down her arm.

"Oh, they're too outrageous. You wouldn't be interested," continued Pinky, swaying as Tony stroked her neck.

"These people are crazy. I can imagine Jesse thinking how primitive we are. It's embarrassing. She's so diplomatic. The kids are always giggling around her, the old women too. And the men are so *guapo*," Pinky said as she looked mischievously at Tony.

"As much as me?" he asked.

Pinky flirted with her eyes in response.

"But what about this gold?" he insisted.

"They were just making *tsismis*, Tony. All this talk about gold statues is silly."

"What gold were they talking about? He asked her. "Is it about the treasure that might have been hidden after the war? I've heard rumors that the Japanese buried gold in Kalinga as well as Ifugao."

"You want to talk gold, not sex, Tony? Okay. Let's talk gold. If I this gold does exist, Tony, how much do you think it will be worth?"

"Who knows how much gold the Japanese buried in tunnels on Leyte or around Manila? Tony took out the calculator from his pocket. "But even if just a small amount made its way to the north... say 5 million, and you multiply it by today's prices. IIt might be worth about 500 million, and that's a conservative estimate, but it could be so much more. People might go to great lengths to locate a treasure like that."

"But couldn't the soldiers have shipped it on to Japan?" Tony's serious focus on the gold was turning her on. She loved to look at him when he was excited about something. Her eyes blazed as black and shiny as the hair she pulled over one shoulder.

"What if the Japanese couldn't ship it to Tokyo? Maybe it had to be quickly hidden."

"But there must have been witnesses," she said, egging him on. "Where are they?"

"That's simple to figure. The Japanese killed everyone involved in burying the treasure at each site."

"Maybe they were buried alive or machine-gunned," concluded Pinky. "I heard one old man say that they he came across many bodies. Maybe all the witnesses are dead. And the *tsismis* about Yamashita's treasure was that spirits still haunt it. Do you remember the stories about the guy from Baguio? Didn't Marcos steal his Buddha? Do you think the treasure is cursed, Tony?"

"What does your friend Jesse say?"

"I don't know. We never really discussed it and the night the old man told his story I was kind of drunk."

Tony stood up and helped Pinky out of her chair. "I still can't believe you went to such a dangerous place. I'd like to have a serious talk with your friend Jesse. She nearly endangered your life. You, I know, don't think like that. But Jesse is aware that the rebels stay there. They could have kidnapped you," he said sounding very concerned and protective.

"No lectures, Tony. Promise me that."

"Why don't we all have dinner together this week? I'd like to hear from Jesse what was going on and if you were fooling around with those native boys."

Pinky was pleased. Her plan had worked. "Sure, I'll arrange it for Friday night. We'll have dinner at Mario's. She can tell you all about her adventures in the mountains. Let's order now. I'm starving for good food."

# Chapter 14

## Don Silvero

Don Silvero's suite at the Castaneda building in Makati was as tastefully decorated as any CEO's office in New York. The reception area was starkly modern—gray walls and three black leather chairs against the wall. Behind a chrome and slate desk sat a young *mestiza* (mixed-race person) with bright red lips. She buzzed Don Silvero before ushering Jesse into his austere office.

There was no question that Don Silvero was a very successful man; the gray silk Italian suit he wore when he stood up to greet her was perfectly tailored. Ignoring her extended hand, Don Silvero kissed Jesse paternally on both cheeks. Then he sat down in a leather armchair behind the massive desk with its marbled pen and blotter set and gestured her to sit on the leather chair opposite him.

Although the puffiness in his face and sagging jowls betrayed a fondness for alcohol, Don Silvero possessed the self-assurance of a man who was used to being in command. She imagined he would feel nothing more than the recoil of the gun after killing a rival, friend, or enemy.

Two large photographs were prominently displayed on the wall; one of Silvero with Ferdinand and Imelda Marcos, and the other of him shaking hands with Cory Aquino. Silvero caught her amused glance at the silver-framed pictures.

"You know, we businessmen have to know how to play," he remarked. "The lives of our companies and our employees depend on that. When Imelda was the First Lady, the parties were memorable affairs." He pointed to one photo. "Her birthday party. Your

Ambassador Bosworth was there and that handsome actor George Hamilton. They say he was having an affair with Ma'am." Silvero winked at Jesse.

"So, *hija*, what would you like to ask me? We'll have to make this a very short meeting," he continued. "I have to prepare for a board meeting this afternoon."

Don Silvero had the reputation of being a Lothario, so Jesse noticed his eyes appraising her as he took control of the situation. Without skipping a beat, she answered in a flat-toned voice. "As you know, Don Silvero, I've spent a lot of time in the Cordillera." She turned on her tape recorder, pulled out her camera, and attached a flash. "Weren't you involved in the Chico River Basin Development Project?"

"A project that has been completely misunderstood," replied Silvero. "Our aim was to produce almost one hundred million kilowatt-hours of electricity. Enough for the whole region."

"Don Silvero, one of the reasons the tribes opposed the construction of the dam was that it would flood their rice terraces." She continued to look directly into his eyes. "Their ancient burial grounds would have been underwater. After protesting the 'legal' machinations of the government project, weren't they met with military harassment?" Jesse could see Don Silvero's nose flaring, and she quickly shot a close-up.

"You've been talking to troublemakers. Don't listen to those Communists. They're a bunch of power-hungry criminals."

Nothing to gain by provoking him, she thought and pointed to the black leather couch across the room. "Don Silvero, I need to take some other pictures. If you would sit over there, I'll only take a few more minutes of your time." Jesse produced her warmest smile and held it on him until Silvero wolfishly grinned. She snapped another roll of film, enjoying a moment of pleasure by shooting from below to accentuate his jowls. While taking the last few shots, she couldn't help asking another pointed question that perhaps would also satisfy Tess.

"Militarization is most apparent in areas where there are financial interests at stake. The Cordillera, coincidentally, happens to be the region richest in natural resources. Did you try dealing with the indigenous groups at all?"

"Maybe you can help me," Silvero replied in a patronizing tone. "I've been told that certain rebel groups are willing to deal with the new government. And we would certainly like to meet with them."

Jesse was unable to hide her astonishment. "*Talalga*. Really? Why, Don Silvero?" she asked. "Are you willing to hike the mountain for a meeting?"

Silvero chuckled. "Hike? I'm sure we could arrange a secure place that would accommodate all our needs. Business is business. If someone is willing to talk, we'll talk."

She was about to ask his opinion whether there was any truth to the rumors of treasure buried in the Cordillera, when there was a knock at the door. Don Silvero's secretary brought in a tray with two iced glasses of Coca-Cola.

"Have a drink," he said, offering her a glass. "You see, we do not have a business just for ourselves. *Aba*, I don't need these problems. I have other businesses in the country and investments abroad. The Chico River Dam will not benefit me personally; it will help all those poor people who live in the area. It is the only road to progress. *Hija*, we cannot afford to be sentimental about burial grounds," he said, speaking to her in a concerned tone, as if she might believe that he cared about the welfare of the indigenous people.

Jesse interrupted him. "Sentimental! *Talaga*! And how many tribal people will lose their land in the process? And who will profit from the dam? Really Don Silvero," she retorted with an incredulous voice. "It's the people in the lowlands that will benefit most from the electricity!"

"Those people are going to be relocated to a better place. The problem is, that they don't want to move." He replied indignantly. "We try to provide them with everything for their betterment, and they don't want it. Do you know how many jobs have been created by these projects? And who do you think is filling up those jobs? The very same people who are complaining. They don't want to work hard, and they have no ambitions at all. I think they are just plain lazy!"

Silvero stood up and walked so close to Jesse that the musky aroma of his aftershave made her momentarily faint. He crossed his arms and towered over her while staring with a practiced, intimidating gaze that would ensure his power as the stronger animal.

"Jesse, there is something you must understand about this country. We cannot run it the way you run yours. Here, we need a powerful government that will tell the people exactly what to do. Marcos had the right idea. Left to their own devices, these people will just sit and wait. We must have a strong partnership between politicians and businessmen to make things move. The problem with you Americans is that you want to restrict progress exclusively to your own country. We cannot have that! *Aba*, we have to take care of ourselves too!"

"But isn't it true…" The buzzer interrupted Jesse's question.

"Sir, it's Mr. Carandang on the phone."

"Put him through." Silvero signaled to Jesse to wait as he picked up the phone. "Tony, how did it go? Have you arranged the meeting with the union officials?" he said before lowering his voice. "I want no more delays on this. Tell those bastards we can easily replace them! And our meeting with Santos is 12:30 at Cafe Burgos. Be there. If you can break yourself away from Pinky," he added, smiling in Jesse's direction.

"You just don't know how many problems we're having because of those friends of yours," Silvero complained, after putting down the phone and returning his full attention to the American woman. "I bet whoever is behind them is fooling those natives!"

Jesse bit her tongue. The telephone call had offered enough distraction for her to regain her self-assurance.

"*Hija*, much as I always enjoy the company of such a pretty girl, I must go." He looked at his gold Rolex. "I have to attend to numerous matters for a meeting this afternoon. By the way, how much longer are you staying? You should visit my farm in Batangas. Do you like the beach? We have a beautiful house, and you're always welcome. Just tell Pinky. She and Tony spend a lot of time there. You must see another side of the Philippines. It's not all about sad stories, poverty, and tribal people, you know."

While respectfully thanking him for his time, she rose to leave. At least Tess's information was confirmed. But she still didn't know what Silvero wanted to accomplish by meeting with the rebels. And it was frustrating that she didn't get a chance to ask him about the treasure. However, Tony Carandang's interrupting phone call was interesting. How she wished she could be a fly on the wall at Cafe Burgos. Suddenly she felt drained. Don Silvero was clever, turning the interview into a stern lecture.

Pinky was having a manicure when Jesse walked into the Santos living room. "Well, how did it go?" she asked.

"I would have liked to ask *Tito* Silvero more questions. He had another meeting, so our appointment was cut short."

Pinky blew on her nails to dry them. "Tony wants to take you out for dinner Friday. I think he'll propose marriage very soon. The plan worked, Jesse. He missed me when I went with you to the mountains. I am very satisfied," she added triumphantly.

*I'd like to meet with Tony Carandang too,* thought Jesse. I can question him about the family business. "Sure Pinky, it'll be sweet to see you happy with Tony for a change," she answered. It was time to start looking for another place to stay.

# Chapter 15

## Café Bugos, Manila

Cafe Burgos was just beginning to fill up with the lunchtime crowd. Businessmen from the nearby Makati financial district were filtering in, greeted at the door by a tuxedoed headwaiter. Don Silvero was sitting at his favorite table, discreetly placed to one side to ensure privacy, and drinking a Martini. When General Santos and Tony Carandang walked in, he beckoned a waiter and, with a wave of the hand, signaled them to sit down.

"Primo," he said to the General, "how is everything at Camp Crame? The coffee shops are rife with rumors of a coup. I hear the popularity of the RAM boys is growing."

General Santos frowned. "Some of the men have been grumbling lately. I've heard talk that certain members of the military are not satisfied with their commander-in-chief."

"That's why they call themselves Reformers of the Armed Forces," joked Silvero. "Cory should pay more attention to her relatives. Everyone in Manila knows who's manipulating behind the scenes but her."

"She should also be concerned about her officers upholding civilian supremacy," the General whispered.

Silvero laughed. "General, now you are sounding like one of the RAM boys."

"Even if she calls them 'my soldiers,' they might not be ready to go back to the barracks. You can be sure that after twenty years of Marcos, the officers are not going to let civilians take power from them again. After all, the aim of the February 'revolution' was to reform the nation." Santos took a large gulp of his cola and continued talking. "Filipinos never seem to be satisfied. In the beginning, everybody liked Marcos; then they grew tired of him, and everyone was in love with Cory. Now, it's as if they're all dying to see Cory out. I think we are fond of spectacles."

Don Silvero laughed. "You know what they say, *kuwentong kutsero lahat*—it's all gossip. So Tony, what do you think?"

"You know that politics are similar everywhere, sir. The same people who are spreading rumors of a coup or who are cheering for one are probably the same people sleeping with the government. Politics is one big circus. Today our handsome ringmaster is Gringo Honasan, the leader of the RAM boys. I hear he spends most of his time signing autographs for adoring fans. Anyway, I've always enjoyed the theatricality of circuses!"

"That's what I like about this young man. He'll make a great politician," said Don Silvero while turning to the General. "Primo, we might have great material here for the presidency. Who knows, you might yet have to serve your future son-in-law!"

"Ah, when that happens, then you'll know who'll run the show. *Walang panama si Imelda kay Pinky*—Imelda is no match for Pinky," said Santos.

Don Silvero ordered another round of drinks and consulted the menu. "*Lengua estofada, calderetang bibi* (Ox tongue braised in tomato sauce, duck stew) and fish roe pâté to start," he barked at the waiter.

"Well, now to business. The other day an old friend came to see me, an American businessman who recently opened an office in Manila. I met him in Hawaii last January, at the Joint U.S. Military Assistance Conference. The story he's been giving the press, even to Cory, is that he's looking for the hidden gold of Yamashita."

"American businessman. Very funny. I'll bet you that 'businessman' is more interested in selling guns to the loyalists and anti-insurgency groups than he is a long-ago story about gold. Cory should watch out. I've heard he's also been talking to the opposition," said the General.

"It's probably the same deal as that he offered me; a 'shopping list,' with a warning that we needed more weapons to protect ourselves against the Communists."

"*Talaga*! The CIA is at it again," joked Don Silvero. "Talk about weapons. It is lucky for our American friends that the RAM boys don't take control of Subic and hold their nuclear weapons for ransom. After all," he said laughing, "our new constitution restricts this kind of long-term storage. It would not look good if someone discovered that these weapons are permanent residents. Perhaps it's time to call Washington. There's more than one reporter who would pay to hear this story."

"I'm more concerned just how much this American businessman really knows about our plans," said the General. "Now, all of a sudden, the treasure's back in the news. *Bakit?*" (Why?)

"The Marcos camp is busy digging up some new maps that they say point to possible locations for the gold," Don Silvero said. I've alerted our people in D.C. to get on the case." He turned to Tony. "What about your contacts?" he asked.

"I'll speak to a friend of mine in the State Department. He's provided reliable information before. I'll mention a leak in the Subic story and see what I can expect in return."

The General broke off a piece of bread from the basket in front of him and slathered it with a hunk of pâté. "I'll have my men ask some questions. We have more than a few mayors and *barangay* captains in our pay up there."

"Sir, maybe this is a strange coincidence," interrupted Tony. "Pinky told me a curious story the other day that I wanted to discuss with you. Two weeks ago, without my permission or knowledge, she went up to Kalinga with her American photographer friend, Jesse Beckerman."

Santos turned red, choking on the large chunk of bread in his mouth, and grabbed his drink, swallowing the lumpy mixture with a burp.

"General, I know you thought she was in Baguio then," Tony

continued. "But sometimes you underestimate your daughter's zeal. We had a little misunderstanding, and before I knew it, she was gone. General, when Pinky told me what she'd done, believe me, I was angry. I told her she could've been taken hostage by the communists and assaulted. There's no saying what those people would do for revenge if they got your daughter," he added. "Thank God she's fine. But while she was in Kalinga, she heard an old man claim that he saw a Golden Buddha left behind by the Japanese. And now Pinky's asking me what I might know about a treasure."

"What did you tell her?" Don Silvero leaned forward, locking onto Tony's eyes.

"Oh, we played with imaginary figures about the treasure's monetary worth, and I scaled the amount down. You know how she can make *tsismis*. With Pinky, it's just so much gossip... like the coup headlines. General, I never asked you about the real story behind the Golden Buddhas. Weren't you there in '71 when one was found?"

The General buttered another piece of bread, pushed it into his mouth, and leaned back in his chair. "No, I was stationed in the Visayas. But some of my men tell me that they've seen it. Dencio, my driver, claims he was with the group that picked up a large Buddha statue from that treasure hunter, Roxas. Imagine, Roxas spends seven months digging in tunnels with a bunch of his Igorot helpers, finds the treasure, only to have it taken from him by Marcos. Dencio swears that what they brought back weeks later was a different one.

"That Marcos... what a thief... he was always so clever," continued the General, raising his glass as if making a toast. "His *Tito* Pio Marcos was the judge in Baguio at the time, so he had Roxas arrested, and then made the switch."

"So, where's the real Buddha now?"

"Who knows? I've heard that Marcos' mother, Josefa, has it. But that was only one of the five rumored to be buried in the Cordillera. It's probably been carted away or melted down and is now sitting somewhere in Switzerland. It could have turned into 3000 pairs of shoes. We know one thing for sure. Marcos found some of the billions of dollars of gold bars that were hidden during the war."

"And here's to our finding more of it," Tony said, lifting his glass.

The white-gloved waiter carefully set the gourmet dishes on the table. "Please eat," said Silvero to his partners. "I'm not hungry, but I ordered these delicacies for you. And how is business going in the mines?" he asked, passing a plate to Tony Carandang.

"Technically, we still are showing a loss," said Tony. "The accountants that I hired are good at their job. What about that old man I sent to the mines last month? He was also boasting he had information about a treasure. What did you think about his version?"

"His map was as phony as his story. *Sayang*—too bad," said Silvero. "So far, our excavations haven't turned up a thing. You know we've got to be careful of booby traps. Those Japanese were very clever. Up till now, it's been easy to cover up the accidents and make them look like natural mining disasters. But the union is getting to be a problem."

"My men tell me that they've been able to quiet things down a bit," added the General, taking another helping of *lengua*. "This food is delicious." He turned to Silvero, who seemed preoccupied inspecting his manicured fingernails.

"*Ah, leche!*(Ah, shit!) Those union leaders are nothing but troublemakers, pushing the workers to a strike," Silvero complained. "And those university students from Baguio are egging them on. Every day, there's a story about conditions in the mines. Just let them get on with their strike. *Aba*, they are the ones who will go hungry! I don't need this."

"Would you like me to send in more troops," the General said. "You only have to ask."

"I'll let you know, General. Maybe we will. Digging has started outside the area of the mines. That means dealing with the rebels and some of the tribal groups. Tony, have you been spreading the money around that I gave you?"

"We contacted some of the tribal leaders. These groups have hostilities that date back hundreds of years. My men passed the money, and in some cases, a few M-16's and some bullets. We're giving to all sides. Keeps the old conflicts going. If necessary, someone gets killed. That's often enough to start a tribal incident."

"If we keep them busy fighting each other, they'll be too preoccupied to care when we move our mining operations around on their land," said Silvero. "I think we have the situation under control." He turned to the General.

"Now, about this American friend of Pinky's. This photographer is getting to be a nuisance. First, she takes your daughter to the rebel area in the mountains and then comes to me for an interview. What do you know about her? Who is she working for? Why is she spending so much time in the mountains?"

The General looked at the younger man. "How much do you think she knows, Tony?"

"Pinky thinks her friend, Jesse, is having an affair with one of the rebels. She says the American woman 'blooms' every time she returns from her travels with them. *Ginayuma na naman*—they bewitched her with a love potion."

"*Gayuma*, the General laughed, "a love potion? No. I think she's just a naïve, idealistic, and very foolish girl. Don Silvero, we've been extremely vigilant in setting up this operation. Taking every precaution. I can promise you that this girl will not get in our way."

"She's been asking too many questions," interrupted Silvero, "and it's obvious she's sympathetic to the rebels. Despite what you think, General, it's clear to me that the American may soon be putting some of the clues together. We certainly can't let that happen."

"How can I help? Tell me what to do," Tony asked earnestly.

Silvero turned to Tony. "Get closer to her. I want to know exactly who sent the girl here and what she knows about the gold. The information must come directly from her, not through Pinky. I'm worried that the Marcos people could be using her."

Tony, flattered that Don Silvero recognized his charm, nodded his acceptance of the assignment.

"General," said Silvero, "Perhaps a big enough scare would send her running back to America."

"Sure, Primo." He stood up and placed his hand on Tony's shoulder. "Whatever you say. It can be arranged. I'll call you next week when I get to Baguio. I'm flying to the mines with Tony to check things out."

# Chapter 16

## The General

General Rogelio Santos was looking out the window when he saw Jesse Beckerman walking across the cement yard towards his office. Cesar Bautista, his trusted aide, was standing by his side.

"These journalists think they can fly into our country, glorify those damn insurgents as heroes and leave without scars," Santos remarked. "And then they insult us when they get home. She may be a friend of my daughter's, but I think it is time to teach Miss Beckerman a lesson."

"Yes, sir. I'll take care of the situation for you," Bautista replied and headed for the door. He had the necessary skills the job required. During the Marcos years, he'd often been called *berdugos*—the executioner, for his ability to exact confessions from political detainees.

"Set it up for tomorrow night," added Santos crisply.

The General hid his annoyance when Jesse entered the room. "*Hija*, please sit down," he said and pulled out the chair opposite his large desk. "How are you doing? Pinky tells me you've found an apartment. Do you know that she was crying when you left us? We haven't done anything to provoke your departure?"

Jesse flashed her warmest smile. "Of course not. I didn't want to impose on your family any longer; you've been more than generous since I arrived. Besides, I'm working on a story about the bar girls, and it's more convenient if I'm available to talk to people day and night. I'll need a private place to meet some of the people I'm photographing. I'm sure you can understand. I've already explained it to Pinky."

"Pinky told me where you will be staying. Mabini is no place for a woman to live."

"I do appreciate your concern for my safety, General," she said in a more girlish voice, hoping that he'd see her response as flattery. "I don't think it's a dangerous area. Please don't worry. Through my years living in New York City, I did learn to be street smart."

The General stood up, walked over to the window, and looked out as if he could view Mabini through the glass. "I'd like to see that whole area cleaned out and the 'hospitality' girls sent back to the provinces where they came from." He turned back to Jesse with a stern look. "I hope your report won't glamorize the subject. Unfortunately, these stories seem to make the red-light district more appealing to foreigners."

"Foreign men, you mean?" She pulled a spiral notebook from her camera bag. "Press coverage can be a double-edged sword. General, do you have time for a few questions?"

The General nodded and sat back down behind his desk. He offered Jesse a Marlboro, lighting it with a yellow disposable plastic lighter imprinted with the words 'PEOPLE POWER.' "We had a collection of these souvenirs after the election," he joked, flicking it on and off several times.

Jesse exhaled a puff of smoke. "General, I'm curious if the military leadership has changed much since Mrs. Aquino became President?"

Santos laughed. "Didn't you hear the speech I gave last week at the Academy, urging the soldiers to be on their best behavior? We want to show that we are now a peace-loving and law-abiding military. We must regain the trust of our people."

"Yes sir. That was an admirable statement. What do you think is the soldiers' new role under the democratic government?

Santos answered without hesitation. "Our men were discouraged when they were represented as statistics while the Communists received extensive coverage. You people in the media love to do interviews with the guerrillas." His expression hardened, "But it's time to see our officers and enlisted men depicted as popular heroes."

"So, you asked your troops to 'respect the rights of the people.' It makes sense. After all, one of Cory's campaign promises was to curb the military's human rights abuses. I was wondering, General, how this would affect the situation in the north?" Jesse asked, and in the silence that followed, while Santos did his best to fix a smile on his face, she exhaled a small perfect smoke-ring.

"Of course, we are concerned about the conditions in the Cordillera," he answered. "Yet the military was strongly opposed to Aquino's peace overtures with the Communists. Didn't you support a strict deadline for talks with the rebels?"

"Personally, I will never trust those communists, but Cory wants to meet with them, and she is our commander-in-chief. I'm more interested in the guerrillas who have expressed an interest in coming down from the mountains," he said. "What can you tell me from your perspective?"

Santos stood up, turned around to the curtain covering the wall behind his desk, and pulled a black nylon cord, revealing a large map of Luzon. TOP SECRET was written in large block letters on top. Areas of the Cordillera were flagged and outlined in red marker. Santos continued to smile tautly, picked up a thin wooden stick, and pointed inside the red lines.

"*Hija*, you are familiar with this area where the rebels are active. I believe you've spent a good deal of time in the village of Tanduhan." He pointed to a blue flagged pin on the map.

"What makes you so sure that's a center of rebel territory?" Jesse asked in a controlled, even tone.

"*Hija*, we all agree on that fact. From what I've been told, you've had a number of experiences with the military operations in the area."

"You're talking about last December, when I filed a story about the 54th Infantry's search for rebel soldiers in Tanduhan. *Alam mo*, none were discovered."

"But you've been back there many times. Even with my daughter," he said, hardly concealing his disapproval. "What did you talk to the guerrillas about when you first met with them?"

"We talked about the peace negotiations. I heard stories about the government's policies regarding land rights. You've seen my published photos, General."

Santos picked up a stack of papers from his desk and shuffled through them. "You've met Nicasio Juachon? I believe you know him as Ka Noel."

Jesse's expression remained neutral.

The General waited for a moment and then continued. "How can you be so sure, *hija*, that these people that you've talked to were telling you the truth?"

"Let me ask you a question, General," she responded calmly. "When was the last time that you were in one of these villages and spoke face-to-face with any of the people?"

Now it was the General's turn to stare blankly. He hated the smug expression of foreigners, as if they had the right to question him. In his thirty-five years of military service, he had been called upon many times by those in power to act as both judge and executioner. "Santos, handle the situation," he had been told, and no more questions had been asked. He had acted as a loyal soldier. He had aligned himself with Don Silvero and the clans in power while eliminating his rivals. He could point a finger and crush this woman in an instant.

A few minutes passed before he answered stiffly, "That is why President Aquino sent representatives of her government to the peace talks. I've heard that you have met with some of our delegates and experts on Cordillera affairs."

"Most of your experts are political appointees. What could they know about the real situation, General? Have they ever been to the region?" Jesse realized she was getting strident and had better soften her tone. "*Alam mo*, your office should have the record of our discussions. All of the meetings were taped."

"*Hija*, what I think is that you have naïvely fallen under the spell of some misguided individuals who want to use you for their own selfish purposes."

In this back-and-forth sparring, Jesse knew it was to her advantage to let the General play out his domineering role. She would not take his critique to heart. Reaching into her bag for another smoke, she offered him one.

Santos declined, lit her Marlboro, and continued his stern lecture. "That's right, *hija*. This 'exposure' you had was pure propaganda, staged specifically for a gullible foreign journalist. My office can organize a tour to just as many towns and villages where people are contentedly working on their own land." He put down the pointer, walked behind the chair where Jesse was seated, placed his hand on her shoulder, and held it there.

"*Hija*, I'm telling you this because you're my daughter's friend." Santos gripped her shoulder tightly with his fingers until Jesse twisted her neck to look up at him. "Don't trust these people. We know them much better than you ever will. They may very well harm you."

Jesse swung her head away from his piercing gaze.

"It was reported that you were warned to stay away from the mountains," he continued. "Don't you understand that these supposed friends would kill you if they thought it would help their cause?" Continuing with an authoritative tone, he intimated concern for her well-being. "We know all about the NPA's threats toward you. In fact, your friend Nicasio Juachon specifically warned you not to return to Tanduhan."

Jesse stubbed out her cigarette and willed herself to not flinch. She was startled that he was so familiar with her personal history. She looked at her watch and put the camera bag on her shoulder.

"General. Sir. I see what time it is, and I realize I have to go now. I have another appointment."

"*Hija*, I'm here to help you. If you have any problems, please, come to me first." Santos put his arm around Jesse and escorted her to the door. "After all, we are always ready to accommodate our friends from the United States."

# Chapter 17

## The Gray Cafe

In the corner booth at the Gray Cafe, Jesse, Pinky, and Marina ordered another round of San Miguel. Pinky was sulking.

"Oh, come on, Pinky, you know I didn't mean to insult you," Jesse pleaded. She had never expected that Pinky would treat her moving out as a personal rejection.

"But what did I do that made you leave?" Pinky repeated.

"You must have asked me that fifty times and I keep telling you... nothing. I had to get an apartment because of the story that I'm working on."

The excuse was partially correct. Although Jesse had sent all her undeveloped film of the rebels to her agency in New York, she still had information about them jotted into her notebook. Someone in the Santos household was likely to snoop through her belongings. She didn't distrust Pinky but understood that her friend's loyalty was to her family. As of now, the General had no proof of her close relationship with Nicasio Juachon.

"Why?" Pinky asked again as she sipped her beer. "Why there? *Bakit doon*? That's where all the girlie-girlie girls stay."

"Pinky, we've been over this. Living on Mabini Street makes it easier to take photographs day and night."

"But decent girls don't go there," Marina scolded.

"It's okay for me to live in Ermita," Jesse replied. "After all, I'm a foreigner, not a convent girl," she teased. "You should come with me when I meet some of the girls."

Pinky didn't laugh. "No way. I'd never go into any of those places. To the customers, I'm just a Filipina like the others. I'd never want a man to look at me that way. Even Tony thinks you're crazy for moving there." She stared into her beer. "He asked me what I did that made you leave as if it was my fault."

"This has nothing to do with your hospitality."

Jesse wondered when Pinky's moping would end and she could exit graciously. She looked around the room. The Cafe, a popular hangout for artists—Filipino, American, and European, and young executives from the Asian Development Bank—reminded her of trendy bars in lower Manhattan. Large surrealistic black and white photographs dominated the walls, and a boisterous crowd danced to the latest tapes. The new wave music usually blasted away some of her loneliness when she got sentimental.

"Would you like to try *'yung Piña Colada namin*? It's very delicious. *Talagang masarap.*"

Jesse looked up at Gigi, the waitress. "I'd really like to, but I can't. I still have work to do tonight." The B-52s' boisterous song, 'Rock Lobster,' made conversation difficult, forcing her to raise her voice. "I was at Camp Crame today, Pinky. I had a talk with your father."

"*Pag may kilala ka sa Crame, walang kaso*—if you know somebody at Crame, everything is fine," said Marina, pointing to Pinky. "I bet you didn't know that I was arrested in '75, during martial law. *Talaga.* So many of us were. I stayed out after curfew. But my uncle knew someone at Crame, and I was released the next day. Crame still means prison to me. Just hearing the word gives me a chill."

Pinky looked at Jesse. "In the Philippines, it's all about who you know. That's what makes the difference," she warned.

"I'm sure I can count on your family to keep me safe," Jesse joked before glancing at her watch. It was after midnight, and she was tired. "I've got to go," she told the group, kissed each one good-bye on the cheek, and slipped out the door.

She hurried towards her new apartment. Despite Pinky's complaints, Jesse would miss her daily dose of *tsismis*. Even though her friend behaved like a spoiled rich girl, she enjoyed listening to the gossip, and had learned a lot from Pinky about the relationships between the wealthy families and clans who controlled the country.

For a few hours, the congenial atmosphere of the club—the dancing, the laughing, and the music—had taken her thoughts off the rebel commander. It was disturbing how much she was thinking about Noel. He was on her mind often enough to now be categorized as an obsession.

I can't be falling for this guy. It's out of the question. Admire his courage: His passionate dedication and willingness to risk his life for his ideals. But get those sexual thoughts out of your head, she ordered herself. I'd better call Davidson in the morning. She could count on his cynical jabs to set her straight.

Jesse strolled past Remedios Circle and down Adriatico, ignoring the children on the street and the mothers with their babies huddled in front of the small fires, cooking barbecue. She shivered and pulled her arms around her chest as if to ward off the unseen spirits hovering around. The air was thick with the musky fragrance of *dama de noche*, the white perfumed flowers that bloom only in the evening.

Noel, she thought, touching the handmade necklace he had given her. What will be the reward for your sacrifice? Is it enough that you'll be remembered?

It happened so fast that she had no time to scream. Two men emerged from the shadows of the doorway, blocked the path, and roughly pushed her against the wall of the building.

"Get away," she yelled before one man held her arms, and the other put his hand over her mouth, shoving the muzzle of his gun into her cheek.

"*Putang ina mo umuwikana*—go home son of a bitch," snarled the man behind her as he twisted her arm harder. "A message from your friends. They don't want to see your white face in the mountains again." He threw her to the ground before they ran.

If her hands weren't scraped raw from breaking the fall, she would hardly have believed what had happened. No one nearby seemed to notice the attack. Jesse picked herself up, walked the short distance down Mabini, and still breathing heavily, she let herself into the front gate. The door to her place was open.

"Holy shit," she screamed angrily, followed by "Goddamn them!" Her apartment had been ransacked. Painted in big red letters, covering her 11" x 14" photos on the wall, were the words AMERICAN GO HOME and CIA WHORE. The drawers had been dumped out, and the clothes spread all over the floor. She picked up a ripped bra by the strap and, trembling at the sight of the deliberate knife cuts, flung it across the room. The small apartment seemed to have been attacked by a squadron of madmen. A cold shiver ran up her neck and down her arms as she remembered the warning that General Santos had given her.

*Get a grip on yourself.* But she couldn't stop the tears. "Fucking cowards," she cursed, choking on the words. It seemed as if a giant wave had crashed over her and that she was alternately drowning then gasping for air. Her anger cresting, she pulled off the necklace Noel had given her and threw it down, and stomped on it "I hate you all," she cried in frustration.

Who could she trust? Certainly not the local police. What could she do except pour a glass of cheap Philippine vodka, followed by another and another? She mechanically put things away, checking around her room. Nothing seemed to be missing; her tape cassette was buried under towels in the back of the closet. She felt for her cameras. Two burglaries in New York had taught her to protectively hide her equipment on a high shelf. She relaxed when her fingers hit the familiar shape.

Soon the alcohol began to take effect. Though her mind was becoming muddled, she knew one thing for certain; this wasn't a robbery. Nor was the incident in the street a random mugging. Someone had hired thugs to scare her. They'd done a good job.

She fearfully checked the lock on her door. Although it had been forced, it wasn't broken, and after locking herself in, she pushed a heavy chair in front of the door as a barricade. She shoved aside the mess on her disheveled bed, sat down stiffly, and lit a cigarette. She alternately took a puff and then a deep in-and-out breath to regain her focus. She reached for her phone, dialed the international operator, and repeated Jonathan's number at the office. The connection was terrible, but hearing his voice stopped her furious tears. Speaking fast while gesturing wildly, she filled him in on the details of the last few weeks. It took almost twenty minutes to begin to slow down.

"Yeah, I understand you're worried about me. Don't think I'm not freaked out trying to figure out who did this and if they are coming back. You know how hotheaded I am. At first, I thought the rebels sent someone to scare me. But then I realized... why would they do it? Why would they want to frighten me away at this time? And the mutilated bra is not their style. No, it's got to be someone else. I started thinking about Don Silvero and General Santos. I sent you pictures of the businessman." She took another gulp of vodka. "There's something going on here. I know what you're going to say. Okay. Yes. I'm listening." She paused while Davidson spoke, holding the receiver away from her ear.

"No. My imagination's not working overtime. Listen to me! Every place I go, I hear rumors about buried treasure. General Singlaub is here. Even Singlaub's saying that he's looking for Yamashita's gold. There are just too many coincidences. Jonathan, just listen to me," she pleaded while pacing the room, folding up clothes and stuffing them into drawers. "I'm sure some of the gold is still buried in the Cordillera, maybe near the mines. And that may be another reason Marcos wanted the people off their land. Who knows? But I think someone is getting close to finding this Golden Buddha and..."

"Forget that story," Davidson said, interrupting her. "I've got another for you, and I've lined up a foreign sale of your terrific ambush pictures... created quite a controversy."

She had a hard time hearing him through the static. "Controversy? What do you mean?"

"The editors at *TIME* wanted to know whether you knew about the ambush beforehand," he answered.

"They questioned what I was doing out on patrol with the rebels? Do they think that I planned the ambush?" Jesse was indignant at the assumption. "Davidson, I nearly got killed." She looked around her disheveled apartment.

"We'll discuss it when you get back, Jesse, "he told her. "I've got an assignment for you in D.C."

"In Washington? You think I should leave? Right now? Jonathan, I really need a few more weeks to follow up on some things. And then I'll come home. I'll be careful. I promise," she said before hanging up.

All night Jesse continued to fight her panic. She threw up the vodka twice. Her head pounded even as she dozed, and then she woke up struggling to fight off a ghost-like assailant. Who had sent those men? Were they military? If they had wanted to frighten her into leaving, they'd done a damn good job. She had the nagging suspicion that they could be a part of a sparrow unit; the urban guerrillas were known to operate in small groups and sometimes attack Americans. Could some rebels still believe she had sold them out? Impossible. What about Tess? No. Tess would not betray her. She had to find someone here who she could trust. She had to, or she'd go crazy.

# Chapter 18

## The Cordillera

Jesse looked at her watch. It was just after two in the afternoon, and she was still trying to erase the vision of her ransacked apartment. She couldn't blot it out of her mind, or rest on the bus, or watch the passing scenery as the jeep sped through the mountains. Wispy figures had appeared in flashes. And it didn't matter if her eyes were opened or shut.

As the jeep backed up before stopping, she saw Abel leaning casually against the concrete marker at the outpost with an M-16 cradled in his arms. A runty black dog barked shrilly near his feet. Across the river, Tanduhan was shrouded in mist.

On other visits, Jesse had stopped at the *sari-sari* store for a Coke before descending the mountain. There was no time for that now. Barely acknowledging the rebel soldier, she snapped the straps to her backpack and started down the steep path. She counted out loud the steps, "...one hundred one, one hundred two, one hundred three, one hundred four..."

Her eyes were fixed on a small hut across the river. She didn't pay any attention to the swaying of the bridge as she ran across and climbed the path up towards the village with the weary confidence of a veteran traveler. Tess was delighted when Jesse appeared in her doorway; she was not expecting the American to return so soon. Jesse was sweating profusely, and she looked at Tess with red-rimmed lids, her story exploding in rapid sentences. Tess listened apprehensively, her eyes widening with each detail describing the ransacked apartment and Santos' ominous warning.

"I feel so vulnerable," Jesse admitted. She had to clench her lips to keep them from trembling. "First, the NPA threatens me... and now, who knows... maybe it's the military who hates my guts. I can't figure out what's going on here. But Tess, I wanted you to know that the attack did not scare me into leaving. It wasn't that I was intimidated." She noted the look of dismay on her friend's face. "I've got another assignment in the States, and I'll be going home in a few weeks. I'd hoped to be able to find out more information for you... about Silvero and his interests in the area, and I couldn't go without saying good-bye."

"Good-bye?"

Tess's obvious concern reflected her dilemma. Her plan for locating the Golden Buddha would be jeopardized without Jesse's participation. So many days had been spent convincing Noel and the elders that it was the best option they had. Even Jos-we had convincingly participated; he had set Jesse up to learn about the treasure. Tess hoped she had judged the woman's character accurately; the hazards might be more than the American was willing to endure.

"You can't go yet," she said brusquely. "Don't you want to find out who's responsible?"

"Do you have an idea? Please, Tess. Tell me. We know it's not the NPA... is it?"

Tess answered after some deliberation. "I think you are right. The military is behind these attacks." She waited to gauge Jesse's reaction.

"What have I done that they'd single me out from the other journalists? Is it because I lied to them about seeing rebels in the village?"

Tess shook her head. "They may have believed you were telling the truth. I don't think that's the reason you were attacked."

Jesse shivered as if an icy wind had crawled through the hairs on her arms and hugged herself to ward off the chill. Her skin was covered with goosebumps.

"You stay here for a few days. You have to talk to Ka Noel." Tess said as if it were an order. Tess had made up her mind to tell Jesse some of the treasure story. How much she still had not decided.

"What's Noel got to do with this?" Jesse had rushed here with the conviction that Tess would be her confidant, the one person in the country she could trust to watch her back. During the bus ride up, she had reexamined and compared the differences in their background. Just as compelling was their similar head-strong passion for social justice and human rights. It was the driving force behind their actions. Tess was committed to the welfare of her people and her duty to preserve the land and traditions. Jesse believed in the righteousness of the indigenous struggle for their land. She had made it her job to get these stories told and hoped that publishing her pictures would make a difference to the people here. Perhaps she would also win some acclaim for her projects along the way.

"Damn it, Tess, I'm depending on you to tell me what's going on."

"Wait for a moment, I'll be right back," Tess replied, slipping out the door before Jesse could protest.

Jesse watched Tess through the window, gesturing to one of the boys outside. She didn't want to consider that Tess would be involved in the Manila break-in. As she gulped the coffee, her imagination raced between hidden agendas and malevolent conspiracies. She slouched onto the floor, resting her head on her elbow. She was too exhausted to expend any energy and sank down in a stupor.

Tess climbed the hill until she reached a small white cross marking the ground where her brother had been ambushed. She was overcome with a sense of bereavement for the past. As children, Ruben would play the warrior, using his bolo to slash a path for her through the bamboo and vines. If she were thirsty, he would scale the tallest palm to toss a juicy coconut, proving his prowess and natural-born affinity with the trees. She could picture his infectious smile as he openly shared his delights and discoveries. Their days seemed so safely rooted in the Kalinga way of life. We did not need to say we belonged here, thought Tess as she ran her hand along the rough wood cross, feeling that she had failed him.

With one more backward glance, she continued up to the rebel camp and whistled a signal to the sentry. Noel was sitting by the fire, talking with Abel when she squatted down.

"There's been some bad trouble," said Tess in a grave voice. "Jesse was attacked by two men in Manila. When she went home, she discovered her apartment ransacked. Now she's come to my house to say goodbye before leaving the country."

Tess stood back up and then turned again to look down at Noel. "Jesse needs answers, and I don't know what to say. Noel, I worry about the danger of getting her more involved."

"You weren't so worried when you came up with the idea," he replied. "All you talked about were your superstitions and the treasure. Don't come to me now and plead for her welfare and security."

"You know how much I sacrificed for the struggle," she spoke back sharply, raising her voice. "My parents. My brother. We have no more children in my family."

"Don't you think I'm haunted too?" he said. The slight quiver to his voice betrayed his raw emotions. "Look what happened to Leila; I've never even seen my son." His widened eyes flamed with orange sparks that mirrored the burning coals. "After Leila was tortured, I swore I would not get involved with another woman."

"Maybe that is why you are sometimes depressed, then explode in temperamental outbursts," Abel spoke up and told the commander.

"It cannot be," the commander insisted.

"*Talaga*?" said Tess. "You've been attracted to Jesse since she first arrived. I think you can't resist her soft white skin, or maybe you see her as your plane ticket out of here."

"And how do you view the naïve American?" He asked and answered his own question. "Is she a comrade who will give her life for our revolution?" Noel retorted angrily. "Don't pretend innocence with me. Not after what we've seen. You will do whatever it takes to protect your inheritance. Even you will use Jesse." He lit a cigarette and inhaled sharply. "It is true that I appreciate Jesse's beauty. I admire her humor and her intelligence. When I talk to her, I can see that she is different from the other journalists. I don't want to see her get hurt."

"I agree, Noel. I'm asking that you promise to watch out for Jesse while she's in the mountains. I'll bring her up here, and we'll tell her the whole story. Let her decide. If she wants to help us. Then you do your best to protect her. Okay?"

Assured of the guerrilla commander's promise, Tess hurried back. The sky had turned dark, and while Jesse lay listless on the floor, she had fixed a plate of rice and vegetables, then placed the dish and a bottle of *Ginebra* next to Jesse. After gently waking her up, Tess poured the clear liquid into two glasses.

Jesse raised hers in a mock toast, gulped down the rough grain alcohol, made a sour face and refilled her glass. They ate in silence. After the last bits of food were finished, Jesse lit a cigarette and shook the empty bottle.

"Think we can get another?" Her head was already swimming, wounded emotionally from the ordeal in Manila. Her goal now was to drink until her thoughts and body were numb. When Tess returned from Rosie's store, Jesse drank the second *Ginebra* straight from the upended bottle.

"I had a fantasy once," Jesse said, her words coming out slow and slurred. "I'd take pictures, and people would see 'em and things would change. That's what I thought was suppose' to h,appen. See, what I really wanna do is help."

"If you knew that you..." Tess hesitated and looked intently into Jesse's sodden face, "...had the power to make a very real contribution, would you do it?"

Jesse shook her head and set the bottle down. "I dunno. What d'ya want me to do?"

"Can you trust me enough to wait one more day? Tomorrow we will have a meeting with Noel."

Jesse looked at the native woman. Two figures were swaying in front of her. Even the flickering shadows cast by the kerosene lamp were doubled. She rubbed her eyes and let her shoulders sag. "I just wanna help," she repeated and put her head down on the floor. "Let's rest now. Okay?" She yawned once and fell instantly asleep.

Tess took out the mat and gently rolled Jesse over so that her body lay on top of it, then covered her body with a blanket. She blew out the lamp, got down beside her, and covered their bodies with a blanket. Before drifting off to sleep, she put one arm under Jesse's head and the other around her chest to guard her against any evil spirits lurking nearby.

Jesse spent the next day quietly recovering from her drunken indulgence. She hardly spoke to Tess while she played with Katya and Marie, repeating the Kalinga words that they taught her. At dinner, she put a small portion of rice and fried greens on her plate, but didn't put a thing into her mouth. Instead, she stared numbly at the floor, silently brooding. "What's wrong?" asked Tess.

"I don't care about leaving Manila, especially after what happened, but I'll miss you. *Miss na miss na kita*—I'm missing you with love. And I'll miss the village...miss your family and friends. I had hoped to get more testimonies from them about what the military did here. Listen to their stories if anything's changed now that Cory's President. Take some more photographs to finish my Cordillera essay."

After clearing up the dishes, Jesse followed Tess along a winding path behind the village. In the distance, sitting around a small campfire, she spotted four dimly lit figures. Simultaneously a warning echoed in her head. *Puta (whore)!* Keep your face out of the mountains!

Her pent-up fear and frustration spilled out in anger when she saw Noel ten yards away. "Do you know what happened to me in Manila?" she yelled and raised her arms as if to strike him.

Tess grabbed her from behind and held onto Jesse's quivering arms, pulling her down to a seat on a thick log.

Jesse jumped up, too distraught to sit, and kept pacing around the fire, clenching and unclenching her fists. "Tess told me that the military was behind it, but I want to hear the words from you."

Noel looked at Tess and lit a cigarette. He offered Jesse one from the pack and lit it for her. Then he fixed his eyes on the mountains in the distance.

"Do you remember," Tess asked, "the night you were here with Pinky Santos and Gan-ao's husband told us a story about the Japanese occupation?"

Jesse frowned and nodded her head.

"Noel has more to add to the story." Tess beckoned for Jesse to sit down next to him. Noel tossed away the stub of his cigarette. He rubbed his knuckles, stared at the ground, and began to speak so softly that Jesse had to shift her body closer.

"After my father died, I was taken to my mother's village. Her younger brother, Nestor, would visit and tell stories to the children. One day he told me about the golden statue he had seen as a child." Noel reached into his crumpled pack for another cigarette.

Jesse looked from Noel to Tess. "Uncle Nestor? Then you and Tess are cousins. Damn! Feliciano said you had a cousin in Tanduhan, but I never considered it was Tess."

"Jesse, it was best if you didn't know about our family," said Tess.

"Why? Is it dangerous information for me to know that you are related? Everyone else seems to know all the facts. Didn't you think you could trust me?"

Tess looked at Noel and didn't answer.

"Did you think I would say something to the military if I knew you were cousins?" Jesse continued after an uncomfortably long silence. "Any other secrets you want to tell me?" She ran her fingers through her hair, twisting the curls angrily. Being lied to stoked her defensive behavior. Now it triggered images from childhood where issues were never spoken about or were covered up with the explanation that 'she wouldn't understand.'

She instantaneously blamed herself, then took a breath to clear her thoughts. Maybe Tess and Noel had a hidden agenda. She'd get to that next. First, she was curious about the treasure stories. After a short silence, she asked, "It seems... that the hidden treasure is now the big story, up here and in Manila. Do you know if any more of this treasure has been found?"

Tess nodded. "Years ago, Marcos, along with his cronies General Santos and Don Silvero, became involved in the search for the treasure. Marcos found some, and we think that's why the government gave Silvero the mining contract. They probably had a deal. There are rumors that some of the gold is located in boarded-up tunnels near the mines. Silvero can have all the machinery necessary for excavations, and no one would question it. And if anyone does... his partner, General Santos can take care of them."

"Silvero and Santos... of course. Brilliant! That's what I needed to hear, Tess." The threads of the story started to make sense. "And they see me as a threat, an interference in their plans," Jesse concluded and impulsively threw her arms around Tess, squeezing her. She turned to Noel and hugged him too, then kissed his cheek.

He didn't push away from her embrace. She could feel his heart pounding against her chest. Jesse hugged him once more then began to pace. When she spoke, her voice sounded husky.

"Give me a heroic challenge... and an assignment that's based around human rights, and I'll push myself harder and harder, loving the sweat, even the punishment it demands." She stopped, looked directly into Noel's eyes, and took hold of his hands.

"But I'm scared," she confessed. "And I don't know who to turn to." She tried to keep her body from shaking. "Damn it. I wasn't born here! I don't know your rules about loyalty. About family. About trust. You didn't trust me with the truth about your family," she pointed out sarcastically.

Noel shook his head and said, "Jesse, I..."

"What do I know about your ancestors? Or mine for that matter," she continued. "My parents arrived in America as immigrants; the family that stayed in Europe were killed in pogroms and concentration camps. The customs officials changed my father's family name when he got off the boat. I have no roots. I have no ancestors. I have no one watching my back. I don't understand what it means to have a tribal history or a clan or a bond to the land. I can't even say I'm from someplace." Jesse took a deep breath and slowly let it out. "I've had to invent my life, seemingly from scratch, day by day. People here never doubt that they belong to a culture that has existed for centuries. But I feel like I'm always running. That I'm caught up searching for something tangible to hold on to."

"The elders say that if you do not look back to your roots, you will never reach your destination," said Tess before slipping away from the fire.

Taking Jesse's hand, Noel led her to the edge of a hill overlooking the river. The moon was almost full, the mountains were silhouetted by the glow of its light. Out beyond the hills, they could hear the water racing through the valley and the trilling of the cicadas in the trees. The damp mist served to isolate and blanket them from the village activity below.

Noel put his arms around Jesse and hugged her to his chest. "Look out there," he said, "at the expanse of mountains." As she rocked back into the crook of his arm, he added, "I was born in these mountains, and years later, reborn as a guerrilla. With each step, I dug my soul into the mud like a tree digs its roots, until even the raging wind, rain, and loneliness could not shake my determination to survive. I learned how to live and to die. I've sacrificed everything I have for the land." His soothing voice was hypnotic. When he stopped for a moment, she held her breath, wanting him to speak again. Instead, his lips covered her mouth as she moved her body into his.

"Do not be afraid, Jesse," he told her.

She looked at Noel, then at the stars in the night sky. Her body seemed to float as if she were lighter than air.

"Do not be afraid to listen to your heart, to trust your heart, to feel the power that flows through this land," Noel whispered. His lips followed his hands onto her shoulders.

Jesse lifted his chin with her hand and looked into his eyes. "Can you know what I feel?"

"Jesse," he murmured as he kissed her neck and repeated her name again. His mouth touched her breasts. "Let yourself be loved."

He continued to stroke her.

Jesse felt her body respond to his caresses. She had no more barriers or resistance and placed her open lips on his, licking him with her tongue. While her toes seemed to spread, grow thick and hug the ground, her spirit moved deep down into the earth through eons of dirt and rock, emerging to float with the wind. Into the water she swam; through the streams and the waterfalls; melting into the flames, red-hot as the fire.

He continued to caress her body, spreading the layers, like the petals of a rose, touching deeper and deeper towards a primal memory that reached to the beginning. Her long dammed up tears washed down her face like a swollen river during a storm. She wiped away the wetness with her hand, and used the moisture on her palm as she tightly encircled Noel's hardness, rubbing up and down, stretching its length, and finally guiding him inside her. They were partnered in a rhythmic movement, one body constantly battered by waves of feeling that shook with each vibration. He kissed her, wetting her lips with his tongue. He kissed her neck and the tender skin surrounding her nipples. Her internal muscles held him tighter, thrusting upwards with her hips. Together they cried and screamed and finally shuddered with the release of his final thrust. He continued to kiss her, cooing softly as to a dearly loved child, comforting her, wrapping her within his strong and tender arms until she fell deeply asleep.

# Chapter 19

## Point 7 in the 'Code of Behavior

As Jesse slept, Noel stroked her cheeks and wound her hair, like strands of copper filament, the other reporters he had met during his years underground. Most of them had idealized his actions, while Jesse's perceptive questions both challenged and intrigued him. Between kisses during the night, he had called her by her nom de guerre, Ka Flame, and exacted a promise that she would grow her curly hair to the waist.

Jesse opened her eyes, smiled, and put her arms around his neck. She could feel the cords in his neck tensing. "What's wrong?" she asked as he pulled away from her grasp.

"I shouldn't do this," he answered tersely. "You don't understand how it is here—my loyalty to the *kasamas*. We depend on each other without reserve. Without compromise."

"Am I a liability?"

Noel thought about his wife and his son. "I cannot be torn apart again by my desires."

Jesse had no idea that he had a family. She assumed his reticence had to do only with her, so she taunted him. "Are you scared to be with me? Afraid that your friends won't approve?"

"Goddamn it, Jesse," he flared. "You know nothing about our lives. I didn't choose to fight this war. All my life, I've been ruled by my duty. To my family. To my cadre. To my wife."

"You're married?"

"I am. We were together for only a short time," he answered

bitterly.

"*Talaga*?" Instead of sympathy, she felt deceived. "What other surprises have you got for me?"

"No surprises. Leila became pregnant, and I married her. You Americans cannot understand the way it is here."

"Understand what? That you were married? That you didn't tell me. Or that you only married her because it was your duty?"

"Jesse, do you know about *punte siete*? Point seven in the 'Code of Behavior' states that rebel soldiers cannot take liberties with women."

"I've heard about these rules," she replied while reaching for her cigarettes. "And what happens if you do 'take liberties?'"

"Disciplinary action. Demotion... and with it, the loss of rank and prestige. I've spent too many years underground to let that happen. But I never lied to her, Jesse. I never told her that I loved her."

"So, you sacrificed your honor and married someone you didn't love for the sake of your ambition. I suppose there was no disciplinary action or demotion." Jesse struck a match, lit her cigarette, and looked sharply into Noel's eyes before she lit his.

"Nothing."

"So where is Leila now?" she asked sharply.

He ignored her question and continued his story. "I was assigned to another area with my cadre. I wasn't with her when she gave birth to my son. It was too risky to go; the military was watching for me. It would have endangered the village."

"What about your son?"

"*Sayang.* I've never seen my son. After the birth, the military arrested Leila."

Jesse's neck stiffened as she shivered and drew back. She tossed away the match as if shaking her wrist could rush some warmth into her clenched fingers.

"Her relatives took the baby to a safer place. What I heard was that she died two days later in prison. From hemorrhaging, they said.

After they told me, I didn't want to know anymore where the boy was living." He rubbed his mouth roughly back and forth with his fingers. "I won't put another life in jeopardy."

"But don't you think he wants to know who his father is and why he's not with him? Don't you owe him that?"

"You Americans. You think life is like your Hollywood movies. Here, there are no heroes. There can be no happy endings while Filipinos kill each other. The children see their parent's struggle. They play with guns instead of toys. They learn to lie to the military, making up stories with such beguiling certainty that no one knows what is true. Even the youngest risk their lives carrying food and messages to the *kasamas,* and what is their reward? Instead of dolls, they smell death on the frontlines. My people are starving and struggling for the barest necessities. Every day people are dying," he said, standing up and turning his back on Jesse, "and you cannot imagine how tired I am of this war."

Noel looked out the window at the sky and whispered, "After my son's birth, I told myself, no more. I won't stay with a woman again." He turned back to face her. How much more did he have to sacrifice to prove his dedication to the struggle? "I told you before, Jesse. I'm selfish."

"What about last night? What about *punte siete*?" she asked sarcastically.

"If I am punished. I don't care. Not anymore," he whispered as he dropped down to his knees and pressed his lips against hers, forcing open her mouth with his tongue.

They kissed as if each lick and bite were part of a final meal together, exploring each deeply arousing flavor with an edgy intoxication.

"*Ang sarap mo,*" he whispered first.

She laughed, repeating back to him in English, "You're totally delicious too," and licked him lightly on his lips, his chin, down his neck, and along the hollow of his chest.

When he broke away an hour later, it was to tell her he had to leave; that she should return to Tess's place and he would join her there later.

Jesse strolled airily down the path. She stopped at the water pump and washed her face. It seemed as if she had been doing that simple motion every morning of her life. She flushed as a wave of passion swept from her knees to her clitoris, and she had to grab hold of the metal pipe to steady herself. More than anything, she wanted to touch his lips again, to feel Noel's strength inside her. She didn't care that he once had a wife. She couldn't think about his son.

Tess was preparing the morning rice when Jesse returned. She looked up and saw the glazed expression on Jesse's face. "After we eat, I'll take you to the hot springs," she said. If she noticed that anything momentous had happened between Jesse and the rebel commander, she gave no indication.

When they arrived at the stream, a few of the older women were already there. Jesse gathered her soap and shampoo. As the warm water bubbled up around her, she took off her batik *malong* and lowered her body onto a rock. Tess picked up a smooth stone and rubbed the dirt off Jesse's back. A toothless elder with shrunken flat breasts picked up a flattened stone and gently rubbed Jesse's thighs, her calves, and then her feet.

Jesse turned, letting the women do as they would. After her hair was washed, she slowly eased herself fully into the hot stream. The steam rose around her, completely enveloping her body. Tess pulled her up, wrapping her hair in a towel and her body into an older clean *malong*. She took her by hand and brought her back to the hut.

"Sleep now," she told her and was still seated by her side, humming a melancholy tune when Jesse awoke. Her palm rested on Jesse's forehead, and every so often, she would rub her fingers across it, as if to smooth away the last of Jesse's doubts.

"Jesse, our people need your help," Tess said softly. "We had to be sure we could trust you." She squeezed her hand. "But what we ask... it might be dangerous."

Startled, Jesse sat up and blinked her eyes. "What do you mean?" she stammered. The intensity of her experiences in the last twenty-four hours seemed altogether too surreal.

"We must get some information from your country before our enemies can find it. You are our only hope."

Jesse looked sharply at Tess. "What do you want me to do?"

"We have to locate an American soldier. Jos-we mentioned Mister Joseph in his stories. He was hidden here during the war. He may be the one to help us find the treasure that was buried nearby by the Japanese soldiers." Tess unwrapped the forty-year-old drawing and faded sepia-toned photograph for Jesse to examine.

"But why didn't one of you try to find Mister Joseph?" she asked, as she studied the documents. "Surely you have friends in the States you can trust?"

"We never had his family name. We can't wait any longer. Silvero and Santos are determined to do everything in their power to stop us from finding the statue, including hurting you!"

"Even if this man was still alive, how will I know where he lives? How will I find him?"

Tess smiled. "You will know. Last night you joined our clan, our history, and our dreams."

# Chapter 20

## New York. May 1987

Jesse groped in her pocket for a cigarette as she waited on the customs line. She couldn't smoke in the airport, but wanted one ready when she hit the outdoors. Small comfort for an exhausting thirteen-hour trip, she thought and tugged at her camera bag to keep it from slipping off her shoulder, yanking at the hair caught under the strap.

She had fretfully passed hours on the plane while she peered past the window, beyond her own reflected image, and into Noel's face. With her fingers touching the glass, she had traced out almond-shaped eyes and full lips in a half-smile. Then she had put her fingers under the blanket and squeezed her thighs tight around them, feeling the throbbing that had become an aching reminder of their separation. She could feel the indentation where his hands had once pressed into her back like a fiery brand.

Now she watched the couple in front of her holding hands and wondered how Noel's cadre would treat the impropriety of their affair. Jesse began the familiar mental minuet: so there are rules about rebels becoming sexually involved with women. But he told me not to worry. Should I believe him? I believe in the righteousness of the war he's fighting. How could I not love him? But what kind of future can we have? Play Bonnie to his Clyde? Guerrilla wife with a gun?

She stopped at the duty-free shop and sniffed the men's cologne. Gotta buy some 'Halston' for Alex, she thought. She pushed her luggage cart through the double doors at Kennedy Airport, past the mobs of families screaming hellos and limousine drivers holding placards with block printed names. Lost in the bedlam of the incoming passengers, she elbowed her way through the crowd to get outside and grab a cab.

When the taxi hit the top of the overpass before the Midtown Tunnel, she gasped at the sight of the New York City skyline. The neon orange on the skyscrapers flamed against the dots of fluorescent office lights and blue sky in the twilight.

The yellow cab raced down Second Avenue. Jesse's eyes hungrily skimmed the sidewalks, looking at the once familiar sights. "You're going to see many more people living on the street now," Davidson had told her. "I'm used to it," she replied, but was shocked by the truth of his prediction.

"Hey pal, out of the way," yelled the cabbie to the bearded man in a dirty purple ski jacket and soiled pants asking for money. "I'll watch you go in, sweetheart," he offered.

The man thrust a paper cup jangling with coins in her face after the taxi let her off at Third Avenue and Eighteenth Street in front of Alex's apartment. She'd never get used to the homeless people living on the streets; she was incapable of cutting off that part of herself that heard their silent screams.

Alex had also been keeping her updated about the changes in the city. Now, the devastating effects of AIDS—the death of two of his closest friends and the ravages of the disease on many of the others— had altered his carefree lifestyle.

His last letter to her was somber: "...*you see a man you know on the subway, and two weeks later, you hear that he died.*"

Still numb from the haunting experience of attending a multitude of funerals, Alex had told her that he no longer roamed the gay bars for a one-night stand. Instead, he had seriously settled down with Gregory. She wondered how his new love affair would affect their friendship.

Even with her bags, Jesse hopped up the stairs two at a time. "Bubbala! You look great," Alex announced when he threw open the door. She touched the top of his spiky blonde haircut, thankful his handsome face and lean body still radiated good health. That settled one of her immediate fears. Alex took the camera bag from her shoulder and placed it down on the floor. He stood back for a moment, grinned, then smothered her with a warm embrace and long kiss.

"Looks like you've turned punk, darlin'," she told him. "Married life must agree with you."

"You lied. Telling me you'd only be gone four months," he admonished, squeezing her so tightly that her spine cracked twice, releasing all its tension. "God... know how much I've missed you? Waiting for your letters drove me absolutely crazy. I'm dying to hear all about your adventures... every tawdry and sex-filled detail. But go wash your face," he ordered, "and then we'll chat."

While he poured the Chardonnay into two crystal, gold-rimmed goblets, Jesse pulled out a *malong* and tee-shirt from her duffel and changed. Alex watched as she stepped into the batik wrap and admired how expertly she tied it around her waist.

"How feminine you've become. Girl, did you have an affair with one of those handsome young rebel boys? Come on... tell me everything."

Laughing, Jesse made an exaggerated pout with her lips. "I've got something for you." She reached down to the bag at her feet, pulled out a piece of indigo and yellow patterned batik, and held it up. "The men look very *guapo* in these," she teased as she secured the fabric around his waist. "You would've been in heaven. All those lean and muscular bodies. All the guys wearing *malong*s... or less. Of course, I dressed in jeans."

"So, Mistress Jesse," he interrupted, "how did you get by without your black leather jacket and whip?"

"C'mon, Alex. How could I have a serious conversation with guerrilla soldiers in a skirt? You know I'm more comfortable without all the feminine trappings," she said. "But I got a rash on my legs from wearing tight jeans, so the women took me aside. They said I needed to air out my body. I began to wear my *malong* for an hour a day. One hour stretched into three; soon, I was wearing it most of the time."

"Jesse, you do seem changed. Much softer," Alex said. He gracefully swirled around the room like a model on a runway.

"Being in the Philippines was good for me." She sat down on a chair, picking up her legs and tucking them under her. "Even Jonathan said that my pictures seemed fresher and more honest than anything I've done before. He noticed an off-balance quality in the composition. And why not? It was all so new. Living with tribal people. Traveling with guerrilla soldiers."

"And darling, I'm sure you were quite the wild woman."

"Hardly wild. But I did get mixed up with a few savory characters." Jesse held out her glass for a toast. "A toast to my *kasamas*. To Tess and Noel. To their strength, courage, and convictions."

"Look at that smile. You had an affair in Manila? Tell the truth, sweetums."

"No," Jesse answered, closing her eyes and seeing Noel. "Not in Manila. But what about Gregory? And how are you?"

"Don't get me started. I don't want to bring you down yet. You know I was never political, but so many of our friends are sick. I'm angry enough now to join ACT-UP. Reagan and his cohorts have been avoiding even saying the A word. They're wasting time, and people are dying. What little medication's available for AIDS is experimental; no one knows about doses or side effects. Jesse, every time I sneezed, I thought I was dying."

Jesse looked carefully at Alex, her concern obvious.

"I'm okay; otherwise, I would've bought myself a one-way ticket to Tahiti, or set out to find you and a fabulous beach in the Philippines. Instead, I fell in love with Greg. He's perfect. Caring. Loyal. Good body."

"So, you're no longer the great slut?"

Alex clasped his hands to his chest as if he were praying. "Hallelujah. I've reformed, Mistress J."

She held up her wine glass. "I look forward to meeting the man who could tame you!"

"Tomorrow, if it's your wish. Greg stayed at his Mom's place so that we could have our reunion." Alex saw Jesse's eyes starting to close. "Honey, why don't you take a rest and lie down for a while."

"I'm fading fast, Alex. I'll tell you more in the morning." She put her feet up on the couch as Alex covered her with a knit blanket. "You know you're my best friend, and I'd do anything for you. I really love you. I hope you know that," she said before falling asleep.

It was the ringing that woke her. Jesse had no desire to move as Alex sleepily handed her the phone. "It's starting," he said, and headed back to bed.

"Jonathan, am I glad to hear your voice. I have so much to tell you. One hour. I'll be there."

She showered, dressed, grabbed a box of prints, a bag of undeveloped film, gave Alex a quick kiss good-bye, and quietly closed the door.

Jesse felt electrified by the streets, almost light-headed with the excitement of being back in her old neighborhood. The avenue seemed wider than she had remembered it. She stared into the windows of stores, reeling from the abundance of things for sale.

The receptionist at the front desk greeted her warmly. "The boss has been waiting for you," she said and pointed to her watch. Jonathan was on the phone, his back to the door as Jesse walked into his office. She put her hands over his eyes. He swiveled his chair around, gesturing for her to sit down and wait. She could hardly contain her enthusiasm, feeling her own energy bouncing off the walls.

"So, how's the prima donna?"

Jesse raised her arm high, and when Davidson copied her gesture, she slapped his hand hard, in a high five. "Excellent," she exclaimed.

"You had me worried," Jonathan answered. He stood up, gave a half-hearted punch to her arm, followed by a strong hug. "You're determined to drive me crazy."

"Hey, wait a minute," she said, pulling away. "You've gotta give me an argument the minute you see me?"

"When you told me about being mugged, that your apartment was ransacked, then said you needed a few more weeks, and I knew from your voice you were going up to the mountains again... I could have killed you myself."

"What words of love you speak." Jesse enjoyed his rage. It was a verbal game they had played many times before, and she knew it covered his concern for her. "Hey. I'm back in one piece and ready to work."

"You are meshugganah," Jonathan said, shaking his head.

"So you always say. But what about the last photos I did? Show me tear sheets of the ambush shots. And the ones of Silvero. And the military threatening civilians in Tanduhan."

"They were somewhere here." He shifted around the stacks of photos and magazines on his desk.

Jesse winced. "How come you can never find my work? So much for making me feel good, Jonathan. I nearly got killed taking some of those shots." She tried to cover her disappointment. It wasn't as if she'd expected Davidson to have large blow-ups of the photographs by his desk, but his lack of regard for her pictures was humiliating.

"Forget the pictures for now. Let's get breakfast. I want to hear all about the trouble you've gotten into." Jonathan grabbed his leather briefcase and coat and shoved her through the door.

At the local coffee shop, Jesse ordered a toasted bagel, lox and cream cheese, and a cappuccino. "During the last year, I would have killed for a bagel," she admitted, looking at Jonathan quizzically as he opened his and fastidiously scraped away half the cream cheese.

"I'm watching what I eat and going to the gym every day," he admitted.

"That doesn't seem to be much of a problem where I just came from."

"The exercise helps to keep my blood pressure down. With maniacs like you in my life, I might not live so long. Now tell me about this conspiracy theory you have. What were their names?"

"Silvero and Santos. The Golden Buddha story is incredible." Over half a pack of cigarettes and four refills of coffee, Jesse outlined her research concerning the Japanese presence in the Philippines during the war. She repeated Jos-we's first-hand account and concluded with her theory about Silvero and Santos's involvement with the buried treasure.

She had decided not to talk about her relationship with Ka Noel or Tess Gadag's plea to search for the missing American soldier. There would be plenty of time to fill him in on that later.

Jonathan remained quiet as she raced through the story until Jesse described the two men who had attacked her in Manila. He turned pale, gripping the edge of the wooden table.

"Are you insane?" he exploded, shaking his head. "It's said that God watches over fools and small children. You're not a child so I have to put you in the other category. Fooling around with the military that way. If they wanted to, those men could kill you at any time. Do you think because you're an American, or a woman, that it would stop them?"

"Jonathan, here I'm telling you a great story—a plot by an amoral general and an unscrupulous businessman who will stop at nothing to get the Golden Buddha while rebel soldiers defend the struggle of indigenous people fighting for their land—and you're calling me a fool."

"Don't bullshit me, Beckerman. Separate the B minus movie from the real-life story of a reckless girl involved in her first affair with a guerrilla soldier. And I'm sure it's one of the rebels who put you up to this craziness? Right?"

"Dammit, Jonathan. Why does my behavior have to be linked up with a guy? You know me better than that."

"Because you're playing revolutionary in a very real situation. Some powerful people probably think that you're sticking your gullible nose into their business, and I'm sure they don't like it. All you have to do is take a few salable pictures and get out of the place. What's with you?"

Jesse resented his condescending tone. "First, you don't find my pictures, and then you put me down the minute I get back." She pushed her plate away, drained the last sip of coffee in her cup, and lit a cigarette. She blew a large cloud of smoke between them.

Jonathan drummed his fingers on the table, twisting his gold wedding band nervously. "Need I remind you that you are a journalist? You are calling a General in the Philippine military and this businessman unscrupulous and amoral. What kind of objectivity is that? Are you so caught up with these people that you have lost your powers of reason? Didn't I encourage you to go for it, go deeper, get the whole story?"

Jesse shrank back into her chair under the barrage of questions.

"But I didn't mean for you to lose your rationality and join in their fight."

"I'm not like one of those parachutist reporters, Jonathan. I didn't just drop into the Philippines for the flavor of the month story. I...," she stopped and looked at him blankly; her energy and enthusiasm dissipated. Before she had been bursting. Now she felt small like she was shriveling up.

Looking at her stricken face, he softened his voice. "Jesse, you're doing such good work. The unique balance of ruggedness and compassion shows everywhere in your pictures. It's the way people let you photograph their intimate moments. And you are right in their face. Maybe it's that receptive smile that fools them."

Jesse felt herself blushing. Although he had just torn her apart, it was just as difficult to deal with his compliments.

"So, what I want you to do," he continued, "is to rest for a few days. Spend some time with your family and friends. And next week, get down to Washington. Photograph the people who visit the Vietnam Memorial—those who touch the names on the black stone and the remembrances that they leave behind at the wall. It's an assignment for the LONDON TIMES."

"How many pages will the spread be?" Jesse asked, coming back to life after feeling she had been beaten into a corner.

"Don't ask me about pages. Just do it," he ordered. He pulled a pair of bifocals from his pocket to study the check, quickly took them off, and put down a twenty-dollar bill.

*Jonathan, you amaze me*, Jesse thought as he left the restaurant. After finishing another cup of coffee, she headed back to Alex's place.

Jesse took giant steps, stretching her legs, two stairs at a time, till she reached the third floor. She fumbled with the tangle of keys, unfamiliar with the three locks on his door. The couch was still disheveled; on the pillow was a drawing of two birds. The bird on the ground had a spiky hairdo and was looking up; the other was flying downwards with wings outstretched. Their long beaks were touching. Alex had also drawn a sun, with a 'be happy' smiling face. Jesse fingered the paper and grinned.

Endora, a burnt-orange and white tabby cat she had found three years ago and given to Alex, rubbed against her ankle. She picked up the cat and squeezed her. "You fat thing," she said as Endora purred, "you still remember me." She scratched her behind her ears.

Jesse pushed the buttons on the phone, tapping out the familiar numbers. Her sister answered on the third ring. "Guess who?" she asked, trying not to scream with joy at the sound of Jan's voice through the receiver.

"Jesse... I'm so glad you're home. Wait a moment. David wants to talk to his Auntie."

"I can't believe he can talk, Jan. He was just beginning to crawl when I left."

"Hello Auntie Jesse," David said in a soft lisping voice. She heard her sister in the background prompting the boy's speech. "Are you going to come to my house today?" he asked.

"Sure I will, honey," Jesse answered, unbidden tears running down her face. "Put your Mommy back on the phone." Letting go of the cat, Jesse wiped her moist face. "Jan, I missed you the most. I have so much to tell you. I'll take the train to Brooklyn. No, wait. I'll take a cab. I really have to see you as soon as possible. I mean, I've just come halfway around the world. This is easy. I'll be there in an hour."

# Chapter 21

## Sisters - sharing laughter, wiping tears

Jesse walked up to the house on Dean Street, happily soaked in the familiar neighborhood ambiance, then ran up the red brick stoop. As she pushed the buzzer, her first thought was how safe this place is, followed by I wish Tess were here, and goddamn, what if Noel could meet Jan. The intense love Jesse had for her sister made her light-headed. It was as if she had just run a marathon and then smoked a menthol cigarette.

"Damn, sis, it's good to see you," Jesse said when the door opened. She was momentarily startled. Jan's blond hair had turned gray. But nothing could stop the smiles, bright with the warmth of a lifetime of shared feelings that followed the kisses and hugs.

After putting Amanda in her room for a nap, they sat down in the kitchen. "So how is it being back? Is Alex okay? I was worried, what with AIDS and all. I've missed talking to your friends while you were gone."

"Alex seems fine. Married to a nice Jewish guy. He's been catching me up on the politics of the disease and how it's changed his life. Alex is a one-man man now."

"I'll never understand the male desire for indiscriminate sex."

"As I remember it, Jan, you were a hot little number yourself at one time," Jesse teased.

Jan blushed. "You mentioned during one of those expensive long-distance calls that you'd met someone. So, tell me about this new friend of yours."

Jesse shook her head. "I don't even know where to begin. I never expected anything like this to happen. There are too many problems, and I don't know how I feel," she said. "Can we talk about men later?

I want to hear about you."

"Why? I'm the boring, stay-at-home sister." She stood up, went over to a cabinet filled with crystal glasses, reached inside, and rummaged through the shelf. "I think I have a bottle of wine around here. I don't usually drink in the afternoon, but this is an occasion," Jan said, pulling out a Cabernet Sauvignon. "This okay? I'm sorry the house is such a mess." She poured them each a glass of red wine. "It's impossible to find anything. We're redecorating."

Jesse looked around. The rust-colored ceramic tile counter with its teal blue trim, the gleaming copper pots hanging from the ceiling, and the crystal wine glasses on the marble-topped dining table gave a distinct impression that Jan had converted to a Yuppie lifestyle. "I see you've been keeping up your subscription to *Architectural Digest*."

"Oh, it's not that fancy," said Jan. She walked over to the small mirror in the hall and tried to pat down the loose strands of hair while studying her reflection. "I keep trying new styles, but none seem to ever look right. Eric says that the gray is very contemporary. I think it just makes me look old. What do you think?

Jesse laughed. "Are you talking about your hair color or the leather couches? I'm not fond of gray hair myself, but you look... distinguished. The couch, however, is classic." She noticed that Jan's hips and stomach had grown wider and that the tight black dress she was wearing was probably one size too small. Even the skin around her chin seemed stretched as if it contained a balloon that had been repeatedly blown up and deflated. Only her gray-green eyes still gleamed with the same brilliance.

"Oh, never mind. We were talking about the house. I did ask the advice of a decorator."

Jesse was surprised and slightly shocked by her sister's appearance. Jan used to be so weight conscious—counting calories, fat grams, and measuring her food in ounces. And what had happened to Jan's eclectic sense of design? "Remember how we used to go to the Goodwill on 125th Street for all our stuff? You found that gray and salmon pink table with the chrome legs and amoeba pattern. Where do you shop now, Bloomingdales?"

"We were kids then, Jesse. It was all we could afford. Besides, it was an 'in thing' to have second-hand furniture."

"Excuse me," Jesse joked and poured herself more wine.

Jan appeared worried. "I'm sorry Eric won't be home till after ten tonight. He's been so busy lately, I hardly see him."

"Why are you apologizing for Eric? Is everything all right between you two?" Jesse asked. "After nine years of togetherness, I thought you guys had the perfect marriage." She saw her sister's face begin to tremble.

"Living with someone is a continual compromise. But that's not the immediate problem. And I'm sorry if I seem distracted; I wanted the house to be finished before you arrived. The painters were supposed to do Mandy's room. You'd think that they'd want the work." She walked over to the sink and absentmindedly rinsed the dishes before placing them in the dishwasher.

Jesse put her arm around Jan's waist. "Tell me what's going on, Jan. You didn't go into the details of why you quit your job when I last spoke to you from Manila. I thought the promotion to senior editor made you happy."

Jan continued to rinse the dishes. "Do you like this black china? I couldn't decide between... oh what the hell." She sat down, cradling her head in her arms. "Sure, I loved my job. But it was so hard, trying to do it all."

"We agreed how important it was for a woman to maintain her independence, even in marriage..."

"...And maintain her self-sufficiency," said Jan, completing the sentence.

"I thought Eric supported you in that."

"Oh, he did. He still does. But lately... I've been tired, and the kids need me more. David is five now and in school, and I put Mandy in playschool three mornings a week. I have a nanny helping me. She was full time when I still went to the office."

"So why did you quit?" Jesse asked again. Jan had often lectured her about the importance of maintaining a job. In fact, she had been the one who pushed her the hardest.

"I fought on so many fronts for the last few years; at work, on the school board, even with Mom. Maybe I just want to be taken care of for a while. Its easy once you stop working, to let go of that sense of self-determination." Jan lifted her glass of wine.

"Here's to you, kid. Maybe you can find another way for a woman to have it all. I've retired from the race."

"I always hoped I'd have a companion... and stability like you," said Jesse. "I can't believe you've given up your goals. Is Eric responsible for the state you're in?"

"He's one of the good guys, Jesse. Don't knock every man cause you've made bad choices."

"Oh yeah? What does Eric want? The sweet little woman cooking dinner when he arrives home from work? Is that what's making you overweight and gray. Pardon me, but Jesus fucking Christ!" Jesse exploded.

"Well, I see your Philippine adventure hasn't mellowed your feminist streak. What about this mysterious man you've mentioned? Are you his one and only?" asked Jan, raising her glass of wine again.

Jesse took a gulp of wine and lit a cigarette. "I didn't tell you this before, Jan, but he's a commander with the rebels."

"A commander?"

"A commander who's not supposed to have a relationship outside the movement, especially with an American."

"How could you, Jesse? What did you say to him when he came on to you... is that a gun in your pocket, or are you just glad to see me?"

Jesse couldn't help giggling, especially when Jan joined in. Tears rolled down her face as she choked back the laughter. "Stop teasing," she said, and wiped them away with the back of her hand. "The guerrillas take their code of discipline and abstinence seriously."

"Sure they do, sis," Jan replied cynically, no longer smiling. "And I suppose that stopped your rebel friend from fucking you?"

Jesse shivered, twisting her head to the side, as if she could feel Noel's fingers stroking through her hair. She took a sip from her glass of wine. "Drinking alcohol is banned," she said, blinking back the tears.

"You're not answering my question. What about sex?"

"You're supposed to ask your cadre first," Jesse answered flatly, "if you're not married."

"Revolutionary rhetoric," Jan snapped.

"Jan, something happened to me there. Remember how I always said I wasn't going to marry or have children? For the first time in my life, I even thought about having a baby. I know that sounds crazy. But it seemed like everyone was always carrying a child. It got so, when I'd be leaving a village, I'd feel cold because I was used to holding a baby against my chest."

"Don't tell me that you're pregnant?" Jesse shook her head as Jan took her hand and stroked it. "Jesse, you're doing so well in your career. You're traveling, contributing something, doing important stories."

"Important to who? While I was in the mountains, I realized that my photos contributed more to my own ambitions than to the immediate needs of the people involved. And I didn't realize how alone I felt until I met Noel, how much I'd barricaded myself until he touched me. For the first time in my life, I felt really connected. He was one of the best lovers I ever had, Jan. He knew what to do. Not so much from experience, but it had to do with who he is—his sensitivity and dedication, how he cares about the people and their struggle. He puts all those feelings into loving a woman." Jesse stared directly into Jan's eyes.

"But now that I'm back here, I don't know," she faltered. "It seemed so natural when I was lying next to Noel; when I was in his arms. So perfect."

"Have some more wine," said Jan and refilled her glass.

Jesse stared into the crimson liquid. *How funny*, she thought. Once she was home, she'd imagined she'd feel safe, but now she was wondering if she was crazy. Was her affair with Noel and her friendship with Tess more imagined than real? "He told me, Jan, that it was possible for a foreigner to join the rebels," she stammered.

"And you said..."

"I said that I liked chocolate chip ice cream, cappuccino, and movies too much to spend the rest of my life in the mountains."

Her eyes began to sting. She saw the looming shape of Noel cradling an M-16 in his arms, replaced by Tess's figure squatting near the cooking fire with a spoon, stirring the rice. Jonathan's condescending voice played over the bursts of images, harshly repeating the words, 'you're crazy,' and 'you think you are so terribly smart.' She put her head down on the kitchen table and whispered, "I'm so sorry, Jan. I thought... for once I'd prove that I'd gotten my life together, and you'd be proud of me." Her sister stood behind her, stroking her hair.

"It's okay, baby, you're just tired. You have jet lag. Go up to my room and lie down. We can talk later. Don't think for a second that I'm not proud of you. I think you are amazing."

Jesse pulled the quilt over her head. *If I bury myself deep enough under these covers, this movie will stop playing in my head.* She could feel herself floating over the rice terraces. She could hear music — soulful ballads mixed with romantic love songs, guitars serenading her, and the clanging rhythm of gongs. She squeezed her eyes tighter. Now the sounds of bullets whizzed past her head. Then bombs were falling. Sadek was shot. Noel was shot. She pulled the covers tightly around her, trying to muffle the screams. Hernandez held up a torn and bloody ear. Was it hers? She pulled her knees up to her chest into a fetal position and rocked back and forth under the quilt. Tess was talking to her about a mission: 'Find the American soldier.' Jesse heard a loud boom and then another blast that shook the bed. A far-away voice said, "Jesse honey, wake up," as she tried to curl up tighter and hide.

Jesse opened her eyes and saw Jan and the children standing by the side of the bed. "We heard you scream. You scared Mandy," Jan said.

Mandy was staring at her. "Here is my Cabbage Patch Doll, Auntie

Jesse. Her name is Ruby. Do you want to hold her?" she asked.

Jesse shook her head. Her mouth was dry, her body burning hot. And then she started to shiver. "I don't know what happened," she said in a raspy voice.

Jan's eyes widened. "You let out a scream. Are you sure you don't have malaria or some parasite? Eric has a doctor friend, an internist. Maybe you should see him tomorrow. Tell me the truth. Has this happened before?"

"No, I'm fine. Really. I'm just tired from the trip."

Mandy handed her the doll. "You hold her, Auntie Jesse," she said, turning around and running out of the room.

"Auntie Jesse. I want you to sleep in my bed," said David, while Jan sat down on the edge of the comforter.

"No, David. Auntie Jesse will sleep in my room tonight," Jan replied. "Now go downstairs and help Amanda clean up the playroom." She waited for her son to leave before turning to Jesse. "Do you want to talk about it?" she asked in a voice that reflected her concern.

Jesse lay still, staring into space. "You don't know what it's like being so far away and doing these stories and having no one to listen to them, and now I'm back in the States, and it is so weird. I mean, who cares? I have no idea what people are concerned with."

"Right now, I'm concerned about you. Try to forget about the Philippines for a while. Come and eat something, you'll feel better. I'm making dinner, so wash up and come downstairs."

Jan was putting the dish of spinach fettuccine with clam sauce on the table when Jesse entered the kitchen.

"Eric called an hour ago to talk to you. He wanted to apologize for not being here on your first night back. See. He is a good guy." Jan handed her the wooden bowl filled with salad. "I fed the kids and put them to bed. Mom called. She wants to know when you're going to visit her."

Jesse didn't reply. She picked at the small clams on her plate.

"Jan, remember how we used to argue at dinner?"

"You were never easy on Mom. Even before I left for school, you used to moralize until she screamed."

"Hey. Whose side are you on? I thought we shared the same sentiments."

"Sure. But I didn't confront her with my opinions like you did. You never understood that there was more than one way to win an argument."

"And you didn't realize that Mom favored you no matter what you said or did," Jesse snapped.

Jan was silent for a moment. "It was painful for me too. I couldn't eat."

"Is that why you were so thin, and I got so *mataba*!" replied Jesse in a less strained voice.

Jan laughed. "*Mataba*? Does that mean fat?" Jesse nodded. "You used to go to the candy store and buy those chocolate bars after school. Now I'm the one who is gaining weight."

Jesse smiled at her sister. "So, how is Mom?"

"Getting older. Worried about you."

"Is she still pissed at me for staying away so long?"

"Mom said she wrote you a letter telling you to come home, but you didn't answer."

"Because when I called her, she ordered me to come home. Can you imagine, Jan. I'm thirty-two years old, and she's still trying to tell me what to do. I didn't open her letter because I could feel the anger coming through the envelope. I needed support. Not anger. That's why I kept in touch with you."

"After you sent her that copy of *ASIAWEEK*, the one with ten pages of your photos of the rebels with the rifles...she freaked. You've got to understand. Maybe because of the kids, I do. It's been hard for her. After I left for school, she had to cope with Daddy being so sick. You two were constantly at each other's throats."

"Yeah, right. You were so popular and pretty, and she didn't pick on you for everything you did. 'Don't hang around with troublemakers,' she'd tell me. 'You want people to think you're a good-for-nothing, like those boys with the long hair?' She's was always after me to play it safe."

"Let go of the past, Jesse. You have to understand that she's alone, and all she's got to think about is what crazy things you're doing. You could've been killed."

"Now you're beginning to sound like a cross between Davidson and Mom!"

"Well, be prepared, sis. She's gonna want to know what you accomplished, and whether you made any money." Jan spooned some more sauce over Jesse's half-eaten fettuccine. "So, did you?" she asked.

"I didn't make a real profit, if that's what you mean. There's not a tremendous market for photos of starving kids in third world countries or of tribal people defending their land. It's not like I was taking celebrity portraits," Jesse shot back.

"Hey, it's me, your sister. You don't have to be so defensive." She went over to the chrome and glass wall unit, pulled out a scrapbook, and placed it in front of Jesse. "See how proud I am. Here are your clippings." Jan poured her a glass of wine. "You know that Mom just wants you to have an easier life."

"All of you should just stop worrying," Jesse replied sullenly. "I can take care of myself. All I really want is for her to be proud of me." Jesse stared miserably into her food. "I guess that'll never happen unless I settle down and get married, no matter what I accomplish."

Jan waited a moment before answering. "Marriage isn't the answer," she admitted. "We both know that. She just can't understand why anyone would take the risks that you do for so little money. She can't relate to your idealism."

"So, you're not idealistic anymore?" Jesse stared at Jan, picking at her food.

"It's hard with two kids, a husband, and large bills to pay. My family comes first. You only have yourself to take care of. This isn't the '70's anymore. I wanted to change the world too. But now I feel 'right on' if I can remember to recycle my bottles and cans."

"What's that supposed to mean?" Jesse asked, startled at the change in her sister's demeanor. She looked closely and saw tiny wrinkles around her eyes and lines in her forehead.

"Let's not get into it now. Anyway, I'd rather hear about you. About your plans." Jan stood up and took the plates off the table, running water over the dishes already stacked in the sink. Jesse followed, holding her glass of wine.

"I'm taking pictures at the Vietnam Memorial; portraits of the people who come there to touch the names and the mementos that they leave behind. I'll be gone for a week."

"Hmm, you know I have this friend, Timothy Connors, in D.C. He's a guy I went to Columbia with. I think he's writing for a magazine there. Do you remember him at all?"

"Are you trying another of your matchmaking schemes?" Jesse asked.

"Tim was a good writer. I had heard he was divorced from his wife. She was also a classmate from Columbia."

"Didn't you go with him for a short time?"

"Only a couple of months. He was seeing my friend Lizabeth, and during one of their break-ups, I dated him." For a second, her eyes sparkled. "We were an incestuous group, yet so serious about the correct political behavior. There was a time when the straight newspapers were hounding the student leaders for interviews. Tim wasn't a big wheel in the movement yet."

"He always seemed charismatic," Jesse said.

"Not at that point. He was quiet and kept in the background. But once he found his voice he leapt into the spotlight. We had designated one person to deal with the press, and there was a misunderstanding— one of the profiles quoted Tim as the spokesperson. His comments espoused a much more radical position than we had agreed on, and Lizabeth was furious. One thing is certain. It shot him to the front-line of the leadership. He was always giving interviews after that."

Jan took a sip of her wine. "I'd just like to know the gossip—how he is, what he's doing now. Think you can do that for me?" Jan turned around to face her sister. She held open her arms, waiting, and folded them around Jesse as they hugged.

"For you, I'd do anything. Let's open another bottle of wine and get seriously plastered," said Jesse, pulling her sister into the living room. "And what about music? This house is dull. I want to hear some music."

# Chapter 22

## Washington, D.C.

Jesse remembered Timothy Conners from the political rallies at Columbia University. Now, the smells came back to her—the burning Patchouli incense permeating Jan's college room—and an instant recollection of the cramped space, overflowing with books, records, and large colored posters of Che Guevara, Jimi Hendrix, and Janis Joplin.

She had been at one demonstration, standing near Low Memorial Library with Jan's friends, while Tim gave an impassioned speech in front of the sundial. He was part of the radical group haranguing the students gathered there to take over a building on campus. The moribund crowd had come to life during his speech, and more than five hundred students had moved to occupy Hamilton Hall. The riot cops attacked in the middle of the night and beat the shit out of the demonstrators with nightsticks. Blood was splattered on the floors and walls. It was everywhere. Later, even the Mayor of New York admitted that excessive force was used. Jesse still had a small scar from the stick that cracked down on her head.

She didn't know how he would respond to her call, but after a short reminiscence about friends, Tim had invited her to a party near Dupont Circle. He gave her Roger Silva's address. "I'll meet you at 8:15 sharp," he instructed.

Still on Filipino time, Jesse arrived thirty minutes later than their appointment. She anxiously searched the room before Mrs. Silva walked over and introduced herself.

"Timothy Connors is my sister's college friend," Jesse explained.

"He asked me to meet him here."

"Tim's probably cruising the ladies at another cocktail party," said Geena Silva with the kind of sly, sisterly grin that made it clear Tim was more than a buddy. "He'll be here eventually. He always makes at least three dates for an evening." Seeing Jesse's perplexed look, she added, "Oh, don't let that bother you; he'll be very attentive when he arrives."

As she walked around the room, Jesse noticed a few men glancing admiringly in her direction. It must be the short dress and make-up, she thought. One of Pinky's designer friends had sewn it, and told her to wear red lipstick and smoky eye shadow for the full effect. She had followed his advice but now felt uncomfortable with the attention.

Jesse was sampling the hors d'oeuvres when she heard a familiar voice call out, "Beckerman, is that you?"

"Oh, no," she muttered crossly. "Hugh Bonner." Making an abrupt turn to face the large man, she replied, "Yeah, Bonner, it's me."

If there was a standard mold for outfitting male photojournalists, Hugh Bonner could have been cast as the archetypal model. He wore a faded khaki photo vest and jeans, a blue denim work shirt, with a Leica M4 slung casually over his shoulders.

His brown beard and mustache were neatly trimmed for a change, Jesse observed, but it didn't hide his jowls and thick lips. And he seemed to have put on some weight; his zippered vest was bulging over his belt.

"My, my. Don't we look pretty," Hugh Bonner remarked. "The Philippines must have agreed with you, Beckerman."

"Bonner, get off my case," she replied insolently. "I was having a good time until I saw you." She disliked Hugh Bonner from the moment she had joined Dispatch Photo. He was a good-standing member in the agency's 'Boys Club.' For a moment, she wondered if Jonathan had changed his mind about her assignment and sent Bonner instead.

She swore at Davidson under her breath, remembering how he had turned down her first request for a foreign assignment and given it to Bonner. She had desperately wanted to go to Africa in '84 to photograph the effects of the famine in Ethiopia. Davidson had explained to her that, "Bonner had impressive credentials: years of experience working in Africa and reliable contacts established during his travels."

She also knew that Bonner was considered part of Davidson's inner circle. He was known for charming his way into prized assignments by socializing with the editors. Her fury intensified as she recalled Bonner's smirk when he whispered 'cock-teaser' at the office Christmas party. Since then, he had continued his brand of flattery, his hands 'accidentally' brushing across her breasts and jokes about getting more assignments if she would use her body to her advantage.

Jesse knew that in the world of international photojournalism, there were many fewer women than men on contract with the agencies. Of the forty or so photographers connected to Dispatch, there were only two other women—one in her seventies and one fifty-five-year-old who spent most of her time teaching.

"Now, if you dressed like this more often, we'd get along a whole lot better," Bonner continued. "Davidson says you've been in deep with the Filipino communists in the north. My expertise is identifying all the weapons. Learned a lot from my years in the military. What with the U.S. supplying the M-16s and the old Russian AKs, there's plenty of hardware around. What would you say you specialize in Beckerman?" Bonner put his hand on her shoulder and turned her around so that she was up against his body. He continued to hold onto her with a tight grip.

"Let go," she said and pushed his hand away, startled by his roughness and being physically close to a man she so disliked.

"I bet the insurgents think their behavior's sanctified because they're the good guys. Right? Come on babe," he said, his face now inches away from hers. "What really distinguishes their violence from that of the military?"

"How could you ask that," she retorted. "Maybe the continuing violence hasn't made life better for the majority of Filipinos, but I'd still side with those fighting to stop the injustices. One of the guerrilla leaders, a priest, explained guns to me in a spiritual way. He said that the gun was considered an instrument used to achieve a higher value—the dignity of man."

"And you fell for that line? What incredible bullshit! Don't your rebel friends think they're above the law? I bet your heroes would take money to fight their revolution from anyone who offered it. Maybe the first time, they would debate it endlessly, but by the second time, their hands would be out, and by the third time, it would be easy— especially if they rationalize their behavior by saying that it's for the good of the people."

"It is for the good of the people!" She expected Jonathan, the businessman, to talk like this but not one of the staff photographers. "When did you get so cynical?"

"Your innocence is a real turn on, Beckerman. Keep it up. Did you hear I won the Newspaper Guild Award for my South African photos?" When she didn't respond, he laughed. "You'd better get a move on babe, if you want to play catch with the pros."

"Shove it up your ass, Bonner," she snapped, and moved in the direction of the bathroom. She wasn't get let him get to her. When I'm done with this story, I'll get my awards. And if Connors doesn't show up in five minutes, I'm out of here, she promised herself.

She stared at her reflection in the bathroom mirror. After wearing jeans and tee-shirts for so long, she barely recognized herself in girly clothes. Leaning in towards the mirror, Jesse made faces and marveled that the copycat woman appeared tanned, slim and attractive. She wondered what had prompted this other self to dress so sexy. It was a far cry from her usual androgynous style. She pulled her hair back from her face and braided it, reapplied lipstick, and carefully blotted her lips. She turned half-around to see the back of her dress, nervously pulled out the braid, and with a final shrug to the woman in the mirror, went back to the party. She was happily nibbling at the chopped liver when someone behind her clasped his hands around her waist and kissed the back of her neck.

"Jesse! Remember me," said Timothy Connors, spinning her around and raising his left fist up in the Black Panther salute they'd all once adopted. Tim looked the same as the last time she had seen him, more than ten years before. His brown hair was pulled back into a small ponytail. He still had the crinkly smile that lit up his eyes.

"I can't believe you recognized me after all this time," she answered, before Tim kissed her full on the mouth.

"I never forget a beautiful woman. The last time I saw you, we were smoking a j..."

Jesse laughed, glad to be around someone who had shared a bit of her past. "No more of that. I've been hard at work in the Philippines."

"Definitely cool," he replied and led her into a corner. He ran his fingers through her curly hair, fanning it out. "There's a wildness about you." He stood back and appraised her. "Gorgeous," he said, staring at her body. "You've really grown up. No more little sister."

His compliments made Jesse cringe. Another asshole, she thought. So far, the whole evening has been a mistake. This guy is only out for a hot date. I'm gonna kill Jan for setting me up with him.

"I'm sure we can find something more interesting to do," continued Tim with a smile. "I'll make an excuse to Mrs. Silva, and we'll get out of here. I want to hear all about your sister."

"Jan is fine." You owe me one, thought Jesse. "Sure you don't want to stay here, Tim? The party might get lively."

"Let's go," he said, pulling her hand. She was feeling ambivalent but being dressed up was such an occasion that she let herself be led outside.

"Nice car," she commented as he popped open the door of his steel-gray convertible. The top was down, and Jesse began to relax and enjoy him driving her around the city. "Smells new. Did you just get it?"

"Few months ago," he remarked casually, "and really Jesse, nice? This is a Mercedes!"

She laughed and smiled at the sky. It was easy sharing common references with friends. The great lawn between the Lincoln Memorial and the Obelisk awakened another reminder—the days spent marching in anti-war rallies with her sister. Tim parked near the reflecting pool and they walked up the steps towards the giant statue of Abraham Lincoln holding hands.

Jesse stared across the lawn to the lights on the Capitol building. "Tim, remember the rally in '67? The official statistics reported something like fifty thousand people gathered at the Lincoln Memorial. It seemed liked a hundred thousand when we walked across Memorial Bridge to the Pentagon. It was the first time I ever saw paratroopers armed with rifles and bayonets. It really opened my eyes." She paused and thought how it also alienated her from her other thirteen-year-old friends, who would not believe the stories she later told them.

"Dissent was the key to the counterculture," Tim remarked as he led her back to the car. "Protesting students juiced by acid-rock, peace, and brotherhood. Sit-ins. Riots. Great pot. Lots of sex and a hardline hatred of 'the Establishment.' I remember those days really well." Before he pulled away from the curb, he turned to Jesse and pointed his finger near her face.

"You were such a serious little girl."

"Hey, give me a break. I was only thirteen and very impressionable. Don't you remember telling me that youth was the revolution? It seems romantic in retrospect, but I really believed that our camaraderie and passionate idealism was strong enough to make a revolution happen. That we had the power to change the government's actions in Vietnam, and our ideas about economic equality would spread into the world."

"Sure," he remarked, raising his fist. "Ho Ho Ho Chi Minh, Columbia strike is going to win!" As Tim reached for Jesse's hand, he lightly brushed her thigh.

She looked at him and smiled, enjoying the spirited conversation and his flirtatious attention.

"So now you've brought your idealism into the world," he teased, "And how about your sister? Is she still blond and beautiful? She became an editor, right? Janice went after what she wanted, just like you."

For a second, a vestige of jealousy for Jan's popularity resurfaced, and Jesse wanted to tell him that her sister was overweight and overwhelmed with Yuppie responsibilities. She caught herself, replying instead with a shrug of her shoulders.

"How about the Philippines, little sister? See any action?"

"Some." With his encouragement, Jesse couldn't help boasting about her exploits. "I took some photos during an encounter between the military and the guerrillas."

"You spent some time with the rebels. Very cool. Didn't some of their leaders go to China for education?"

Jesse stared at him. "You surprise me. I didn't think people here would know so much about the Filipino revolutionary struggle."

"I've always been interested in third-world politics. You'd be surprised if you knew how fast stories travel inside Washington. Right now, the possibility of a military coup in the Philippines is a very hot topic."

"Ever since Cory Aquino became President, the papers have been filled with reports of an impending coup," she replied. "The hot joke going around Manila is... that there couldn't be a coup because people gossip, make *tsismas* so much, the government would find out before it happened."

Tim's laugh was so warm and encouraging that Jesse couldn't help smiling.

"So, you've been with the communists. What's happening to the National Democratic Front? Are they still following Mao's Red Book, hoping to wage a guerrilla war from the countryside, or are they arguing among themselves?"

"Now, I'm impressed. You're very well informed. The peace talks are on again—off again. They can't even agree on an agenda to follow. The military continues to harass civilians, and the rebels are still fighting in the provinces."

"Any idea how the comrades get their arms, ammo, and money?"

Jesse shook her head. "I don't think that the New People's Army gets financing from any foreign government. It's a pretty rag-tag group. The Muslims in Mindanao have the exotic firepower. The Moro National Liberation Front may get their arms from other Arab countries. And there's been a lot of in-fighting among the NDF leadership, so the funding from Europe has dropped off."

"I remember when your sister had faith that things were going to change in the movement. Equality for all was our chant. But within our little group, there were also power struggles for leadership. Janice got out of it before people turned on her."

He stopped the car outside a building on J Street. "Come on, sweet girl, smile. You're home with your friends, and I'd be really pleased if you were having a good time. I want to hear more of your exciting stories. Let's go up to my place." Tim locked the car door and moved around to her side. He took her willing hand and led her past the uniformed doorman into a mirrored elevator.

The stark modernity of the building made her feel oddly out of place after their passionate talk about the Philippines and his hints of seductive charm. Jesse ran her fingers along the monochrome wallpaper below the mirrored walls as they walked along the carpeted hall to his apartment.

Tim opened the door. "Welcome to my world," he said and gestured for her to look around.

His apartment seems as colorless as the corridor, thought Jesse. The couch, chairs, and kitchen table in the two-room apartment looked barely used, as if they had been bought out of a catalogue and arranged exactly as they appeared in the picture.

He went into the tiny kitchen, returning with a cold bottle of Dom Perignon and two glasses. "Sit," he commanded, leading her over to the couch, "I'll be right back." Then he disappeared into the bedroom. She could hear him playing back his telephone messages.

"Miss me?" he joked with a grin when he returned.

"You weren't gone long enough for my heartstrings to flutter," she flirted back with an easy repartee.

After popping the cork and pouring the bubbling wine, he pulled out a small vial and sat down on the couch next to Jesse, spreading out two lines of coke on the glass coffee table. He offered her the aluminum tube.

"No," she said, "I'm having a good time without that. Coke was never my drug of choice. It makes me jumpy."

"What can I do to help you lighten up?" he asked, snorting up one line then putting away the rest of the white powder. "How about a joint? You used to love to get high."

"It's been a long time since I did," she confessed, taking the tightly rolled stick of pot in her fingers. Tim pulled out a lighter as Jesse put it to her lips. "What the hell," she exclaimed and inhaled, sucking in deeply.

"That's my girl," he said, and walked over to his stereo and turned on a Peter Gabriel tape. The music sounded tinny as it bounced off the bare walls.

Jesse kicked off her shoes. "These are killing me," she admitted. "All I've worn in the last few years are sneakers and flip flops. High heels must have been invented by some sadistic guy. True, they make your legs look great, but oy... it's painful doing this female thing," she said, putting her feet up on his table.

Tim sat on the edge of the couch arm. "Some women marry and then expect men to pay their keep the rest of their lives." When he saw her glare, he smiled and added, "Don't jump down my throat. I'm teasing. But not every woman's like you, Jesse. You're different. Special. An adventurer, and I admire your style." Pretending he had a machine gun, he silently mouthed a rat-a-tat-tat. Jesse burst into giggles. "Tell me more stories about what you've been covering. You're exciting me."

It's the effects of the pot, she thought, surprised by how easily she had let him get away with a sexist remark and cheap flattery. But the giddiness evaporated as soon as her thoughts turned to her past assignments. Tim was knowledgeable and interesting to talk to, and the smoking made her feel like sharing some of her adventures.

"My first time out of the States, I went to El Salvador for three weeks. I did an essay on the *Co-Madres*."

"The women who marched around with posters of missing kids?"

"Kids, brothers, sisters, and parents. I got friendly with some of the women, stayed in their houses, and taped their stories. Flavia and Carmen are a little older than me, and have fifteen-year-old sons who are friends. Both boys disappeared on the same day after they left school. It was rumored that they had been forcibly taken to serve in the army.

"I photographed their group—these defiant, middle-aged women with scarves tied like bandanas across their faces, demonstrating in front of shielded, armed soldiers at military headquarters. Flavia was carrying her youngest in case the mothers get arrested, and her eight-month-old baby was breastfeeding and clutching at her shoulder. Meanwhile, Carmen's holding out a Walkman to record the incident. I narrowly escaped arrest when the military hassled me. One of the soldiers pointed his gun at my chest and demanded the film from my camera. I had to scramble quickly to hand over a substitute roll."

"You are so good," he complimented her while clapping his hands.

Jesse faced Tim with pursed lips. "I want my agency to submit those pictures and the ones I did in the Philippines for an award. I'd like to get some support for my personal work. I have so many ideas," she told him. "I started a series on battered women and..."

"You can't be making much money from news stories," he interrupted. "Why don't you move to Washington. Live in a nice apartment. You could cover the White House."

"That's not what I had in mind," she said. "I like being in the field. I've covered stories from the U.N., and all you get is the same headshots that are on TV."

"I've been with you just a few hours, Jesse, and I'm already seriously worried about your safety. Are you one of those adrenaline junkies who get high from danger? What did you think about when the bullets were going by your head? Did you get off on the excitement?"

Jesse took the joint Tim offered and stared at it in her fingers before laying it down on the table.

"Honestly, Tim, it's hard for me to deal with. The seductiveness of working in the middle of life-threatening situations can be... almost intoxicating. Yet I work in the midst of a civil war, and I can't understand how anyone wants to inflict death or torture on another human being."

"What if cruelty is just part of the human condition?"

"Premeditated cruelty. I just can't stomach it. It's hard to watch and just let it happen. I witnessed the military intimidate an entire village. I saw my friends being shot at. What would you do? If you were offered an opportunity, would you do something to help them?"

Tim's face took on a hardened expression as his brow wrinkled tensely and his lips tightened. "Maybe once I would have done something, but I'm much more selfish now. I admit it. But I admire your devotion to the cause. You're like Saint Joan, leading the troops to war." He took her hand in his, tapping his fingers on her palm, and broke into a smile. "Or you can be the good witch, waving her magic wand, feeding all the munchkins, and making Oz a better place to live in. The only problem is that righteous behavior has no value in our marketplace." He poured her another glass of champagne and saw her face darken. "Never fear, my darling," he added gallantly, "I'm on your side. Now relax," he whispered, and close your eyes."

"I wish I could, Tim, but I've gotta work tomorrow," she replied stiffly. She reached forwards and tried to give her arms and shoulders a long stretch. "I was shooting reflections all morning at the Vietnam War monument. What a surreal juxtaposition: the etched names of hundreds of thousands of dead running across a black mirror image of their wives, children, parents, and friends. Some of the women were crying and running fingers over the names of their loved ones. It was a moment of finality and acceptance of death. I was stunned by the honesty of the memorial and salute the architect, Maya Lin, for her integrity and brilliant design."

Jesse picked up a copy of *NEWSWEEK* from the table and flipped absentmindedly through it for a minute. "Kind of outdated," she remarked, noticing it was four months old.

"I don't spend much time here. Like you, Jesse, I'm always working."

"Your place doesn't look inhabited. Bet ya five dollars there's no food in the fridge."

"Don't bother getting up; you won the bet. You must be hungry. Let's order some in." He stood up and went over to the phone. "Chinese?"

"I really should be going," she said, glancing at her watch. "I have a lot to do tomorrow."

Tim walked over to her, got down on his knees behind the couch where she was sitting, and began to massage her neck. His fingers were soft and smooth. He's never done any manual labor, she thought. The lids of her eyes were getting heavy.

"That feels great," she admitted. "I might not get up."

"My plan exactly. Just keep those eyes closed and relax." He continued to massage her neck and shoulders until he could feel her resistance ebbing. He moved around slowly to the couch next to her, sitting in a corner and pulling her body against his so that he could continue to rub her shoulders and arms. Very slowly, he started to move his fingers down her chest.

"My life is boring compared to yours," he said, touching her breasts lightly as his breath skimmed her neck. "I'm just a government hack. I'd like to help you in your work. Drive you around. I'd be glad to."

She wished his touch didn't feel so good. It seemed disloyal to Noel, yet her body was responding. She clenched her teeth, trying hard to thwart her involuntary reactions until the sensation became almost painful. She shifted her weight and felt him growing hard beneath her. "Damn," she said, "why did I smoke? Let me up; I have to go to sleep. Alone."

He looked at her quizzically. "Anything you say. You're the boss. But I'm here for you if you want it."

"Not tonight," she said in a softer tone. This situation is too confusing, she told herself, as haunting memories of the rebel commander came flooding through her thoughts. "Tomorrow, I need to check some material at the Archives," she offered as an excuse.

"No problem. I have friends working there. Let me help you. And sleep in the bedroom. I'll take the couch."

****

The sun streaming through the blinds woke Jesse up, and it took a moment to figure out where she was. Her head was thick. "Champagne and pot," she muttered, "always gives me a hangover." She saw her dress tossed over a chair and a black terry cloth robe hanging on a hook behind the bedroom door. Next to the dresser, Jesse caught a reflection of her naked body as she slipped on his robe. She walked into the living room and tried to remember the events of the night before. Tim was sitting at the blue Formica table, drinking coffee, and making notes on a pad. With one hand, she poured herself some coffee from the pot sitting on the table and used the other to hug the robe tightly around her body.

"About last night," she said, faltering, still trying to remember what had happened; she recalled feeling aroused by his touch, and then stopping him and lying down in bed.

"No problem. I understand. You've got some reentry problems." He got up from the table and put his arms on her shoulders. "I'd like to take care of you," he offered. "Why stay in a hotel? You should stay here." His low voice had a lulling authoritative quality to it. Jesse found it hard to resist.

"It isn't necessary," she said, half-heartedly.

"Just let big brother take care of you." He tightened his arms around her shoulders, pulling her face closer to his. "Now, where do you have to go?"

She walked over to the window and stared into the apartment across the way. "The National Archives."

"I'll drop you off. I have to go in that direction anyway."

# Chapter 23

## The National Archives

Staring down the long rows of card catalogues filled with hundreds of thousands of titles seemed as daunting to Jesse as scaling miles of stone walls along the massive Cordillera rice terraces. She made her way through the aisle, marking titles of books and articles on index cards and wondering if the information in the dark wooden cabinets would reveal a Pandora's box of secrets.

Under the subject heading: IGOROTS, a few historical texts from the early 1900s written by American government officials and missionaries seemed intriguing. Then she looked up YAMASHITA: PHILIPPINES, and found numerous books on the Japanese occupation of Luzon. There were no listings for PHILIPPINES: GOLD other than titles that dealt with folklore and legends.

Overwhelmed by her stack of requisitioned books and magazines, Jesse sat down at the large oak table. She checked through her cards and noticed one missing edition—the sole book listing a treasure map. Her eyes burned. She rubbed them and massaged her temples, trying to clear away the lingering effects of champagne.

She wondered if she had stayed overnight with Tim because Jan would approve of a relationship between them. He was attractive, intelligent, and fun to be with. His curiosity about the Philippines had sparked some challenging conversations, she told herself. But it couldn't compare to the intimacy she had shared with Noel. So why was she flirting with the first man who showed interest, while her rebel hero was fighting the war?

Jesse closed her eyes for a brief rest to think about Tim. She wondered who his friends were and how his public relations job—writing press releases for a government agency—had influenced his opinions. She told herself that checking into a hotel remained a viable option, then opened the top book from the mound in front of her.

It was a biography of the American-born Japanese war crimes investigator who had interviewed more than three hundred witnesses about the treasure left behind by retreating Japanese soldiers. Jesse copiously jotted notes as she read about Fukumitsu Minoru. He was supposedly given access to secret documents while working with the cooperation of the Japanese government, and had made over 600 trips to the Philippines since 1951.

In a book about the Cordillera, she was able to trace Yamashita's journey through the mountains until his surrender in Kiangan. She read documents concerning the forty-year statutory period provided in the post-war International Treaty. The ownership of relocated war treasures ended in 1986, giving anyone the chance to try to recover the treasure.

She opened an oversized art history book about the evolution of the Buddha image in Asia and scanned the chapters with photos of statues made of bronze or gold. Jesse marked off the major styles and brought the book over to be xeroxed.

After threading a spool of microfilm marked 1943 into the display screen, she scanned newspaper clips from the 'Baguio Gold Ore.' Shifting the pages from left to right, she carefully read a story about American soldiers who were believed to be missing in the mountain area. When she passed a familiar name, Jesse took a deep breath and read it again.

"Yes," she said so loudly that the elderly woman sitting next to her dropped a propped-up book onto the table while giving her a disdainful glare. On the bottom of the right-hand page was a story about a soldier with the 121st infantry who had disappeared into the Ifugao-Kalinga area after escaping from the Bataan 'Death March' in June 1942. Lt. Colonel Benjamin Moses was presumed to have been captured in a Japanese-controlled area of Kalinga twelve months later.

Perhaps Mister Joseph was also part of the 121st. If she could find a complete listing of all the men who had served in the Cordillera region during those years, she'd find someone who knew him. The clue gave her a place to start searching, and miraculously cleared away her headache. She turned off the machine, exhausted yet thrilled by her one discovery. When she left the library, she headed directly to the apartment, intending to get her bag and cab over to a hotel.

After the doorman announced her, Tim was waiting with a pitcher of frozen margaritas, and a long-stemmed red rose between his teeth. Jesse had to laugh and gave him a friendly kiss.

"Sorry for my behavior last night," he said, presenting her with the flower. He led her to the couch, pulled off her shoes, and handed her an iced glass.

"I apologize for coming on too strong. I've been messed up since my wife and I split, and it's been a while since I've been out with a real friend. Let me make it up to you. Your sister meant a lot to me, and if there's anything I can do, just name it."

"There is," she answered without skipping a beat. "If you had to find out the name of someone who served in a particular unit in the Philippines during WW II, what would be the quickest way to locate him?"

Tim's eyes glittered. "That's easy, he answered. "I know people at the Veteran's Administration. What's the man's name?"

She sipped the tequila and decided that Tim would have no reason to guess whom she was looking for or why. "Could you get me a list of all the men in the 121st infantry?" To cover herself, she added, "It's been almost forty years since the end of the war, and one of the magazines I work for is doing a story about some of the men who fought in the mountains. The editors thought I'd be good for the job since I spent so much time in that region."

"Consider it done. I'll find out for you in the morning. Now, how about some dinner?"

****

Turning over, Jesse looked at the clock: 8:30 a.m. The vividness of her dreams had awakened her more than once during the night. She groaned, remembering how she had tried to ignore Tim's persistent stroking until finally her body had stopped resisting him, and they'd had sex, or at least he did. He came quickly, and then it was over.

Jesse heard the thud of his feet pacing the floor in the other room and his voice talking on the phone. When she came out of the bedroom, he put down the receiver.

"Come here, babe," he told her, holding out his arms for an embrace. "I'm sorry I didn't keep going last night. You were so hot."

"Don't remind me," she countered, after a brief kiss. "I feel a little guilty because I'm involved with a guy I met in the Philippines, and there are certain complications involved in this specific long-distance romance."

"Take your time," he told her, then brushed her knuckles with a light kiss. "I've got something better than sex for you, Jesse. How about your list of soldiers?"

"How did you..."

"Uncle Tim can handle anything for his girl. I'll pick you up at the wall around noon."

"Excellent," she said, getting excited. "See you later. Davidson will scream if I don't get over there and shoot more photos."

****

Jesse glanced over the typed list that Tim had given her. The sheet included the city where each man had enlisted, but there was no one with the family name of Joseph. Given names were only listed with an initial.

Her first six calls were a bust, but the Boulder, Colorado operator had a number for J. Gilmartin. After saying hello to his wife, Jesse repeated her story about photographing the veterans who had fought in the Cordillera.

"My husband's always interested in talking about the war," said Mrs. Gilmartin, and gave her the number at the law office where John worked half days. Wrong name, thought Jesse as she dialed. For luck, she stroked the Buddha charm on her neck.

"Did you know a man named Joseph?" she asked Gilmartin after repeating her story once more. "I don't know his family name. He was wounded in '45 and hid in a cave near the village of Tanduhan." There was silence on the other end. She clutched her gold charm and prayed she'd be lucky enough to hit the jackpot.

"You might be referring to Joseph Montgomery. I met him at a reunion about twenty years ago. Those of us who served in the mountains felt like family to each other."

"Bingo," she whistled. "Do you know where Mr. Montgomery lives?"

"I believe it's somewhere in Florida," Gilmartin answered. "I remember, like it was yesterday, that we were talking about retirement, and he said he'd settled in the place he was born. Yes, I'm sure it was somewhere in Florida. I have a reunion booklet at home. It might say where he lives in Florida."

"I'll call you back tonight, sir," Jesse said, holding her breath until he agreed.

"It says here... Joseph Montgomery... Davie, Florida. Does that help, Miss Beckerman?"

"Mr. Gilmartin, you've been great. And I promise I'll get back in touch when my editors are ready to do the story."

Jesse hung up the phone, shaking her head in amazement, and touched her lucky Buddha. Florida was inscribed on the back of the photo that Tess had given her. Girlfriend, just keep on guiding me, she prayed. Now that she had his last name, Davie was the place to start her search. She dialed the number of the Dispatch office and asked for her boss.

"I shot some good pictures today, Jonathan. It was a good representation of American ethnic and class diversity—people wearing everything from baseball caps to mink hats. Children, brothers, sisters, parents, grandparents, and friends all rubbing their fingers over the names. I photographed the tears as each touch of the stone seemed to finalize a loved one's death. I couldn't miss."

She sighed then added, "And by the way, I'm going to Florida after finishing my work in Washington."

"Jesse, are you out of your mind?" Davidson yelled. "There's talk of a coup any day now in the Philippines, and I want to send you to Manila. You need a vacation?" When she didn't answer, he said, "What's so dammed important in Florida?"

"Jonathan. This is personal. Something I've got to do. I'll give you the number of my hotel, and I'll be ready to leave for the Philippines on a dime. Don't worry," she assured him.

"I'm always worried where you're concerned," he replied before slamming down the phone.

.

# Chapter 24

## Florida

The hot gust of damp tropical air at the Fort Lauderdale airport reminded Jesse of Manila after a noontime rain. She stared wistfully at the coconut palms, then fastened her hair back in a tight bun.

Although there was no listing for Joseph Montgomery in the Davie phone book, she was sure that if he was alive, the old soldier still resided in this vicinity. The breeze whipped her hair as she drove the white Nissan convertible towards Davie—passing horse farms, orange groves, shopping malls, and a giant Winn-Dixie supermarket. The main street of Davie was almost deserted.

Jesse pulled her rental car into the lot near an old-fashioned diner. A couple of lanky young men wearing cowboy boots, jeans, and tee-shirts sat at the counter, a table of middle-aged women were smoking in the back corner while the sultry voice of Patsy Cline singing 'Crazy,' blared from the radio. She wondered just how much hair spray the bleached-blonde waitress had used to get her hair teased up that high. After drinking her third cup of black coffee, Jesse showed the 40-year-old photo to the waitress and pointed to the out-of-focus church in the background. "Anywhere around here?" she asked bluntly.

The woman blinked through her thick blue mascaraed lashes and answered, "You lookin' to go to the colored neighborhood, honey?"

"I'm trying to locate someone. I'm working for an insurance company, and this man I'm looking for, well... he just inherited some money."

The waitress nodded. "I always play the lottery. I never win nothin'.

Let me get the directions for ya." She took the photo over to a man fixing hamburgers by the griddle.

When the woman returned, she nodded in the direction of the cook. "Elias says that church is over in the colored section, alright. Past the canal. You want me to draw you a map of how to get there? If I were you, I'd be out of there by dark. People get robbed that go over that way."

"Thanks for the advice. I'll be careful," Jesse told the waitress and covered her mouth so the woman wouldn't see the Cheshire cat grin on her face.

The stucco and wood ranch houses were smaller in the black area of town and painted in the aqua, pinks, and yellows that decorated many buildings in the 'Sunshine State.' Jesse passed two giggling teenagers walking down the center of the street arm in arm, stopped, backed up, and asked the girls for directions to the church. She headed towards the steeple. Kids tossed a ball outside the whitewashed old clapboard building.

"Is the Pastor around?" she asked them.

"He's inside," one of the boys answered before diving for a low ball.

Jesse instinctively pulled out her camera and shot a few frames. Eager to find Montgomery, she walked to the doorway and waited for her eyes to adjust to the muted light streaming through the stained-glass windows.

The first thing she noticed when she got inside were the red candles burning in front of the sanctuary. The second was an old man, bending over a stack of books on the opposite side of the room.

"Excuse me," she said quietly, and introduced herself while pulling out the worn photograph. "I'm looking for Mr. Joseph Montgomery. This picture is all I have to go on."

The gray-haired Reverend turned the picture over and looked at the inscription. "Emily-lou has been dead about ten years," he said matter-of-factly. "I married the two of them here in this church, right after the war." He stared at the sepia-toned photo. "She was such a beautiful girl. Up till the day she died."

"Is Joseph Montgomery still alive?" Jesse held her breath while waiting for his reply.

"Lives with his daughter now, over in Bethany. He hasn't been very well, so I hear. Now, what was it you wanted him for?"

Jesse explained, once again, about doing a story about the veterans of WW II.

"Well, I don't know what condition he'll be in. But I'll give you his daughter's number, and you can talk to her. Imagine, coming all the way here from New York to do a story on Joseph. Your magazine must sure have a lot of money."

"I'd pay for it myself if I thought it was important," Jesse replied, glancing once more at the sepia-toned photo of Emily-lou before putting it into her camera bag. "Is there a phone here? I'd like to call his daughter."

The Pastor led the way to a small apartment attached to the back of the church. The telephone book was neatly stacked on a shelf in his tidy kitchen, and after looking up Wanda Montgomery's number, he handed her the phone.

A woman's voice picked up after two rings. By now, the story rolled off her tongue. "I can be there in ten minutes," she pleaded, not giving Wanda Montgomery a chance to say no.

After getting directions from the priest, she raced to her car and drove east. "I can't believe this," she yelled, and then started singing along with the Sam Cooke medley on the radio, "Yeah... bring it on home to me."

Jesse had no trouble finding the Montgomery's. She was parking next to the orange flowers of a blooming Royal Poinciana just as a middle-aged, stocky woman in a print dress and apron opened the screen door and politely greeted her from the wooden porch.

"Hello, Miss. My father just got up from his nap, so you can talk to him now. We're 'bout to have dinner. Why don't you join us?"

"I just ate so, please don't go to any trouble," Jesse replied. "I'll stay till you are ready to eat." She glanced around the living room, noting the simple furnishings—the glass cabinet filled with knick-knacks and the framed photos scattered about. The house had a slight mildew odor that was evocative of her Aunt's house near the beach in Rockaway. Aunt Lena's vitality had seeped into the cushions and walls like the rains that had flooded her house. Wanda disappeared through a lace curtain. Jesse heard her say, "Poppa, the woman's here that I told you 'bout."

Joseph Montgomery looked his full eighty years. He was rail-thin and supported his stooped body with a gnarled wooden cane. His tight white hair, beard, and mustache made a stark contrast to his ebony skin. As he came closer, Jesse saw the deep-cut wrinkles in his face. She helped him to sit down on the couch.

"I can't tell you how great it is to see you, sir. I've been saying my prayers for this meeting." She could see a twinkle in his cloudy eyes.

"Not every day a pretty, young girl comes to see me. Guess I should be flattered. Wanda, bring this girl a glass of lemonade. Or would you rather have a beer?" he asked.

Jesse looked at Wanda, "Don't go to any trouble," then focused her attention on the old man. "I won't stay long, Mr. Montgomery. But I was working in the Philippines," she said, the words rushing out, "in the Cordillera. The elders in Tanduhan told me stories about you and..."

"Tanduhan," he interrupted. "That was a long time ago. And they still remember, you say? I never gave my family name to anyone in those days. Scared to give it to 'em. Didn't want to make more trouble. We had to be real clever."

"It doesn't matter now." She impulsively leaned over and kissed him on the cheek. "My friend's mother nursed you after you were wounded."

Montgomery seemed to drift into his past. He closed his eyes and leaned back into the couch. Before opening them, he asked, "You speak Tagalog?"

Jesse nodded. "Yes," she said.

"Now, what was those words? My memory's not too good. It's a saying, 'bout the debts that you owe."

"*Utang na loob*?" Jesse asked. It means a debt of gratitude.

"That's the words I was lookin' for. *Utang na loob*. I said if I ever got out of that place, I would repay them for savin' my life."

"Mr. Montgomery, there is something you can do," Jesse said quickly. "Your friends are in trouble and need your help. For more than ten years, the military's been waging a war of intimidation and murder to get them off their land. Do you remember the vast expanse of rice terraces? Imagine how valuable that land is now. There are still virgin forests. The trees can be sold for lumber, the rivers dammed for electricity, and the mines plundered for gold and silver. When Marcos was President, he out-and-out tried to steal the land. The people fought back, but now there's a new government. Why should they be sympathetic to the Igorots? Their resources are a salable commodity."

Montgomery cocked his head to the side as if he could hear better from his leading ear. "I got a little money in the bank," he quickly offered. "It's not much, but..."

"No, they don't want your dollars. What they need is for you to remember something. Do you remember the drawing you gave the Kalinga boys, Jos-we and Nestor? It was a statue of a Buddha, and they told you about buried treasure? You know, the gold and statues that were hidden at the end of the war by Yamashita," Jesse said, hoping she could prompt his memory.

The old man looked carefully at Jesse and scratched his head. "I remember hearin' 'bout a golden statue once, but I didn't see it myself."

"Are you sure?" Jesse pleaded. She couldn't mask her disappointment. After the thrill of locating Montgomery, it didn't seem possible that he had no clues to the hidden loot.

"Well... they did give me a statue to take home. But it ain't gold, only wood. The village chief, he gave it to me so I'd remember them. I thought it would bring me luck. Wanda," he called out, "go get that carved wooden piece that I keep on my dresser."

Wanda came back carrying the twelve-inch-high icon. "All these years, my father wouldn't get rid of that thing. No matter what, he said he had to have it in the house."

"A *bulul*," Jesse said as she examined the antique. "It's very old. I've never seen one carved quite like this." She turned the statue around in her hands. The rice god was seated knees up to the chest, his arms squarely folded around his legs. The squatting figure rested on a short wooden base.

Joseph began to nod his head. "I'm feelin' a little tired," he said. "All this excitement of a visitor from the Philippines." He closed his eyes again.

"Perhaps you can come back tomorrow?" asked Wanda shyly. "We're gonna eat now."

"Sure," Jesse replied and stood up. "I've got lots of stories to tell your father. I can find my way out. Thanks for everything. I'll come back in the morning. Is that okay?" She closed the door and skipped over to her car.

Jesse headed west, across Dixie Highway and stopped at the first blinking neon lounge sign. She sat down at the bar and ordered a shot of tequila with a beer chaser, then another.

All this way, and for what? An old man with a fading memory of *utang na loob*. A lot of good I'm doing. *Tess will be so disappointed*, she thought sourly and ordered a third round. The TV news report caught her attention when she heard the words "Philippines" and "major coup."

"Could you turn the sound up?" she yelled to the bartender, busy flirting with a girl two seats away. As the anchorman read the lead story detailing a fifth major coup attempt, the screen rolled with images of fighting in the streets of Manila.

"Holy Moses! Damn! Shit!" she cursed. "Couldn't they wait till I got back? This is the big one! Davidson is gonna kill me," she muttered while placing a twenty under her empty glass.

All the way to the motel ,she frantically planned the arrangements to make. I'll get the first plane out tomorrow. But they said the military rebels had captured Manila International Airport. No matter, I'll fly to Tokyo if necessary, and be ready to go. Once in her room, she called Davidson.

"Get your ass out of there," he screamed, before adding that since the Manila airport was closed, she had bought herself some time. "Tomorrow, you're booked on a flight to Tokyo."

"My thinking exactly," she said before hanging up, dialing Alex's number and leaving a message on his machine: "Please take care of your sweet self. I'm going back into action. I'll call when I get to Manila." She dialed Tim's number and left a message that he should turn on CNN and look for her in the crowd around Malacañang. She'd call when she arrived. Jan wasn't home either, and she repeated her message to the baby-sitter, adding a plea for her sister to return the call.

The following morning, Jesse packed her bag and headed for Joseph Montgomery's house. Her international flight was scheduled to leave from Miami Airport at 2 p.m.

The wooden door to the house was open. Wanda was hunched on the couch next to an older woman who seemed to be comforting her. Wanda's lip was swollen, and the living room was in shambles.

"What happened?" Jesse asked as she looked around at the mess. "Where's your father?"

Wanda Montgomery tearfully recounted what had happened. "About an hour after you left, two men appeared, asking for Poppa. They pushed their way in here. One of them dragged me through the kitchen into the back yard."

"Look at her face where he slapped her," said her friend pointing, out the bruise on her cheek.

"He didn't hurt me," Wanda said as if trying to reassure herself as well as Jesse. "But Poppa... they said at the hospital he had a stroke. When I got back inside, he was lying on the floor." She started to sob. "I don't know what they wanted."

The woman sitting next to her continued the story. "I live two houses down. I didn't hear anything until Wanda started to scream."

"Did you call the police?" Jesse asked the woman.

"Sure. But they don't do anything in this part of town. They said it was an attempted robbery. But what all do we have to rob?" She started crying too and mopped at them with a white handkerchief.

Jesse looked around miserably. *You won't be around to talk about it.* The assailant's harsh words jarred her memory. Could someone have trailed her to Joseph Montgomery's house? They couldn't have found out about Montgomery through me. How would Santos or Silvero know where I went? No! I'm being paranoid and dramatic, she thought.

Jesse sank into the couch and rubbed her eyes with her hands. "I wish there was something I could do." Jesse petted Wanda's arm, trying to comfort her. "I'm so very sorry."

Wanda continued to sob into her handkerchief as Jesse patted her on the shoulder, overwhelmed by a sense of helplessness. After a while, she stood up and walked silently around the room, lingering over the family photographs, inspecting a few china doll figurines from the assorted collection, and then trying to be useful, carrying the empty coffee cups to the kitchen sink.

"I have to go, Wanda. I'm leaving for the Philippines. There was another attempted coup. It was on last night's news, and I've got a flight out in a couple of hours."

Wanda blew her nose and looked at Jesse as if she had just noticed her presence. "Wait a minute," she said, stood up, and went into her father's room. She returned with the *bulul*. "Take this. I think my father would have wanted it to go back to that village. He always talked about returnin' it himself."

Jesse kissed her good-bye, backed out the door, and looked despairingly at the Montgomery house.

Please let Mister Joseph recover, she prayed, "and let this have nothing to do with me. "Damn bastards," she cursed. If this had anything to do with me or the treasure, I'm going to find who did it. Somehow... I will find them," she pledged, "and then get even."

# Chapter 25

## August 31, 1987. Manila

Jesse dropped her bags at Arnel's apartment in Makati. He was a local photojournalist, and it was well known among the international press that his place was always open for a brief stay to those who couldn't afford a hotel.

She headed straight for Fort Bonifacio. She stood next to Freddy Sanchos, a photographer from *THE MANILA TIMES*, as President Aquino laid a wreath at the monument. It was Corazon Aquino's first public appearance since the bloody coup had failed three days before. Dozens of guards with Uzi submachine guns and M-16's stood on full alert nearby, poised for action.

"The size and ruthlessness of the attack, the treachery that marked it, the brutality of the military rebels who fired on civilians and the timing... prove beyond doubt their murderous intentions," the President was saying to hundreds of newly arrived reporters standing under the hot sun. The press photographers had their long lenses trained on Cory and were clicking simultaneous close-ups of her speaking.

Jesse pushed her way through the pack, joking with some of the wire service guys and nodding to the hotshots from the agencies. The coup in Manila had attracted a broad core of international photojournalists. When she saw Freddy again, she poked him in the ribs. "Where's Gringo?" she asked.

Colonel Gregorio "Gringo" Honasan, one of the heroes of the 1986 'People Power' revolution, had led the unsuccessful mutiny. After a daring escape from Fort Aguinaldo by helicopter, he was reported to be somewhere in northern Luzon. His face adorned the front page of every newspaper in the country. Honasan, with his handsome mestizo appearance and thick black mustache, had achieved the charismatic status of a movie star.

"I hear that he's willing to talk to foreign journalists," Freddy whispered.

"Think it can be arranged?" Jesse asked. In the past, Freddy had provided crucial contacts for her, and she welcomed his hints of assistance.

"Maybe," he answered and moved in front of her to snap another photo of Aquino in her trademark yellow dress.

During the next week, Jesse was too busy to think about the Cordillera. Davidson wanted photos of Honasan in hiding, and she checked out every potential lead. He was reportedly seen riding his BMW motorcycle along EDSA, one of the main highways, or in Camp Aguinaldo talking to the soldiers, or eating at a sushi restaurant. She knew it was just a matter of days before she was contacted; her name had been placed on the proper list.

Honasan had been the head of the Security Operations Group at the Ministry of National Defense. Before the failed coup in November, Jesse had photographed him by his office door, below a sign stating:

**MY WIFE YES, MY DOG MAYBE, BUT MY GUN NEVER.**

Two months after this coup, called "God Save the Queen," she had taken photos of Honasan removing his Gahlil rifle from the wall where it was prominently displayed and cheerfully cleaning out his office. Honasan's superiors were sending him to Fort Magsaysay, in the province of Nueva Ecija. They hoped he would have less contact with the other officers of the 'Reform the Armed Forces Movement' and stay out of trouble.

But when she photographed him a third time, at Fort Magsaysay, she noticed the inverted Philippine flag hoisted on the center flagpole near their headquarters. Many of the trainees were wearing tee-shirts emblazoned with the words: KILL WITH NO MERCY. Honasan had casually admitted that he had taken 400 M-16 rifles, 200 Gahlils, and

150 Ultimax machine gun weapons with him from the Ministry.

"This guy's got the chutzpah to try another coup," she wrote to Alex. "It's amazing just how loyal the men in the army are to one of their own." She knew that Honasan was a popular student leader at the Philippine Military Academy and that he'd organized a faithful following among many of the officers and recent graduates. Even officers that didn't approve of his plans for a military takeover of the government did little to stop him.

Life in the capital was still uneasy after the unsuccessful coup. There were soldiers stationed throughout Manila—in front of the four television stations that had briefly fallen into rebel hands and lining the major intersections of Makati, Quiapo, and Cubao. M-35 trucks filled with armed men combed the streets day and night.

Jesse had focused on the wild look in their faces, knowing well that the militia can be more dangerous than the rebel cadres in the mountains. While the guerrillas had a made a personal commitment to fight for the people and an end to a repressive regime, these soldiers were usually poor boys from the provinces, *probinsiyanos*, who were given guns and ammunition. They were out of control, scared, and in their panic, liable to shoot at anyone without reason.

It was almost dark when Jesse answered the knock on the door. She was expecting a messenger to pick up her film or maybe one of Arnel's friends.

"Surprise," Timothy Connors said, handing her a bouquet of white lilies. "Jesse, this long-distance romance is killing me. The Philippine phone system sucks, and it's awful not being able to talk whenever I want to hear your voice. I'm turning into a crazy man," he whispered while putting his arms around her back and giving her a kiss. "Besides, I've really missed you."

"Tim," she gasped as she pulled out of his grip, completely stunned to see him standing there. She had called him a few times to chat and now remembered that she had mentioned where she was staying. Although she enjoyed their long-distance flirtation, she'd never thought he'd surprise her with a visit. "Holy Shit. I can't believe that you're actually here."

He glanced up and down—at her tousled hair, warm rusty tan, the torn undershirt and the batik *malong* wrapped at her waist, and bare feet. "You are gorgeous," he said, accompanied by an approving whistle. "Wild thing. You make my heart sing," he sang to her while patting his heart.

"When did you arrive?" she asked, still staring at him with disbelief. "Why didn't you let me know you were coming?"

He grabbed her tightly, and they kissed again. "If I stopped to ask, I might not have made such a quick decision." He ran his fingers slowly down her back. "And... you might find an excuse. Anyway, I think you're a woman who appreciates surprises. Am I right?"

Jesse gave him one of her shy smiles that he knew meant yes.

"So. Can you take a vacation from your assignments and projects?"

She immediately started thinking of the places that she'd love to show him and the fun they could have.

"I figured how I could combine business and pleasure since my office has a contract with a public relations firm in Bangkok. I've got three weeks on this side of the planet. At some point on this escapade, I have to be in Thailand for a few consecutive days."

Jesse pulled herself away, walked over to the table, and absentmindedly picked up one of her cameras. When she realized she had it in her hand, she put it to her eye, focused, and shot a frame of Tim. "For posterity," she laughed. "It's not often that someone follows me half-way around the world."

"I wanted to make sure you weren't going with someone else. You became special to me very fast."

*He's such a nice guy*, she thought in response, *and I wish there was some potential for a relationship.* Jesse had relegated Washington and her affair with Connors to the category of 'passing fancy.' Damn. She hated feeling jerked in two directions.

"I'm flattered by your attention. And happy to see you," she replied, touching his arm firmly, "but I never expected you would come all the way to Manila."

A heavy silence filled the room. When she turned to face him, she saw the tension in his expression and softened her tone. She lightly squeezed his arm this time. "It's just that I'm so busy. Still, we can plan things to do together." Jesse knew that she often took memorable pictures when wandering, exploring, and observing on her own time.

"It's so damn great to see a familiar face," she assured him. "Tim, you can't imagine how lonely I sometimes get."

"That's what I came here for." His eyes caught the black and white, poster-sized photograph tacked up on the wall behind her. Two young guerrilla soldiers were washing their clothes in the Chico River. A group of children were playing near a rock in the foreground. Leaning against one of the large white boulders was an M-16 rifle, backlit from the sun.

"Pictures of your friends?" he asked.

"Some of the boys I've met in the countryside. Here, sit down," she said, pointing to a chair. "How long will you stay in Manila? Do you have a hotel?"

"It would be more fun if you would come to the hotel and stay with me."

Jesse went over to the refrigerator, got out a beer, and filled two glasses while thinking fast. She couldn't help feeling flattered that he had come all this way to be with her, but what about her privacy? It was essential for her contacts to feel safe. She needed to stay in Arnel's innocuous apartment. Going to a hotel would jeopardize spontaneous visits by her friends in the underground.

"I don't think that's possible," she told him. "I'm working on an assignment about military coups, and I've still got lots to do. Interviews, more pictures, and editing."

Tim walked over to her and put his hands on either side of her face. His hands moved to her back, and then his fingers kneaded her shoulders.

"You caught me at a difficult time. I wish you'd called first," Jesse said, trying to sound convincingly firm, stammering out an excuse. "I would've made some other arrangements with my work."

"You know damn well if I'd called, you'd have found an excuse. You are just freaked out that I made the next move."

She kissed him lightly on his cheek before pulling his hands away. "C'mon. Let's go out and party. I know some really good bars with pool tables, and then we can go to one of the clubs. I'll introduce you to my friends. It'll take me a minute to get ready." She stuffed her cigarettes into her bag and escorted him out the door.

Jesse was locking the front gate when Tim stopped her hand. "Wait up. I left something for you at the hotel. I'll go get it and be back in an hour to pick you up." Before she had a chance to respond, he had jumped into the front seat of a passing taxi.

She was surprised by his frenetic behavior and walked across the street to the *sari-sari* store to buy a few cigarettes. Reopening the iron gates, she climbed the steps to the apartment and carefully closed the door. Jesse paced around the room, picking up her camera and putting it down, then rolling up and putting away some of her clothes piled messily on her bed. She had tried to create a place that felt comfortable because she knew it would inspire her continuing work. Tim's presence should make her feel secure. Why did it send her into a tailspin?

Jesse lit a cigarette and glanced at the wooden *bulul* (carved wooden figure), noticing how the elongated arms tightly wrapped around its legs in an almost fetal position. The *bulul,* with its oversized head and stern monkey face, seemed to be watching her like a silent yet potent guardian. The answer, she decided, was that Tim represented a realistic relationship. Noel was on the opposite end of the spectrum. This terrified her, and so she had treated him shabbily.

She continued staring at the statue. The *bulul*'s magical presence had a calming effect, and like a magnet, drew her closer until she ran her fingers over the crimson-colored patina. A light rapping on her door broke the spell. She thought Tim had changed his mind, and flung the door wide open. A small, bronze-skinned boy in a tattered tee-shirt looked up at her.

"*Mayroon akong sulat para sa iyo*—I have a message for you," he said, pulling out the tightly folded paper from his pants pocket.

He waited in the hallway while she slit the taped packet with her fingernail.

She read the single sheet of paper with a handwritten message from the rebel commander. He wanted to know about her plans to return to the mountains.

"You're going home after all these years," she addressed the statue as if it could hear her. Her heart was pounding as she quickly scribbled a short reply.

*Kumusta ka, Noel. I've got so much to tell you about my trip home. I want to share all the details when we are together. I'm finishing one last assignment in Manila and in three weeks, I'll leave for the Cordillera. I'll be staying with Tess between the 27th and 30th of September. I'm looking forward to seeing you.*

She added the words *miss na miss na kita.* And in red pencil, wrote KA FLAME inside the outline of a heart before folding the paper into a chicklet-sized packet and handing it to the courier.

# Chapter 26

## The Funeral

The warm September night was heavy with the musty smell of four-day-old flowers mingled with an assortment of women's perfumes. Chapel D of the *Funeraria Nacional* was tepid in spite of the steady hum of the air conditioner. The round, bright funeral lamps threw harsh glares on the well-dressed men and women talking in muted tones.

Over the last few days, Chapel D had seen more than a thousand people coming and going to pay their respects to Tony Carandang. His unexpected death had shocked the upper levels of Manila society. Prominent politicians, businessmen, and their wives arrived every night. Women came in their best mourning clothes; some were escorted by their husbands and others by their bakla fashion advisors.

The wake for the eminent geologist and one of the year's Ten Outstanding Young Men had turned into a major social event. The chapel had become the place to view the body, see people, and make *tsismis* about Tony. Pinky's closest friends—Marina, Boy, and Doris were gathered in the back, speculating about the identity of the woman last seen with Carandang.

"It couldn't have been Pinky. He doesn't need to be discreet with her," Boy whispered to the girls.

"I heard he was seen with Maribel Gonzaga that night at the Silahis Hotel," added Marina.

When Jesse appeared, there was an immediate end to the gossip. The mourners exchanged condolences and gestured to Pinky, who stood weeping near Tony's open casket.

"How's Pinky doing?" Jesse asked the group. "Tony seemed so healthy. Did he have any history of heart problems? High blood pressure?" She smoothed down her frizzy curls that had puffed out like a wispy halo in the humid weather. "What do you think happened?"

Boy, Marina, and Doris exchanged glances, raising their eyebrows.

"Does it make you aware of your own mortality when someone our age suddenly dies?" Jesse questioned them.

"Did you ever hear about *bangungot?*" Boy asked. "Dreams that cause death. Bangungot is a phenomenon peculiar to Filipino men."

"Some people say that men can die in their sleep from a bad dream," added Doris, her voice low as if she were sharing a secret.

"*Talaga.* It happened to my *Tito* Momoy," interrupted Marina. "My *Tita* found him. He went to bed just fine. Next morning, he was dead!"

The official story was that Tony had checked into Room 14 of the Blue Velvet Inn as he usually did when he was too drunk to drive home after a night of poker with his *compadres* at a nearby club. However, nobody believed the official story. The Blue Velvet Inn was not a place where one checked in alone. It was common practice for philandering men and their mistresses to spend a few clandestine hours in the pricey, short-term rooms. Most of the motel personnel were expected to keep their eyes and ears closed to the goings-on around them. But even this private place could not avoid publicity when a famous corpse was discovered on its premises.

The previous evening, the bartender in the Gray Cafe had told Jesse one rumor; the front desk clerk heard a loud scream at the motel around 5 a.m. the Sunday Tony's body was found. By the time the clerk could open the locked door to investigate, Carandang was dead. He was alone in bed. His body had turned as blue as the midnight sky, and his belly was swollen like a giant balloon. When the authorities arrived later, the mound in his stomach had disappeared. There were additional rumors of a cover-up by government officials.

"What about these weird stories going around about his body. That it... was blue," Jesse asked, hoping to prod the group for more information. "I was told superstitions like this one when I was in Kalinga. I didn't believe them."

Boy snickered. "Maybe they should ask the lucky woman who was with Carandang what happened."

Jesse pointed to the front pews. "Who are those three solemn ladies?" she asked, taking her camera out of the bag and focusing the lens towards the coffin.

"That's Carandang's mother and sisters. *Kawawa* (pathetic, pitiful, sad)! See those cheap dresses they're wearing. If there was any cover-up, it was of his background."

But it was to Pinky and not his family that people instinctively offered their condolences. And Pinky, surrounded by a coterie of wealthy matrons, basked in the limelight while she had the sympathy of her friends. If she knew the true circumstances surrounding Tony's death, she kept it to herself, hiding her feelings underneath the mask of a grief-stricken fiancée.

It was common knowledge that their relationship had become a partnership of convenience. A bargain between the two most certainly had been struck, based as much on ambition as any true feelings of love. Jesse guessed that the pain caused by Tony's demise actually spared her the embarrassment of being publicly spurned. After all, he had died at a time when Pinky was still considered the primary woman in his life.

Early the following morning, as Jesse waited at the lab for her photos to be developed, she watched a continuous tableau of snapshots rolling across the color drum and continued her weekly letter to Alex.

*For more than an hour, I've been staring at hundreds of 3" x 5" glossy prints of Filipino life. I've seen cute little girls in frilly communion dresses, chubby babies and their smiling Lolas, sentimental family barbecues, and picture-postcard sunsets with and without a beautiful woman, a guapo boy, or a giggling teenager posing against a tree. It's absolute proof that reality exists on multiple levels.*

*What I'm looking at are personal moments in ordinary lives, and each snapshot records the rites of passage of people that seem untouched by the war in the countryside. These Kodachrome moments are surprisingly comforting. Don't gag, Alex. Sometimes I can almost hear Paul Simon singing "all the world's a sunny day."*

*It's a paradox that the photographic image, considered a source of factual information, can reveal elements of both truth and distortion. Looking at these pictures, I have to admit that photos of war-torn villages are only part of the visual story describing reality in the Philippines. There are so many levels of truth, and I haven't even begun to explore the supernatural events that occur here.*

Jesse stopped writing and thought about Tony Carandang's untimely death, and what Agunay had told her months ago about sharing food with someone who is your enemy. That you can be poisoned and your body will turn blue.

*Alex, sometimes I wonder how I can tell it all. Keep in touch, dear boy. I love you. KA FLAME,* she concluded with a flourish.

After the clerk handed her the prints from the wake, Jesse quickly shuffled through the color images—close-ups of Pinky in the act of mourning, wide-angle shots of society ladies gossiping, and overstuffed *mataba* government officials making deals. When she came to a shot of Tony laid out in his expensive white satin-lined coffin, she stopped to study the photograph. His face seemed puffier than she remembered and showed a faint trace of distain, as if the funeral didn't quite match the standards he had set for himself. Surrounding the coffin were dozens of floral wreaths made up of lilies and *dama de noche*. The flowers were draped with long white ribbons. *Tony, I Love You* said one message with Pinky's name in large gold script. On the other side of the casket was an arrangement of flowers in the shape of a cross that read,

### Tony, We love You -The Santos Family

She turned the photo over and scribbled on the back, *September '87. The Final Remains of Tony Carandang's Passage on Earth,* picked out a few other snapshots, folded them into Alex's letter, then slipped the rest into her bag and headed for a phone.

She'd had dinner twice with Tim since his arrival in Manila, plus one day of sightseeing. He had proven to be very understanding about her privacy, and didn't push to see her again immediately liked she feared. He had projects to do for his office, he'd told her. He seemed to understand to not make her feel guilty about her reticence. Now she wanted to see him. She needed him to give her a dose of comforting hugs.

"Damn," she cursed, after the receptionist replied that Mr. Connors wasn't in town. Like her mother had long-ago predicted, this must be one of those times when her art wouldn't keep her bed warm.

# Chapter 27

## Decisions

Pinky Santos stared at herself in the full-length mirror. It was a relief to get out of the black mourning clothes that she had been wearing for the past three weeks. She turned and looked over her shoulder to see how the demure, pale gray linen dress accentuated her ass. Skillfully twisting her silky black hair up on top of her head, she used a mother-of-pearl chopstick to hold the topknot in place. It had become increasingly tedious to act out the role of a grieving fiancée. However, she'd never admit that to her friends.

"I've been upset since the funeral," she had confessed to Jesse during their morning phone call. "I still break down in hysterics every time I think about poor Tony." When Jesse suggested they go out to a club, she had agreed, but was careful to not sound eager. "Perhaps you're right," she said. "It's time for me to get out of the house. I'll have my driver pick you up around nine. Okay?"

"Tim Connors is back in town. I'll tell him to join us there, so you can finally meet him."

Later that evening, as they were drinking Red Horse beer together, it was Jesse who seemed resigned to melancholy.

"Why the sad face?" Pinky asked as Jesse stared distractedly into her glass.

"I'm mixed up, Pinky," she confessed, followed by a long sigh that indicated the depth of her torpor. "When I first got back to Manila, I was so busy photographing the aftermath of the coup that I didn't have time to think about the Cordillera. Then... surprise! Tim Connors shows up. Followed by your jolting news." Pinky's face instantly tightened, and her eyes teared up at the mention of Tony's death.

"I wanted to be here for you, and sit with your family and friends during the wake. My mountain trip became secondary to your loss."

"*Sayang*. It meant a lot to me that you stayed. I know you miss your friends."

"I do. Now I'm feeling paralyzed. I can't seem to motivate myself to do anything."

The longer she waited, the more reluctant Jesse had been to return to the mountains. What possible life could she share with Noel? His future was grim. How much longer could he evade the military? And she couldn't live with the daily threat of his death. No, unless he was willing to leave the country, they could never stay together. She knew that even if he could get a passport, he would never leave his *kasamas*. She had tried only once to tempt him with stories about New York, hoping to stimulate his curiosity, never expecting he'd accept traveling thousands of miles from the Philippine countryside.

"Come back with me," she had flirtatiously asked. "Why not give yourself one chance to live away from this island. You'll meet people from every continent who are involved in political struggles. You've never been to a museum, a concert, the theater, or a dance performance. Think about the culture. Think about tasting all those delicacies from around the world. You've never tasted Indian curries or homemade Italian food with a good bottle of red wine."

"The first thing I'd like is ice cream," he had joked.

She wondered what his favorite flavor would be. Mango? Coconut? Chocolate? The truth was that she had fallen in love with a man who would not be co-opted so easily. The only chance for a relationship to exist would be if she stayed here to be with him.

"Jesse, are you thinking about Tim?" she heard Pinky saying.

"I was... missing New York," Jesse stammered. She couldn't tell Pinky her conflicted thoughts about Noel. And what did she feel for Tim? She picked up her bottle of beer, took a sip, and then answered honestly, "Pinky, I don't know where I want to be." Looking directly into her friend's eyes, she added, "I'll make one more trip to the

Cordillera and then go home."

They were still chatting an hour later when Jesse glanced over to the bar to order another round of drinks and saw Tim Connors' reflection in the mirror. He had his back to her. "That's him, Pinky," she said, pointing with a nod of her head.

He turned around and saw them. "Tim's so *guapo*," she whispered to Jesse. "Why are you resisting him? If you're not interested...."

Jesse looked up just as he reached their table and felt his hand squeeze her shoulder. She leaned back, took hold of it, and passed it over to Pinky to shake.

"Ms. Pinky Santos," she said politely, "Mr. Timothy Connors."

"How perfect," remarked Pinky, her lips curled up in amusement. "Just when you were getting that puppy dog homesick look, along comes one of your countrymen." Her flirtatious smile made it obvious that she was admiring his handsome features. "Jesse's been moaning that she wants to go home. Now that you're here, maybe she'll stay longer."

Tim picked up Jesse's hand and kissed it. "I followed this woman all the way from Washington, Pinky, and she can't decide if she cares for me." He kissed Jesse's hand again, while his eyes flirted back with Pinky.

Pinky laughed. "Another *bolero*. Men are the same liars everywhere."

"Hey you," Jesse said, and stood up to give him a kiss. "This has been a hell of a few weeks. It was a good thing you stayed in Bangkok."

She studied Tim's face while he was talking with Pinky; he was good-looking, but his lips were too tight, and his eyes veiled a steely coldness. He could never compare to Noel, and that was the problem.

"Tim certainly likes you," Pinky told her after he left, "I'm jealous."

Jesse flushed. "He's like the big bad wolf. He's got eyes for all the girls. Tim knew my sister in college. She wouldn't admit it, but I suspect he dropped her as soon as he found the next woman he wanted to screw around with." She stared at the swinging door that had closed behind him.

"I think you're scared. He's perfect husband material and you know it. You're gonna dry up like a raisin if you don't... you know."

Jesse's cheeks reddened briefly. "It does scare me when he talks about love. I wish he hadn't followed me from Washington."

"Maybe he's working for the government," Pinky replied, laughing again. "Maybe he's a CIA spook!"

"And how many times have I heard people here say that I'm CIA?" she said curtly.

Pinky shook her head. "I can see the amusement is over for tonight. You need a trip to the Cordillera. Go visit your handsome rebel friend. And maybe... well, why don't you have some sexy fun while you are there," she added with a saucy grin. "Who would know?"

"You think sex can solve everything," Jesse replied as they walked out the door.

Pinky's gaiety abruptly disappeared as her eyes widened. She turned to Jesse and clutched her arm. "I really miss Tony."

Jesse held Pinky's arm tighter and wished that she had never made the last remark. She couldn't tell the truth to Pinky. Instead, she was covering it up and bad-mouthing Tim.

"I'm sorry," she apologized. "I know you still hurt. You're right about me, though. I should go up to the mountains."

"Why don't you call Tim and see if he wants to go to Baguio?" asked Pinky.

"Tim?" she stammered. It might be a good way to figure out her feelings for both men. "Good idea Pinky. I was going to ask Don Silvero if I can shoot some pictures at the Oro Mine site. I can get my pix, honeymoon with Tim, and see what that's like. Then he can get back to the States, and I could go on to Kalinga. What do you think?"

"I can't keep up with your energy. You amaze me, Jesse."

What she didn't say, that while she was in Baguio, she also planned to look for some concrete information to tie Don Silvero into the treasure story: something to prove that Silvero was not only looking for the gold, but also covering up his operation.

# Chapter 28

## The Traitor

The ten-hour day shift at Oro Consolidated was just finishing, and the mineworkers were preparing to leave. A group of thirty Igorot men were crammed onto the elevator platform as it rode upwards. Fatigued by their long workday, they suffered silently through the final daily indignation. One by one, they opened their rattan and cloth backpacks and turned their heads away as the guard patted up and down their bodies, looking for hidden pieces of gold ore.

Inside the locked, air-conditioned office, Don Silvero was pacing back and forth, the phone wedged between his shoulder and ear. He spoke in a carefully modulated tone that was as persuasive as it was authoritative.

"I can assure you that I'm just as determined to get this matter taken care of," he said to General Santos, then slammed his fist hard on the desk. Yelling into the phone, he angrily said, "do they think that we are amateurs? They want to keep their fingers in every pie. Marcos may have needed help in marketing the gold internationally, but Marcos is gone. We have other plans."

He paced around the desk, circling like a tiger in a steel cage, and looked over at Cesar Bautista, who stood silently in the corner. "I'll deal with this problem. Santos, tell your friends in Washington that we're going to take care of the American." He slammed down the phone. "Idiots!" he exploded.

Cesar Bautista enjoyed watching Don Silvero lose his temper. Some might find it frightening, but he admired a man who had fire in his veins. Despite growing up in poverty in a mining camp in Benguet, Bautista had been determined to make something of his life. He knew that joining the Armed Forces was the surest way of gaining access to upper-class society and had worked hard to pass the entrance exams to the Military Academy. He had to sweat even more to get good grades, and suffer one humiliation after another as the sons of the rich became officers before he did. But he knew how to wheel and deal, and had maneuvered himself into the position of Santos's right-hand man. To see the General, first, you had to meet with Bautista. In the last year, he had also been called upon by Don Silvero, to "fix" things at the mines when there was a problem.

"From time to time, we have special jobs that are confidential," Silvero had told him. "Some people in the government might not understand what we are doing. But the General and I know we can count on you."

He had gained Silvero's trust and prided himself on brilliantly maneuvering through the powerful elite circles. No matter what was asked of him, he knew how to respond: "Yes sir, no sir, anything you say, sir." All the while, he kept stashing away the money he was able to extort. And he had luck. Just when Carandang was becoming suspicious of his collection scheme, Tony had conveniently died.

Bautista knew about everything going on at Oro Consolidated. He had often heard the workers grumbling about conditions in certain long-abandoned mine shafts—the smells and the odd placement of human bones that were uncovered as they dug down below the water table. The Igorots superstitiously thought those places were haunted by the evil spirits of people who had been murdered by the Japanese during the war. It was also rumored that these bones were markers that would lead to buried gold and stolen treasures that the Japanese soldiers had hidden there.

Bautista had heard stories about treasure maps, that gold was in the mine tunnels, sealed with concrete, and that Oro Consolidated was a cover for the real digging that was going on in those particular shafts. He had even heard Don Silvero and General Santos discussing ways to dispose of the gold once it was found. It was said that they were going to melt the gold into new bars to prevent identification and sell it over an extended period of time so that world prices wouldn't plummet.

Oro Consolidated was the perfect cover. The amount of gold extracted from the mine could shift each year, and no one would suspect the actual source. And if any of the workers gave them trouble or got too curious; their bodies were easy to get rid of. Bautista was excellent at that. Now, he waited patiently for the order to take care of that meddling American photographer.

Don Silvero interrupted Bautista's thoughts. "You understand what you are to do?" he sharply asked.

"Of course, sir. *Walang problema*—no problem. It will look like an unfortunate accident."

"Bautista, you are very clever. There must be no way it can be seen as anything but accidental. We don't want to offend our good friends in the United States."

Bautista nodded. "There won't be any mistakes."

They both smiled, simultaneously raising their eyebrows to acknowledge their contempt for the Americans.

"They are arriving on the 4 o'clock flight. I'll give them a tour of the mine at 4:45."

"Everything is prepared, sir," Bautista said. He turned, unlocked the door, and let himself out of the room.

****

"You're so quiet," Jesse told Tim as the plane descended to the Baguio airport. He had been staring so intensely at her that she pulled back, as if to break his magnetic spell.

"I wish we were going home. I want you to think about moving to Washington. Imagine the fascinating and creative life we can have together. After the work you've done here, you can always get international assignments. Think about the possibilities. We'll be in the center of the political arena. You can still do your stories and also be safe with me."

"Are you proposing that we live together? I'm flattered," she admitted while caressing his face with her hand, "that you're so serious. I don't know. It's a tempting proposition."

"You have no idea how serious I am. I want you with me. And I'll help you," he continued. "I know lots of people in DC. Let's go back together after you finish here. Promise me you'll go back with me," he said so earnestly that Jesse kissed him on his lips.

When the plane landed, they walked into the airport hand in hand until Jesse pointed back to the armed military guards on the tarmac.

"Wonder if any of those men were in Manila the day Ninoy Aquino got shot," she remarked.

"It's amazing how martyred men become heroes," he replied. "Aquino was trained by the CIA. He even boasted of his intimacy with the Agency, and took Cory to Langley for their honeymoon."

"That may be true," said Jesse, "but without Ninoy, there would have been no revolution. His assassination was the final straw that broke Marcos's back. When Aquino was so blatantly murdered, the Filipinos were outraged. The streets were swarming with demonstrators - nuns and priests, students and teachers, the workers linking arms with farmers, peasants, and society matrons. Even the conservatives finally said they'd had it with the government's lies and the military dictatorship. It's ironic because the *tsismis* is that the palace magician told Imelda that if Ninoy Aquino ever set foot in the Philippines, it would bring down their government. And when Ninoy's body hit the tarmac, boom! The Filipinos united wholeheartedly against them."

"Did you even ask yourself why Cory needed the protection of US fighter planes during the last coup attempt if she's so popular?" Tim squarely faced Jesse. "Do you really think the Filipinos are better off now that they've elected Cory as President?"

"She was the people's choice, Tim. Give her a chance."

"I'm trying to believe. But you know she comes from one of the wealthiest families in the country. Sure, her husband got killed, but is she giving up her hacienda to help the poor? Take a good look at the world. Today's villains are tomorrow's buddies," he said, leading her towards the rows of taxis that were parked outside the terminal.

"What about human rights, Tim?"

He grabbed Jesse's arm hard enough to spin her around. "You're like your sister, believing on faith that things will change for the better. So why is it that everywhere you look, you see greed, brutality, and destruction? Look," he said to her lowering his voice, "I want to believe in the good guys winning scenario. Being with you, I remember how I used to want to change things." He embraced her with a light squeeze to her shoulders. "I think that's why I'm falling in love with you. Forgive me, sweetie, for sounding cynical."

Jesse's heart had begun to pump faster when Tim mentioned love.

He opened the door for her to a waiting taxi. "I'm disappointed, though. I hoped we'd have more time together while I was here. I thought if we could spend some time together, you would see..." his voice trailed off.

When they were both inside the cab, she gave him a long, hard stare and didn't talk all the way to Don Silvero's office.

Silvero was outside, talking to his Igorot foreman when they arrived. Jesse pulled her camera from her bag and snapped a few wide-angle photos before he had a chance to object.

"I see you mean to start working before we even say hello, Miss Beckerman. And who is this young man with you?"

As Tim Connors stuck out his hand, Silvero grasped it. "Timothy Connors, Jesse's friend from New York City."

"I hope you don't mind that I brought Tim," she added. "I thought this was a good opportunity for him to see Baguio. We came straight from the airport."

"No, not at all." Silvero looked at his watch. "However, it's getting late, and we should start our trip to the mines. Mr. Connors can tag along if he likes." When he saw Jesse shift the heavily weighted camera bag on her shoulders, he added, "Why don't you let Mr. Connors carry your bag."

"No thanks," Jesse responded crisply. "I can manage."

"If you two don't mind," Tim said, "I'd rather stay out here. I'm not fond of dark spaces. I'll just wander around."

"I'd like to take a few more photos outside before the sun goes down," said Jesse. "Wait, take this," she said to Tim and handed him her small duffel bag, crammed with clothes. "I'll be back in five."

Jesse walked behind a large boulder to shoot the ORO CONSOLIDATED sign. The sky was at its Technicolor peak with yellow rays streaming through an opening in the clouds while hot pinks washed across the lavender sky.

"Damn batteries," she said when the flash on her camera didn't charge as she tried to fill-in light on the billboard. "Damn," she repeated as she hurried over to get the new batteries she'd left in her other bag with Tim.

"If Tony were alive, you'd never treat me this way," she heard Tim saying angrily, just as she was about to walk around the rock that was blocking the two men from view.

"If Carandang hadn't recommended you, I would have had your balls by now," she was shocked to hear Silvero reply.

Jesse turned white; an icy wave rippled down her arms as she surreptitiously listened, inching closer but remaining out of sight.

"Listen, Silvero. Didn't I tell you where the old man lived in Florida?"

"You were supposed to stay with Beckerman and report to me every other day. Instead, my men had to follow your nightly escapades. Spending our money at the local bars, drinking, and doing drugs with the hospitality girls. I haven't heard from you in a week."

"I can explain, I ..."

"I'm not interested in your explanations," interrupted Silvero. "You had something to sell, and Carandang bought it. That may have been enough to save your ass in Washington, but not here. Life can be exceedingly cheap in the Philippines. If I see you as a liability, your government will forget you exist. Your girlfriend's getting too close to our project, and we don't need any more of her photographic exposés when Santos and his men clean out the area. Your job was to get her out of here. No thanks to you, we've heard that she's been making arrangements to travel deeper into the Cordillera."

"But you still don't know what she found out from Montgomery, do you?" Tim sputtered. "I can find out for you. You still need me. I'll find out. I swear it," he pleaded.

"That would be good, Connors. But mess it up this time, and you'll find out just how much my men love to eat white meat."

Jesse's breath was stuck so deep in her throat, she thought she would choke. She looked around for where to run, and when she saw Silvero's office, raced the fifty feet to the door. Tears were falling from her eyes. She forced herself to slow up, entered, and looked for the toilet. At the sink, she ran the tepid water over her wrists. *Tim and Silvero knew each other.* She grasped her cramped stomach and wobbled into the cubicle. She couldn't believe what she just heard. *He screwed me and then told me he loved me.* A flood of nausea forced her to bend over and vomit.

"Oh God," she repeated, realizing her egregious error. "That fucking traitor." Curse words were flooding her thoughts. She kept heaving until her stomach was empty, then limped back to the washbasin and stared at herself in the mirror. "That bastard set me up. He's a fucking, fucking, fucking liar. Nothing about him is real."

How could it be? He had been Jan's good friend. She forced herself to remember their first meeting. How soon after that encounter could he have made contact with the Filipinos? And when did he link up with Silvero and his henchmen? Washington is as small a world as Manila. Someone there must have known she was looking for information about the Buddha. Slowly she sank to the tiled floor, resting her head on her knees. She still couldn't accept what she had heard. Only a minute or two had passed when she heard the door slam. She blotted her face with a handkerchief and stood up.

"Must've been something I ate. I got suddenly sick," she told Don Silvero when she stepped out of the toilet, "and threw up."

"My dear. I'm sorry you are not feeling well," he replied, "but you don't have much time if you're going to see the mine. Unless you'd rather cancel?"

"No. No, I'll be okay," Jesse replied, thinking fast. She had to cover her suspicions and had to get safely out of here. She was definitely on to something with Silvero. This might be her only opportunity to look around. She grimly followed Silvero, her camera gripped tightly in her hand, to where Tim was talking with one of the workers. As they reached them, Silvero nodded to Cesar Bautista, who proceeded to dig his fingers into Tim's arm while twisting it harder behind him in a swift motion. She could see a gun shoved into his back.

"I'm afraid there's been a misunderstanding, Miss Beckerman, and we have to take care of some business," Silvero said, pulling a Baretta 380 from his pocket and aiming it at her.

At the same moment that Tim jerked around to struggle with Bautista, there was a shot. Tim crumpled to the ground like a rag doll. He fell backward with his head twisted at a funny angle to his body. Jesse could see blood oozing through his shirt.

She knelt down and whispered, "Tim?" and watched as the light left his eyes. This must be a mistake. Her whole body went cold. Instinctively wanting to breathe life back into him, and put her lips near his mouth.

"Tim?" she said again, this time louder as if she could wake him up.

"Come with me," Silvero commanded.

"No," she rasped. Even if she hated Tim Connors, she couldn't accept this finality. "No way," she cried out hoarsely and jerked away, surprising both Silvero and Bautista. Then she ran as fast as she could towards the thick bushes lining the road, stumbling once when she heard the crack of a shot behind her.

Jesse crawled on her knees through the tangled underbrush and tall grasses, hearing the voices move further away as she changed direction. She silently cursed her clumsiness and at the weight and bulk of her cameras for impeding her movement. The voices were becoming indistinct. She kept on dragging her bag, praying she was making her way parallel to the road. *I've got to get out of here, or they're gonna find me*, she told herself while taking short, shallow breaths. She was afraid to pop her head out of the bushes. Suddenly she heard a clucking sound, and seemingly from out of nowhere crouched one of the Igorot workers.

"I was told to watch for you," was all he whispered and motioned her to give him her bag and follow as he crawled on all fours. When they hit the muddy embankment of a stream, he stood up. Then, taking her hand, he led her through the woods. They walked at a fast pace for more than twenty minutes until a small house appeared in a clearing.

"You rest here," he told her. "I'll find a ride to take you to town."

Jesse barely moved once he left her. She closed her eyes and remembered the promise she had made to Wanda Montgomery. Call it divine retribution, village justice, or a coincidence of fate. Mister Joseph's death had been avenged.

# Chapter 29

## The Impossible Choice

Jesse was drenched in sweat, the scent of death following her into the deserted house. She lay on the floor for more than an hour. Glassy-eyed, she tracked the shadowy movements of a gecko racing across the wall as it darted in and out of the ribbed pattern of moonlight filtering through the slatted windows until the mechanical sound of a ringing bell echoed off the concrete walls. When she jumped up, the lizard scurried out the window.

"Jesse?"

"Yes." Her heart began to pound as soon as he spoke.

"*Kumusta ka?*"

She recognized his voice, although distortion rendered the words almost unintelligible. "I won't ask where you are calling from, but... holy Moses, it's wonderful to hear the sound of your voice." Jesse heard a small laugh on the other end. She bit her lip as she was about to say his name, caught herself and repeated silently: Noel.

"I need to see you immediately," she pleaded. "Something happened today at the Oro Mines, and I'm really scared. There was this guy... an American that I brought up to the mountains who was murdered right in front of me by one of Don Silvero's men. I thought he was my friend, but found out he was working for Silvero. They were going to kill me too." Jesse held her breath until she heard his voice.

"Listen carefully," he instructed. "Our friend, Leung, will be back very soon. I want you to go with him. I've arranged for a private car to bring you here."

Even as he gave the directions, Jesse was moving, opening her bag and checking her cameras. She laced up her sneakers, grabbed her camera bag, and waited until the native returned.

Leung led her down a dark path, crisscrossing through fields and knee-deep streams. "We must move quickly," he ordered when she stumbled while jumping off one of the logs that bridged a small waterfall. "Ka Noel is more than an hour away."

The driver of the black Fierra started the engine as soon as he saw Leung and Jesse coming along the path. They slid into the front seat. The jeep climbed the steep hill outside of Baguio and headed north towards La Union.

In her head, Jesse tried to list the things she needed to tell the rebel commander, organizing the events as they had happened. But logic was no match for her roller coaster of emotions. Anger at Tim for his duplicitous betrayal, combined with the horror of seeing him die, made her clenched jaw so tense that her teeth hurt. Jesse forced herself to swallow and willed her mind to clarity. *There is no room for weakness*, she told herself, but flinched as the Fierra hit a deep rut. The driver turned off the road and headed towards the trees, shutting off the headlights before reaching a dead end.

"We can walk from here," Leung said. He waited for Jesse to climb out of the car and took hold of her arm. "By now, you are used to these late-night walks." He paused and added, "Ka Noel will be happy to see you."

The cold sweat breaking out on her neck was chilling. Her pants, still wet from the stream, made her rubbery legs shake even more. The only sound as they hiked through the underbrush was the slapping sound of her sneakers in the mud. Jesse did not see the *nipa hut* until they were a few yards in front of it; the windows had been covered to hide the light. When the door swung open, a single bulb, attached to the ceiling by a cord, illuminated three figures sitting at a rough wooden plank table.

Jesse's eyes washed over Noel from head to toe, drinking him in as he moved toward her. For a moment, neither of them spoke. She bent over slightly and placed her camera bag on the floor, never taking her eyes off of him. Halfway into the room, they met. Noel held her tightly, kissing her cheeks and forehead and pulling his fingers through her hair. She lifted her mouth to his and waited the few moments it took for his *kasamas* to leave the room.

"*Mahal kita*—I love you," he whispered as he led her to a wood-framed bamboo bed near the wall.

Jesse's eyes darted once around the empty room before her hands caressed his face. Noel stared at the door, placing her hands near his heart. "I wanted to be alone with you."

"What about your men. What will they say?"

"*Wala akong pakialam*—I don't care." He kissed her lips. Her mouth opened wider as they breathed each other in. She pressed him down to the floor and felt his hardness beneath her.

"Silvero tried to kill me," was all she said as she pulled off his pants and tee-shirt, shifting her weight so that she was fully on top, and rubbed her lower body over his. Noel's lean body seemed to have shrunk; the protruding hip bones dug into her abdomen.

Her fingers traced a circle around his face, into the hollows of his temples and under his cheeks. She moved her hand down his chest, using her palm to glide over the sharp ridges defining his ribs and abdomen. The velvety smooth skin was stretched like a drum. She rubbed the inside of her hand along the deep cavity where the tight muscles of his glutes joined his sinewy thigh. It was like the sculptured contours of boulders she had once climbed in a stream bed. Jesse imagined that the smooth indentations had been carved by water rushing over stone.

He rolled her onto her side, pushing up her sweatshirt and held her, one hand on her breast and one hand on the small of her back. As her body arched, Jesse closed her eyes, feeling the trail of his kisses down her neck and on her bare chest.

Memories of the mountains, the waterfalls and their last night making love, flooded back. She responded instantly to his touch.

"*Tumingin ka sa akin*—look at me," he commanded as if she was one of his soldiers. Jesse opened her eyes. His face, not more than six inches away from her, expressed a vulnerability that she had never before seen. It lasted an instant before Noel shook her and said, "I put aside everything in my life... everything... in the fight for our land. After Leila's death, I understood my selfishness. When reporters come to glorify and write stories about Ka Noel, the rebel hero, I want to tell them no. I could not be with my wife when she needed me most."

"You should not blame yourself. You couldn't go to her. You would have been arrested. How can you have such guilt when you have sacrificed so much to fight for all your people?"

"Leila is one more death I am responsible for. From that point on, Jesse, I slammed the door tightly on my personal desires. When Leung reported that you were at the mines and there had been shots. An American had been killed. That you had escaped. I told him to find you and bring you here. I knew I had to see you again." Noel's lips hungrily found her mouth.

"What will happen to you?" she asked between their kisses.

"*Hindi ko alam. Wala akong pakialam*—I don't know. I don't care," he repeated, but this time the tension in his voice betrayed his despair.

She tightened her fingers and massaged him slowly, using her thumb to stroke upwards from base to tip. He grasped her shoulders roughly and pulled her towards him.

She whispered in his ear, "Noel... I love you."

"Don't love me!" Then he shook her hard and pushed her away, as if hurting her would stop the tenderness of her kiss. "Can't you see that I offer nothing in return for your love?"

"Shush," she said, using one hand to momentarily cover his mouth and the other to pull his head closer to her. "You are everything I've wished for and dreamed my lover would be."

His lips and tongue swept her body, alternating between kisses and tiny bites while his hand stroked rhythmically between her legs until the moisture soaked her jeans. He quickly pulled them off, moving his tongue down her legs. When she moved to hold him, he whispered, "No, let me do this," and kissed her on the mouth and on the eyes. In response, she lay back and spread open her arms and legs.

He used his fingers, explored softly inside her, and then moved them deeper. Her newly sensitized body had never exploded in so many places, and all she knew was that she wanted more. She was already flying, soaring aloft as his fingers launched her further into the sky. She was riding air currents, no longer a physical body but elemental like the wind. He was driving her upward, and she flowed like a river in a typhoon-driven frenzy until she could stand it no longer and rolled her body on top of him.

She used her arms to push up and then lowered herself onto him. She looked into his eyes just as they half-closed, and balancing on one leg, moved up and down until he used his hands on either side of her waist to pull her down hard. Her body arched as he came up to meet her. Locked together, she wrapped her feet around his legs as he pushed up, thrusting even higher into her. He rounded his lips, using short breathes to cool her sweating body until his breath turned into short howls that melted into her animal moans. They reached the apex of their flight with a climax that exploded like a roar of waves bursting inside her head. Exhausted, she fell on top of him as he tightly hugged her to him, kissing her face.

Wordlessly they stared at each other. Noel's eyes were red with tears.

"*Naalala mo...* do you remember," he asked, "the night when I gave you the necklace?"

Jesse put one hand on his cheek and murmured, "So that I would never forget you. I always carry it with me, in my camera bag."

His dark eyes narrowed, and he turned his head away. "You should never have become involved. There are some things, Jesse, you can't fix. You don't understand the danger and what they could do to you. These people will kill you next." He pushed her hand away, and bitterly continued, "I have lost too many friends in this goddamn war. I want you to go home."

"Go home? How ironic. Both you and Tim Connors are alike on

this point. How dare you tell me what to do!" She threw his black tee-shirt at him and quickly pulled on her sweatshirt and pants. "Damn your machismo and damn the danger. I don't see it stopping you from fighting." She glared at him, her eyes flashing. "What about the complicity between Tim Conners and Silvero? I've got to find out what they are covering up. What they thought I was going to expose. Is it the gold that Washington is interested in? Or something else? What about Tess? How can you shut me out now!"

Jesse saw Noel glance at the door and stopped her tirade. "I thought you said you didn't care what they thought."

When he didn't answer, she pleaded, "Noel. Look at me. *Tumingin ka sa akin.* I'm sorry." She kissed his lips. "It's not just the story. I believe in what you're fighting for. I want to help. You know you need the money to continue. Tess thinks it's possible to locate the treasure, and I agree with her." She lit a cigarette, stood up, and started pacing the room. "And you're wrong. I can do something. I'm going back to the mines to see what I can find out."

Noel remained seated on the edge of the cot. His face looked gaunt; his mouth hung limply open as he was staring upward. With only the shirt draped over his torso, he appeared to her as the kind of tormented figure that El Greco would have painted—a Christ figure whittled down to the barest bones after his descent from the cross.

"Oh God, I'm sorry," she said, getting down on her knees in front of him. Noel lowered his eyes to look at her, and the pain that she saw in his face made her gasp. She wanted to put her hands inside his body and cradle his heart.

Jesse stroked his face. "I love you, Noel. I want to be with you. Please. Let me help you." In the silence that followed, she held him tightly, then whispered, "Let me love you."

"Go out to the car," he said. "I'll follow soon."

"Kiss me one more time," she whispered, "and then I'll leave." Their hearts pumped as if each beat was dependent on the strength of their embrace. Then Jesse picked up her bag and started to walk out the door. She stopped, pulled her camera from the bag, and walked

,back towards Noel, focusing the lens as she moved.

He was lying on the cot, his arms limp at his sides, his eyes closed. She clicked the shutter. When she stood over him, she took another photo with her wide lens accentuating the angularity of his body. He didn't move at the sound except to open his eyes. She took one last close-up of his face, neck, and rail-thin shoulders, then abruptly turned and walked to the waiting vehicle.

In the back seat of the jeep, next to Leung, was a man who introduced himself as Father Nilo Dammay. It was difficult for Jesse to make out his features in the dark. Within minutes, Noel slid into the front seat and looked at the watch on his wrist.

"We have twenty more minutes before I leave," he said. "Tell us what you know about the American who was killed. What is his connection to Silvero?"

Like a good soldier, Jesse gave a concise and unimpassioned description of their relationship. "I admit we were intimate, but I had no reason to distrust Connors. He was a family friend. He had excellent credentials: a former student activist—a radical. I heard Silvero say something about Tony Carandang, and I don't know the connection, but Tony did his graduate work in Washington. Maybe he met Tim during his school days."

"You were getting close to uncovering something important and..."

"And that insidious bastard sold me out," she said, angrily finishing Noel's sentence. She wanted to scrub herself inside and out when she remembered Tim's words of love and how easily she had responded to his attention. She covered up her shame, forcing herself to focus and report the details of her visit to Florida.

"Before he was attacked, I asked Joseph Montgomery about the statue. He didn't know anything about it or about a map."

When the jeep lurched to a stop, the guerrillas jumped out in unison. Noel was frowning as he leaned back into the window.

"Be careful," he warned Jesse and abruptly turned away.

"You too," she said, aching to kiss him one more time.

# Chapter 30

## The Magnet to Men's Hearts

With a coughing sound, the Fierra started up a steep hill. Jesse was crying so hard that her handkerchief was soaking wet, and she couldn't quell the overflowing tears. It was no longer a test of which one of them was stronger. It had become apparent that Noel needed her, no matter what he said. But there could be no expectations for a relationship. She could not fight by his side. Would she have the courage to wait patiently till this war ended with the hope that he'd live through it?

I'm way too insecure and self-centered, she thought, and we'd always be arguing. It would be her fault when this tug of war between them broke down his strength. Jesse knew she was abandoning Noel, but if she stayed, he would be compromised.

Father Dammay's soft tenor broke the silence as he hummed a Filipino ballad. Then he eased gracefully into the conversation.

"Did you know, Jesse, that four centuries ago, the friars were calling gold, 'the magnet to men's hearts?' They believed that Divine Providence had placed the gold in pagan lands so that men would be inspired to leave their countries. In their wake would come the preachers of the Gospel."

"The Spanish conquistadors and priests had a stake in the Cordillera?"

"Of course. Greed is a powerful force. The rumors of gold in the mountains had attracted the Spaniards as early as the mid-sixteenth century. But our ancestors resisted their attempts to occupy the mines, so the conquistadors sailed to Mexico following their quest elsewhere. Two hundred years later," he continued, "the people of Benguet were still fighting battles to keep the Spanish away from their mines."

"And three hundred years later, the mining concessions are largely in the hands of foreign investors," said Jesse.

Father Dammay shook his head. "Perhaps. Temporarily."

"Don't the Igorots work for Oro Consolidated? They seem to have lost the battle."

"Jesse. Don't forget we are the third-largest gold producer in Asia. With avaricious men like Marcos and Silvero raping their own land, we have battles to fight on many fronts."

"Father, knowing what you do, how can   you really believe that the Igorots can win back the control of their resources?"

The priest remained silent for a minute. "Look out there," he said, pointing to the shapes of Benguet pines silhouetted against the morning sky. "What do you see?" In the same breath, he answered, "The land. The supreme treasure of God's creation. Saint Ambrose said, 'The earth is given to all, not to the rich alone.'

"Did Nicasio... I still call him that by habit, Jesse. Did Nicasio tell you that he spent one year in the seminary—the Society of the Divine Word? When we first met, I was one of the guest lecturers. We were like two fish out of the sea. Both of us from the Cordillera."

"Why did he quit?" Jesse asked. "Noel told me some stories about his student days. He said that he was oppressed by the other students because he was an Igorot."

"There was discrimination at the seminary. He was always asking why the natives were not treated with respect by the lowlanders. Why our customs and laws were not honored by the government. He quit because of a disciplinary incident; the order has a strict rule about not leaving the seminary premises. When the Taal volcano erupted, many seminarians rushed to do relief work. Nicasio stayed away the longest, and his superiors debated whether to expel him. He didn't give them a chance. He wrote that he could not remain in so isolated a society and enrolled at the University of the Philippines."

"Excuse me, Father," said the driver, interrupting Dammay. "We're close to Baguio. Where do you want to be let off?"

Dammay looked out the window. As the sun rose above the mountains, his leathery face, wrinkled from years of exposure in the northern countryside, softened in the dusty yellow light.

"Near the bus station," he said, turning back to Jesse. "Nicasio said you are determined to do a story about Silvero and the buried treasure. Do you understand that you might not be able to tell what you have witnessed? Do you realize how dangerous a published story would be for everyone you care about?"

"I know it's dangerous," she replied. "Look what happened to Joseph Montgomery because of me. I feel responsible for his death. That's why I have to do something."

"Tell me, Jesse. How much are you willing to give? Every day, people risk their lives to fight with the poor. People with the best of intentions are killed in the struggle for freedom. Tess and Nicasio have made this commitment." The priest waited a moment to gauge her reaction. "Are you willing to make such a sacrifice? Think about it." He pulled out a pencil and torn sheet of white paper. He scrawled down a telephone number.

"If you need my help, they know where to find me. Stop here, driver," he said and exited from the Fierra. Dammay turned once around, raised his clenched fist high enough for Jesse to see the gesture, and disappeared into the crowded street.

She stuffed the paper into her pocket and looked at her watch. Stores were opening their gates. Hordes of people were crossing streets on their daily routes to work. Jesse dragged her body into one of the nearby shops to have chicken broth with noodles. She mechanically put the spoon to her mouth, hardly tasting the food.

*Stop thinking about him.* Jesse could still feel Noel's touch as if it were a fiery brand etched into her body. She glanced around the crowded restaurant to see if anyone had noticed her reddening face. Never before had she told a man that she loved him. But how could she give her heart to Noel, and accept that he might be killed at any moment?

Her only resolve was to prove her courage. She had to find the link between Silvero and Tim, expose Silvero's ties to Washington, and figure out who was behind Montgomery's murder.

By ten o'clock, the taxi had dropped her off near the sludge-filled lake where the residue from Oro Consolidated's gold ore processing was dumped. In the distance, she could see the ramshackle miner's homes that perched precariously on the hills. A giant metal crane stood like an iron dinosaur to the side of the road. Next to it was a smaller plow, used to clear mudslides from the roads in the rainy season. Stenciled in black on the sides of the construction equipment was the name ICHII STAR. She wondered whether it was coincidental that the largest foreign contracts for road equipment were given to Japanese companies.

Jesse hugged the bushes with her body and stayed within the shadows near the entrance. She waited, and when she saw no one moving around the area, cautiously headed towards the spot where Tim Connors had been killed. She crouched behind the large boulder, keeping her eyes trained on Silvero's office.

Suddenly, two large barking Dobermans came charging around the rock, followed by Cesar Bautista. He held the chain leash taut as the dogs bared their teeth in front of her. Jesse backed against the rock and eyed the automatic rifle in his hand.

"*Saan ka pupunta*—where are you going?" he demanded gruffly, grabbed her shoulder, and pushed her towards the main office.

Don Silvero was on the phone when Bautista marched Jesse into his office. "I found her outside," he said, continuing the rest of the sentence in Ilocano.

Shaking his head, Silvero motioned for Jesse to sit down. "I didn't expect a return visit so soon. No matter. But you know you must have a guide to take you into the mine."

Jesse nodded, her throat constricted. Cold-blooded. Bastard. Inside the mine is where he wants to get me. I've gotta find a way to stall them, she told herself, until I can figure my next move.

"Good," Silvero said, looking at his watch. "Bautista will take you." He gestured to the man, giving him instructions in Ilocano.

"Tell me one thing before I go, Don Silvero," she said, glaring at Bautista, "how did you link Tim Connors to me so quickly?"

Silvero laughed and, in a patronizing tone, said, "Stupid girl. There are more than a few businessmen in your Congress who understand the necessity to protect their financial interests in the Philippines. Where do you think Marcos got the money for the deforestation projects in the Cordillera? We have had many silent partners funding our lumber concessions. *Sayang.* You had a bigger story than you knew."

"About what's hidden in the mines?" Jesse asked as Bautista put the gun to her back.

Silvero stood up, walked past Jesse, opened the door, and gestured for the American to follow him. "The treasure was more than gold, my dear. Biological weapons were stored at Subic, and President Marcos was paid handsomely for the favor. Some of those weapons mysteriously disappeared. Quite a breach in security. Now where do you think would be a good place to hide them? And how much would such information be worth?"

Jesse shook her head in disbelief.

"Can you see how alike you are to members of your government? How we laugh when you come to the Philippines with your enlightened mentality and personal agenda. You Americans underestimate your 'little brown brothers.'"

Bautista pulled on the dogs' chains seated by his feet and gave Jesse a shove with his rifle.

"No. I don't think you're going to tell your story," Silvero said as the Dobermans yanked against the heavy chains. "Connors was easy to buy."

Bautista pushed her forward—Jesse numbly moved as if her feet were unconnected to her body. They walked along a barren grayish-yellow hill that had been stripped of all timber and life.

"*Nandoon*—over there," he said, pointing to a heap of twisted metal, old tires, and junk that sat in front of a dark hole between two large piles of gravel. Two rotting wooden beams supported the entrance. A piece of decayed aluminum sheeting held up the roof. He tied the dogs to a spike sticking out of a wooden pole. Then he took his flashlight from his belt, turned it on, and gestured for her to enter first.

The inside of the mineshaft was almost black. Bautista's small light focused three feet ahead and barely illuminated the walls. She felt increasingly claustrophobic as they walked deeper and deeper into the interior. The crunching sound of her sneakers grated in her ears.

Jesse was sweating. She put her hand into the camera bag and grabbed the small can of mace packed inside. *Let the bastard make his move.*

When Bautista did, the beam of his light shone upwards and illuminated his face in a blinding flash. His dark eyes were filled with hatred. "*Puta ka!*" he growled through clenched teeth as he dropped the light, grabbed her hair with one hand, and backhanded her face hard with the other.

Jesse's head jerked back; the impact left her ears ringing. "Damn you," she yelled in a voice mixed with hatred and fear. She brought her hand, holding the can up to his face, and sprayed the mace directly into his eyes. Bautista screamed. As he fell backward, she kneed him in the groin with all her fury.

She half-turned to run, but Bautista lunged forward on his knees, blindly grabbed out, and connecting with her ankle, tripped her. Jesse went sprawling forward and kicked back hard with her free foot. The second kick hit squarely in his face, and the third connected with his neck. She was panting hard as she lunged free and scrambled to her feet. Without looking back, she ran up the narrow shaftway.

Jesse saw the shadows of the chained dogs at the entrance. Flattening her body against the stone wall of the cave, she passed just out of the reach of their jaws. They continued to bark frantically as she ran to the road.

It didn't take long before one of the frequent jeepneys that ferried workers to and from the mines passed. She flagged it down, jumped in the back, and rode towards Baguio, with one thought in mind. At the bus station, Jesse reached into her pocket, took out Father Dammay's number, and dialed the phone.

"Is Father Nilo there?" Jesse asked the woman who answered. "I must talk to him immediately."

"*Wala pa dito*—he is not here."

"Tell Father Nilo that Jesse Beckerman called. Tell him I'm in trouble, and I'm taking the next bus to Manila." After leaving the message, she bought a ticket and quickly climbed aboard.

*Forget the story*, she told herself. *Forget the gold. Forget about Noel and Tess. Forget about the prizes. Forget the whole fucking adventure*, she repeated silently. *Just get the hell out of here.*

# Chapter 31

## Manila - Devastating News

Jesse telephoned the priest as soon as she reached Manila. She could not risk going back to her apartment. She asked if he could send someone to get her passport, some money, and if he could help her find a place to stay until she figured out what to do next.

"Father, one more favor," she added. "I have a small statue, a *bulul* that I got in the States, and I promised I'd bring it back to Tanduhan. Could it be delivered for me?"

Dammay assured her he'd make the necessary arrangements and told her to go immediately to the house of a friend. Later that evening, Jesse wrapped the *bulul* in a tee-shirt, packed a few other shirts and a pair of pants into her backpack, and headed for the church.

She flagged down a jeepney on Avenida Rizal. "HOLLYWOOD" was carved in big wooden letters and outlined in Christmas lights above the front window.

The jeepney snaked its way up Avenida Rizal, steering in and out of the tightly packed stream of vehicles and people. While skinny boys caught free rides—jumping on and off the backs of buses—others sold roses, newspapers, Stork menthol candy, chiclets, and single sticks of cigarettes, adding to the dense confusion in the dusty streets. Jesse hung one-handed to the overhead bar as she was slowly inched half out of her seat to make room for more passengers. She felt oversized, taking up the space of two petite Filipinos. She pushed her bulky camera bag and backpack tightly between her knees, making room for one more woman to squeeze in.

"*Mama, bayad,*" Jesse said, trying to make herself heard above the deafening wail of the song blaring from the driver's cassette.

She had ridden enough jeepneys to know the ritual of handing her 65-centavo fare over to the man sitting next to her who, in turn, handed the money to the toothless woman beside him. Absentmindedly, she watched as her fare changed hands down the line until it reached the outstretched hand of the driver who popped the coins in a little wooden box below the image of the Sacred Heart bedecked with *sampaguitas* and dried orange flowers in the middle of the dashboard. To ward off evil spirits, the anting-antings hung from the rear-view mirror.

Out on the street, the headlights of a passing taxi pinpointed a gang of children surrounding an American sailor. Kids she'd photographed, had told her that they would sniff glue and get high with the money from the servicemen; it was a momentary escape from the ever-present hunger. As she thought about their desperation, an overwhelming sadness engulfed her.

The orange twilight soon faded into darkness, and garish red bulbs cast crimson shadows on the faces inside the jeepney. Jesse tried to move her body and ease the throbbing cramps in her legs. She glanced at the old man seated directly across. His thick callused hands and deeply etched face spoke volumes of his long years of hard work. He reminded her of Joseph Montgomery.

Looking up, Jesse's eyes caught the epigram painted ornately on the ceiling of the jeepney amidst paintings of bucolic settings of nipa huts, coconut trees, and blonde women with huge bared breasts— DRIVER SINGLE — POGI ANG DRIVER—said the sign that proclaimed the virility and machismo of the driver.

The jeepney driver was going up an unidentifiable side street, having customized his route as he had his jeepney. Jesse glanced at the small opening through the pile of cassettes that blocked the front window, past the array of gleaming silver horses and mirrors that decorated the hood, to see if she had missed her stop.

"*Mama, para,*" she yelled, rapping her knuckles on the jeep's ceiling to get him to stop. The driver braked in the middle of the street. Gathering her bags, she half crawled to the back, stumbling over the other passengers' legs and belongings. She was still bent over after landing on the pavement when Jesse felt a hand push her right into the path of an oncoming car.

It all happened so fast—the screech of brakes, the shrieks of people nearby. And then she was in the middle of the road, her belongings spread around her. She saw a hand reach out of the crowd, grab her backpack, and disappear. For a brief moment, she seemed suspended in time. With a sickening jolt, the sounds came crashing back.

"Stop him," she yelled before touching the painful bruise on her shoulder. Hands surrounded her and helped her up.

A small boy pointed in the direction where the thief had fled. "*Doon*," he said. Shaking, she mumbled thanks, grabbed her camera bag, and ran in the direction the boy had pointed. But when she reached the street in front of the Quiapo Church, a crowd of half-naked men with towels around their necks blocked her way.

Still unsteady, the men around her pushed Jesse in all directions. The acrid odor of perspiration from a multitude of gleaming torsos assaulted her senses. Although she tried to make her way out of the crowd, she couldn't. Instead, she was pushed forward by the sea of bodies. Black heads swayed rhythmically, first to the left, then to the right, and then lunged forward to the beat of unintelligible groans. On a hand-held platform above the crowd, Jesse saw a giant ebony-colored statue. When she turned around, a thousand pairs of charcoal eyes on the faces of half-naked men stared back.

Far off in the distance was the sound of traffic and rock and roll music. Panicking, Jesse looked up at the sky and gasped for air. The last thing she saw before she passed out was a huge black Jesus Christ on a wooden cross looking down at her.

****

A blunt nose, watery brown eyes, and a large silver cross on a link chain were the things Jesse noticed when her vision cleared. "Don't try to get up yet," Father Nilo admonished from the chair by her side.

Obediently she stayed still, feeling the hard bench beneath her body. Her head hurt when she tried to twist it to see where she was.

Jesse reached her fingers to her mouth, touching her swollen tongue and dried lips.

"Today was the Feast of the Black Nazarene," Dammay told her, reading the question she was trying to form. "You ran into the middle of the celebration. You fainted and were carried to the Sacristy."

Jesse looked up at the high domed whitewashed ceiling. Across the room, sitting on top of an immense wooden dresser with ornate silver handles, were gold candelabras and religious statues. A painted crucifix was built into an arched recess on the opposite wall. She turned to Father Nilo and said, "I remember being pushed..."

"One of our people accompanied you in the jeepney. We made sure that you would not be alone." The priest pointed to a familiar shape. "Your backpack is here."

She stared at him with a wan smile. The priest took hold of her hand, and his face grew somber. He took a deep breath. "Jesse. I have some bad news... some very bad news. There was an ambush early this morning. Nicasio... Ka Noel was killed."

Jesse's heart tightened painfully in her chest. "Oh no!" she gasped, jolting upright. "No. Not that." She squeezed her eyes closed as if the lids could become a protective barrier to shut out the piercing agony. The silence of the room was replaced by a roaring sound in her ears. She placed her hands over them, opened her mouth wide, and inhaled sharply. She was drowning in the noise.

"Why him?" she repeated over and over. "*Bakit? Bakit siya?*" The priest shook his head. "Was it because of me? He took a chance, didn't he? He came out of hiding to try to arrange protection for me."

"No. This has nothing to do with you," answered Father Nilo sharply. "Ka Noel was a soldier. He was doing his duty to the people he loved. His life was dedicated to the struggle in the mountains."

"Don't talk about him in the past," she pleaded. It was inconceivable that she would never see him again, never hear his laugh, or feel his touch on her skin.

"Death claims its victims without bias. You have been here long enough to understand, Jesse. You have witnessed how the Philippines is bleeding. After so many massacres, we are hemorrhaging. Our blood drips through the fields until the rivers flow crimson, and no one is safe from the violence. One day it is a church worker, and the next, the brightest of our student leaders. In the provinces, whole families are taken from their homes and executed. Can you now understand how the passion for God's justice grows stronger in the face of such agony? Why the peoples' courage becomes stronger in the face of death?"

It was like a searing fire had burnt off patches of her skin, leaving her insides raw and painfully exposed. "Father. How can you talk about God's justice when your people are so hungry that they suck the moss off the stones in the bloody rivers? How can you still love God?" she whispered.

"Christianity teaches us about the love of men for each other. Nicasio shared his life with the people. Through that love, his existence had a purpose. Like Christ, he offered his life so that others might live ,and like Jesus, he confronted the powers that be and paid the price. His sacrifice was his final gift to us; the fulfillment of his giving. It was the proof of his love."

"I don't understand," she screamed. Her voice echoed off the marble walls. "Don't give me a priest's sermon. How can Noel share his love if he's dead?"

Father Dammay took her hands and repeated the words of Christ, "Those who hold on to their life will lose it; those who risk their life in the service of the people will find it." He stared directly into her eyes. "When I was ordained, my life's work was to teach men to love God by loving each other. How could I reconcile the role of the church when faced with injustice? So many of my people are suffering. The wealth of this country sits in the hands of a few." His voice became taut. "As a disciple of Christ, I cast my lot with the poor, with the homeless, and the oppressed. I made a vow to truly serve my fellow man. To have nothing. To give everything. To give my life for the liberation of my people. But the military says I must choose. I can feed the hungry, but not those who ask questions. I can visit the poor, but if I visit with those who dare to dream of a just society, then I am marked as a subversive or, worse, a communist. And if I dare to speak out about repression and impoverishment, then I am threatened with prison and death."

Jesse pulled her hands away and clenched her fists, overwhelmed by the iniquity of Noel's death. "What do you tell people, Father, when they say that they are willing to rid the world of the monsters and tyrants, to commit murder, if necessary, for what they believe is right?"

She stood up and walked over to her backpack, feeling the weight of the *bulul* inside. She pulled out the statue, placed it near her heart, and waited for an answer.

"With such hatred in your heart, can you know what is right? What is truth? The military thinks they know the truth. So does the government. So does Silvero. Can you be sure that you know what the truth is?"

Jesse stood absolutely still. She knew the truth, and nothing would ever be the same again in her life. She nodded her head, silently affirming her response.

Dammay stared into her eyes. "Then I say that violence must be met with violence. That the biblical cry for justice is a morally defensible act."

Jesse moved closer to the burning candle behind the priest. She could feel the heat from the flame under her hand and rolled the dripping hot wax between her fingers.

Dammay walked over to Jesse and put his hand on her shoulder. "I asked you once before. Are you willing to give your life?"

Jesse stared at the figure of Jesus nailed to the cross behind the priest's head. Her gaze locked on the crown of thorns and the trickle of blood from his punctures.

"We all have our jobs to do," Dammay said quietly.

"I'm going back to the Cordillera," Jesse said. "I have to take this there... myself."

# Chapter 32

## The Cordillera

Small white wooden crosses dotted the roads and hills throughout the Cordillera; each one a graphic installation marking a bloody encounter during the years of civil war.

As Jesse climbed the rock stairs, she wondered where Noel had fallen, whether someone had placed small stones or flowers on his grave and if the wind had swept them away. She wanted to know every detail of how he'd been killed. Had Ka Georgie or Ka Abel cradled him tenderly, so he was not cold or alone as he died?

There were no rebels stationed at the outpost to ask. She gazed towards Sleeping Beauty. Ta-u-ngay was asleep in her stone coffin, covered by a blanket of green-velvet brush while the muddy terraces, like an earth-filled womb, surrounded the slumbering giant with seedlings. The children did not scream out in chorus, "Americano, Americano," when she entered Tanduhan, and the clusters of squatting men and women smiled briefly as if she were native-born. Tess was crouched by the hearth, boiling coffee. A deeply etched pain streaked her taciturn expression.

Jesse unwrapped the carving and placed it on the floor between them. Then she gave Tess a strong hug.

"I came to bring the *bulul* home and tell you about Mr. Joseph."

"And talk about Ka Noel?" she added bitterly.

"I need to know, Tess. Did Noel get ambushed because he set out to help me?" The words caught in her throat. From the moment Dammay had told her that Noel was dead, it was as if she had split in two. The cool Jesse focused on the job she had to do, and her devastated twin had a skewered heart.

"I know that I was the one to bring you here with my dreams of gold. He told me it was not your business. *Apo.* I was so sure I was right. I worried for your safety... not for his." Tess poured coffee into two cups and handed one to Jesse. "It is hard to understand why the spirits tease me so cruelly. I knew he would die, and there was nothing I could do to prevent it."

Jesse took hold of her hand. "Tess. I'm so sorry. So very sorry."

"No! Don't say you're sorry. You don't know what I can see. Before the peace-talks started, I saw a red-haired witch rising from the river with golden oranges in each hand. A full moon surrounded by a rainbow appeared the night before Ka Noel was killed, a sure sign someone important would die." She stared wide-eyed at the statue before she rubbed her hands over the wood. "When I was a child, *Ina* told me stories about the rice god who lives above the sky-world, in the fifth region of the universe."

"But you go to church each Sunday. How can you still believe in your pantheon of deities?"

"Because we must live! Without rice to eat, we will not survive. I can never ignore the rituals to appease the *arans.* Before planting and harvesting, we must offer food to the spirits to protect the fields, the granaries, and the fertility of our crops. Each generation in their turn knows to respect these ceremonies."

She turned the *bulul*'s face towards Jesse. "It is said, when there is a death, that a *bulul* can be used as a bridge to the sky-world." Her dark eyes glazed, becoming almost transparent.

"Tell me how. If there is a way that I can see him again... what should I do, Tess. I want to believe that it's possible."

Tess gestured for Jesse to hold the statue against her chest. The women withdrew into silence, the words between them unspoken.

Jesse closed her eyes. Under a canopy of lilies swirled a rainbow of faces - Alex, Jan, Tess, her parents. Two figures dressed in black fatigues exchanged bullets instead of rings before a volley of gunshots signaled their kiss.

She could feel the squeeze of a child's hug and the trail of wet kisses on her cheek. Black fuzzy hair pressed against her face, and as the tiny, honey-colored fingers wrapped around her own, she seamlessly blended into the picture as the daughter, the mother, and the wife.

Jesse didn't know whether ten minutes or ten days had passed when Cecilia arrived to accompany them to Gan-ao's house. She walked along the stone path clutching the warm *bulul* to her body as if the pressure would keep her visions intact.

"*Kumain na tayo*—let's eat," commanded Gan-ao, putting down plates of boiled okra and rice.

Jesse forced herself to part with the statue and mechanically wash one hand in the basin of water. No one spoke until Jos-we picked up the sculpture from the bamboo floor. He turned the figure over in his hands.

"I was there when Nestor gave this *bulul* to the American soldier," he said, scrutinizing it with the childlike awe of a new discovery. "Tell us, Jesse, what you can say about Mister Joseph."

Jesse cleared her throat. "Joseph Montgomery treasured your gift and kept it by his bed. He clearly remembered you and Nestor and the time he spent in Tanduhan. We spoke about *utang na loob*, his gratitude, and he told me that when he prays, he still thanks the people for their care and protection." Jesse's voice began to waver. "Wanda, his daughter, said that he always kept this *bulul* near him." She paused, rocked by a wave of grief.

In the darkening room, Tess put her arm around Jesse's shoulder. Jos-we gestured for one of the children to pour coffee and turned his head so as not to notice Jesse's tears.

"Jos-we. Do the Kalinga use *bulul*s in their ceremonies?" Jesse asked the old man after a few minutes had passed. "I thought the rice god was part of Ifugao lore."

Jos-we rocked back on his heels and took out his clay pipe. Then he rolled some tobacco from his pouch, stuck it into the pipe, struck a match on the floor, and lit it.

"Mister Joseph asked for men from all the tribes to fight in the resistance," he answered. "A boy from Ifugao brought the *bulul* with him."

"But why did you give it to Joseph Montgomery?" Jesse questioned the elder.

"As a remembrance. Before the Japanese army retreated, they burned everything in the village, shooting everyone they could find. They murdered villagers, guerrillas, and their lowland prisoners. Nestor's father and a young Ifugao warrior were killed. We hunted them down to avenge their deaths. It was Nestor who found this statue near the corpse of a soldier. When he searched the body, he discovered the drawing. That night, we killed a wild pig. We sacrificed it to the *anitos* and dipped the *bulul* in its blood."

Cecilia interrupted the storytelling. "My father told me that when the war ended, everyone was hungry because the fields were destroyed. When the warriors caught the Japanese, they promised them food, then killed them, taking their heads."

Jesse whispered to Tess, "Remember the jawbone attached to the gong? Didn't you say it was from a Japanese head? I thought you were kidding!"

Jos-we relit his pipe and blew out puffs of smoke. "The enemy's skulls decorated our huts. There are still bones around if you want to see them," he said, looking at Jesse. "It was the time I got this tattoo." Jos-we pointed to the deep blue cross on the bridge of his nose. "The night we dipped it in blood, we gave the *bulul* the name Joseph to remember the American. He fought like a warrior against our enemies. Before he went away, we gave him the statue. We wanted..."

At that moment, an explosion rocked the hut, sending the pigs squealing and the chickens flying.

"Mortars," yelled Tess, "they're firing from across the river."

They heard a whistling sound before a rocket slammed into the stone wall of the terrace below, shaking the house like an earthquake. Then they heard the whirling blades of a chopper.

"Get outside," yelled Jos-we as he pushed Jesse to move and jump from the bamboo porch to the ground beneath the floor.

Crisscrossing beams of light swept on angles across the village. Tess squeezed Jesse's hand tightly as the military passed back and forth overhead, then turned to buzz the coconut palms on Sleeping Beauty's face. They heard a muffled round of mortars on the outskirts of the village before the chopper disappeared into the nitrogen-blue sky.

"They wanted only to scare us," she said angrily, leading the group up the steps. "They could easily have destroyed the village."

For the next few hours, the natives went from house to house, checking the damage and repeating stories of what they had witnessed. Jesse listened silently and took notes. She only spoke before they went to sleep when Tess reminded her to finish her story.

She told her friend all she knew about the Montgomery family, about the lumber concessions, and about the missing biological weapons.

"Do you realize how this could implicate the American government? What hubris! Or maybe it was the Army. I mean, if they really built igloos to hide weapons and your government knew about it..."

"Wait a minute, Jesse," interrupted Tess. "It is not only dangerous if our governments learn we have this information. The weapons are stored here, right? On Kalinga soil? What are these biological weapons? If there is some sort of accident, it could endanger everyone," concluded Tess.

"This story is so staggering. I have to be sure I can substantiate Don Silvero's information. The military might not stop next time," Jesse agreed, "unless we figure how to turn this information around to your advantage."

They talked until the first light of dawn, understanding there was no time left to wait.

# Chapter 33

## The Golden Buddha

Jesse followed Tess up the path to the rice terraces above Tanduhan. Tess clutched the *bulul* in her hand and gazed across the valley. The morning fog, suspended in a band across the top of Patucan Ridge, obscured the outline of Ta-u-ngay.

"When I was a child, I'd stand right here, pick a point in the distance, then run across to the terraces. I'd make my way up, as if walking a giant stairway to the sky, and lie on my back in the very spot I'd seen. It seemed as though I could float between the pines and the mirrored pools of water in the terraces."

Tess squatted and absentmindedly split an *atswete* berry in half. After rubbing the red dye from the seeds onto her lips, she stroked the *bulul*. The grim expression on its monkey face seemed to change into a half-smile as the carved lines filled in with red stain. She broke open another berry and rubbed it along the back of the carving, feeling the smooth contours under her fingertips as she inked in the grooves.

"This is how it must have looked when it was dipped in the blood," she told Jesse.

"Jeez! It's scary. It looks like a ghost!"

Tess held the painted wooden statue at arm's length, twisting and turning it back to front and on its side as if it were a stepping stone offering passage from one world to the next. As the minutes passed, she was no longer caught in the gap between the past and the present, between the *bulul* and the contours of the mountain, between the earth and the sky. Like a sculptor, she saw the form of the statue become the outline of Ta-u-ngay; the carved lines on its back flowed exactly like a waterfall along the opposite ridge.

"*Apo*," Tess cried out, jumping up excitedly. "Look over there, Jesse," she said and pointed across the valley. With her finger, she carefully followed the lines of the backbone down to the base.

"Follow me," she said, ignoring Jesse's puzzled expression. "I've explored every trail on that mountain. As children we used to climb all over the face and body of Ta-u-ngay. I've watched the rhythms of the land—the terraces, fields, waterfalls, and vegetation—change through every season of my life. I know the colors and the shapes of the trees like I know my mother's *salidummay*."

Tess carried the *bulul* in her shawl as they made their way across the valley and up the side of Sleeping Beauty.

"It's buried somewhere here. *Alam ko*. I'm sure of it," Tess exclaimed when they came to the pool of water at the bottom of the falls. She held the *bulul* at arm's length again. "Nestor may have added these carved lines and grooves to the statue. He would know how to identify the spot."

"Tess. Are you kidding? You know where the treasure is hidden?"

Tess nodded and turned in a circle. "See... the falls are this line, and if you put your finger here, right at the base of the statue's back, you'll feel a slight indentation. Look around. Somewhere nearby, there should be a hole or ridge."

Although they both walked step by step, carefully examining the ground, they could not find any unusual dips in the terrain.

"Forty years have passed. Maybe the bushes covered the spot," said Jesse. "Could you be mistaken?"

"No," she said emphatically. "The statue is buried here. I know that."

While Tess continued to scour the area, Jesse sat down on a boulder and lit a cigarette. Her eyes followed her friend as she walked back and forth in frustration.

"Tess," she called out, "I have an idea." Jesse jumped down and walked over to a large rock. "Remember the lotus stone that the

Buddha sat on in your drawing? Maybe there's a marking or a hole in one of these boulders." Together, they began to carefully examine each rock, wiping away dirt and moss as they searched.

It took less than an hour before Tess brushed off the dirt covering an arrow that had been chiseled into the granite. The arrow pointed down. They looked at each other in amazement.

Tess broke a stick off a bush and started to dig. The ground was damp and easy to remove. Jesse found a branch and started another hole a few feet away. Two more hours were spent digging, and all they had to show for their work were mounds of soil and broken fingernails.

"Let's go back and get some tools," Tess said.

"I'll stay and keep digging. I don't want to leave this spot," said Jesse.

Tess laughed at her. "The treasure has been asleep for many years. I think it will wake up by and by. Come on. We need to eat."

They returned after lunch, accompanied by Agunay and Cecilia. Each woman carried a small trowel. Jesse was taking photos of the site when Agunay struck something hard.

"Over here," she yelled. Tess dropped to her knees, using her hands to push away the loosened soil. Cecilia and Agunay joined the frantic digging while Jesse continued to shoot photos.

"I knew it would be near to this rock," Tess exclaimed as she cleared away inches of dirt from the top of a rounded object wrapped in a shredded blanket. She yanked at the old fabric until it fell apart in her fingers.

The flame *ushnisha* on top of the Buddha's head peaked out from its hiding place. Thirty minutes later, the statue was completely free. It took two of them to carefully pull and lift the heavy Buddha out of the ground. The gilt bronze stood almost a foot high and glinted in the afternoon sun.

"Oh my god. *Ang ganda*—It's beautiful," yelled Jesse as she crouched for another angle. "Brighter than any of the pictures I've seen in books!"

Cecilia, Agunay, Tess, and Jesse walked around the statue, spontaneously holding hands as they moved in a circle, beating out the rhythmic steps of a traditional Kalinga dance with their feet. Jesse could almost hear the music of the gongs.

"No one must know that we found it," cautioned Tess when they stopped moving, "until we figure out what to do."

Agunay suggested they call a tribal meeting of the elders, while Cecilia wanted to send a message to the rebel cadre. "Once the government finds out, they're sure to send the military to take it from us," she said.

Jesse kept shooting pictures. "Hallelujah. I can taste the Pulitzer," she gleefully admitted, waving her arms up and down between shots.

"We have to be smart," interrupted Tess. "If we tell anyone, even within our clan, the story will spread. And we'll lose the Buddha. Someone will steal it, and later, the military will certainly bomb the village."

"Outsiders will arrive looking for more of the lost gold," added Cecilia.

"We have to plan wisely if we are going to use it. We have to be smart." At the sound of the clicking of the shutter, Tess glanced at the photographer. "What about you, Jesse. What can you say about loyalty? Can we believe you will keep our secret? Will you do that for our people and for Noel?"

Jesse put down her camera and stared at each woman for a moment. Hearing her lover's name was like the twist of a knife in her heart.

"I've lost my parents, my brother, and now my cousin to this war," Tess pleaded. "I can never forget that their sacrifice was for us, and for our children."

Jesse sighed deeply as if the air could fill the vacuum of sorrow, anger, and loneliness in her chest. "Promise me that you'll use the Buddha to get the money you need. If somehow, it can improve life here or make the military leave you alone, then it's worth it." She waited for Tess to nod, then gave a thumbs up and opened her camera, pulling out the roll of film and exposing it to the light.

After placing the statue back in the hole and covering it with dirt, the women returned to the village. Throughout the night,ord the discussion continued. When the morning light began to fill the sky, Tess outlined her plan. Before separating, they each repeated a pledge:

"To honor this decision, to never speak of our secret, in the name of our ancestors and all those who have died in the struggle to protect our land."

# Chapter 34

## Revenge

Tess placed the Buddha on a rock and quarter-turned it after each shot was completed.

"That does it," said Jesse, putting her camera back in the bag. "We've got all the angles." She watched Tess begin to wrap the statue in a blanket. "My library time in Washington was well spent. I'm almost certain this Buddha came from Thailand. I'd say the thirteenth or fourteenth century. The gesture of the palm pointing downwards is called 'touching the earth.' Siddhartha was meditating during the night of his enlightenment and wanted the earth goddess to witness the merit he had accrued during his lifetimes."

"Did she see his good deeds?" asked Tess.

"He must have done something right because he achieved Buddhahood," Jesse laughingly answered. "Now, the next step on our path towards enlightenment is to get Don Silvero and General Santos to take the bait."

They had spent time going over the details to ensure that their carefully crafted plan would work. Jesse had decided that no other negatives or photocopy of the statue should exist and used her Polaroid camera to record the shots.

"Be sure to contact Father Dammay. Tell him when you will arrive in Manila. And be careful, Jesse," Tess instructed, "when you speak to the General and Don Silvero."

"I'm gambling on their greed," Jesse said, putting the Polaroids into her backpack. "I don't think they will care that much about me."

After embracing Tess, she started down the mountain. As she

walked across the hanging bridge, Jesse felt unencumbered by the heavy emotions of the past week; it seemed like a lead yoke had slipped off her shoulders.

"Yes," she said while raising her hand in a clenched fist, "this is for Noel." She admired the shamelessness of the scheme they had designed. Now it was up to her to see that all the elements fit perfectly.

When Jesse arrived in the foothills of Tabuk, she went directly to the local PILTEL outlet and handed the operator Silvero's number. She waited nervously inside the small booth but hung up in terror after two rings. She lit a cigarette and asked the clerk to redial.

"That's right, Don Silvero, I'm still here. And I've got a deal for you. Listen carefully. We did it. We found one of Yamashita's golden statues. *Talaga.* I'm willing to give it to you... for a price. One, I want to get out of here safely and two, I want to find out more about the illegality of the stored biological weapons. I want some names of the men you did business with. I don't need to quote you as my source. *Alam mo*, the Americans had no intention of upholding your constitution. That's what the press will focus on. And you can have the statue. It's in excellent condition—gilt over bronze. Classic 14th century Thai, seated in the earth touching gesture. After all my research, I can tell that the sculpture's worth a fortune."

Jesse pictured Silvero's swiney face as he received the news—his eyes growing furious, then narrowing while his mind tried to reason and find a way to outsmart her.

"What makes you think I'd be willing to trust that you have the real thing?" he asked.

"I've got photos as proof, and after we complete our arrangements, I'll be happy to send them to your office. General Santos already offered me ten thousand dollars," she bluffed. "We know that it's worth so much more, but my friends want me to make this deal quickly and see that I get safely home with my story. I'm willing to accept his price unless you can make a higher bid and give me the info I need." Jesse counted two beats until Silvero replied.

"Do you really think you're going to get out of this country so easily?" When she didn't answer, he added, "I don't understand what's in this for you. Be smart. Give me the Buddha, forget the story, and you can have more money than you ever imagined. You're young. What could the Philippines mean to you? How can you compare living in the States to a country where you can count the hours of consistent electricity on one hand? This is not your fight. And even if your friends keep the statue, it would only be a short time before we'd find it. You're only stalling the inevitable. Now is your chance to get something tangible for yourself. I've always admired your dedication. Put your idealism in a place where more people can appreciate your talent. We can set up a production studio. You could direct documentaries. You like exotic places. Why not shoot the unspoiled beauty of the rain forests? You could explore Palawan. Work for me, if it's adventure and artistic expression that you want. Oro Consolidated has holdings and subsidiaries in other countries. Travel first class and forget about this statue. You're a smart woman. I'm sure you would appreciate the special bonuses I could give you."

He was offering her so much that Jesse knew it was all a lie, but his greed would be his downfall. She took a deep breath and exhaled slowly before she answered. "You just don't get it, Don Silvero. I'm doing what I want to right now. Stop jerking me around." *You bastard*, she thought. *I'm gonna make you sweat.* Jesse counted to five and replied, "Pinky told me that her father had made plans to be in Hong Kong next week. You know how Pinky loves to make *tsismis*. I heard that the General had already made a deal with a Chinese consortium."

"When can I get the statue," he countered.

"When you supply the information I need, I'll give you the place where you'll find the Buddha. That is, once I'm safely out of the country." Jesse's voice was cool and calculated. She forced a tight smile. Everything depended on her confident behavior.

"And thanks for the job offer. One of my dreams is having the budget to shoot documentaries. It's tempting, but it gives me real pleasure to say no. I don't think we'd agree on the content. I'll call back in an hour," she promised, hanging up the phone. Now to get

Santos hooked.

"Yes, General," she said, "*Talaga*. I'm telling you the truth. Don Silvero made me an offer of twenty thousand dollars for the statue. Despite all I've been through, I owe something to your family. Pinky is my best friend. Don Silvero told me that he was counting on you being in Hong Kong and not finding out about the deal. I'd be willing to sell it to you for ten thousand if you can assure me a safe passage out of the country within 48 hours."

While Jesse waited for the General to speak, she closed her eyes. *You're doing good, girl. Bluff and play them off each other. Santos thinks he's getting a bargain, and Silvero is convinced that the General is selling out to a Chinese consortium for a huge profit.*

Then she called Silvero back, closed the deal, and wrote a note to be hand-delivered with the Polaroids. It instructed him to take his car and driver—she prayed it would be Bautista—to Mount Data Lodge in Benguet. She knew Don Silvero would feel comfortable doing business from the expensive inn.

Of course, there were a few details that Silvero didn't know. Somewhere along the narrow road to Mount Data, his vehicle would be stopped. Perhaps a landslide. There would be another jeep waiting, filled with laborers from the mines. His car would go over, an accident which frequently happens on the treacherous mountain roads.

They had arranged another plan for General Santos. Roxas, the treasure hunter who had found a Golden Buddha in '71, had been contacted. He was more than willing to sell his brass copy of the statue for $500—a small fortune for a man from Baguio, who had been cheated out of his discovery by the Marcos family. Fuzzy snapshots had been taken of the fake and delivered to Santos's office.

By the time the General tried to sell the copy, she planned to be long gone from the country. A phone call from the States would assure him that his name would be left out of her article if he agreed to halt the military's action against the natives. She was sure he'd be agreeable; the ensuing scandal could easily affect the stability of the new government. Tess would bury the original so that it could not be discovered. There would be no proof that there was a 'new' Golden

Buddha. Even if Don Silvero's Polaroids were found, they would be totally faded because the prints had not been properly coated.

It was dangerous, but instead of fear, she felt elation—in control of the situation and determined to succeed. She went over her timing, planning how to get back to the village that afternoon, then down to Manila within two days.

After calling the airport to check her reservation, Jesse walked rapidly to the station and took her seat inside the next jeep leaving for Tanduhan. She lit a cigarette and put a tape in her cassette. The music of the brass gongs filled her ears.

# Chapter 35

## Yamashita's Treasure

Jesse climbed to the top of Patucan ridge, letting her eyes swept across the immeasurable stretch of terraces. Thin shoots of emerald seedlings were poking through the mud. Dotting the fields were scarecrows, basketwork figures that looked like large gulls with distended wings waving in the breeze. The bogus flock appeared to fly, dipping and turning in unison to scare away the smaller birds from eating the young plants.

As a light wind wafted along the canyon, Jesse longed to stay suspended in this moment—hovering between the spirits in the sky-world and the mauve-green valley. Like a palpable beat echoing across the mountains, she could feel the rhythm of the Cordillera heartland and focused her camera for a few last photos.

"*Kumusta ka,*" Tess said, in a low voice that swirled from the haunting breeze.

"*Mabuti,*" Jesse answered automatically.

"*Masydong tahimik dito*—it is so peaceful here. Will you be sorry to leave?"

Jesse felt a deepening gloom settling over her. She licked her index finger and held it up to the wind. "I'm tasting the air and sucking in the view. I've got to saturate my vision with the forests and the rivers. When I get home, I'll need to remember how every detail meshed so gracefully. I only hope that my images will provide as clear a picture."

She took two steps back, looked through the wide-angle lens at Tess with Sleeping Beauty as her backdrop, and clicked the shutter.

"It was naive of me to think that my photographs would change things. Ironically Tess, it was only by giving up my ambitions that I was able to help you at all."

"What do you mean?"

"I can hear Noel's voice in the whisper of the trees. I think about him constantly, and it's made me crazy. I ask myself whether he was driven by vengeance. After he died, my passion... my love... turned to hatred and a burning desire for revenge. The only thing that mattered was getting back at Silvero and Santos. That's why I told Father Nilo I didn't care about publishing the story about the hidden gold. It seemed a small sacrifice. Noel was dead, and I was out of my mind with grief. I would've sworn anything to honor my lover. But now that I'm going home, I realize just how magnanimous my promise was." A bitter laugh escaped from her lips.

Tess was startled. "Jesse. Do you intend to reveal that it was found?"

Jesse picked up a rock, threw it over the side of the mountain, and followed its path as it spun downwards to the Chico River.

"For over forty years, people have been searching for Yamashita's treasure. It's hard to believe that we found a piece of it, and yet no one outside Tanduhan will know." She was beginning to feel sorry for herself. "If the story was printed, I would receive the credit, and maybe, for one brief glorious moment, I'd bask in the stardom." Her voice began to waver. "Think of the exposure... the talk shows and interviews."

"Is that so important?" Tess asked.

"You couldn't understand what individual success means in America. Without it, you're on the very bottom of the heap. Without it, you have no identity. Even my family sees it that way. People are critically judged by what they've last accomplished. With this story, I would have won the blessings of my agency. My journalist career would be assured. Now I can't help feeling like a failure."

Tess was shocked by Jesse's candor. "Is that what you really care about? The rewards? I don't understand how you can forget the sacrifices we've all made. The price we have paid in lives."

Seeing the crestfallen look on the tribal woman's face, Jesse carefully tempered her reply to reassure her of their deepening friendship. "Tess, I don't want to disappoint you. I was in love with Noel, and I love you too. You're like a sister to me."

"And you have become part of my family. You should stay here with us."

Jesse stooped down and picked up another rock and threw it out, over the edge of the cliff. "It's not that simple. If Noel were alive, I don't know that I could leave. But now I'm going home, and the values there are so different. I'm being honest about wanting success. Yamashita's story could bring me one notch higher on the ladder."

Tess took a step back, as if to break the intimacy. Her guarded eyes reflected a growing apprehension. "Do you still believe the sacrifice was worth it?"

"Look at the breathtaking beauty of this valley. Down there," Jesse said, "an old man is wading through the water while his caribou is pulling a wooden hoe. It's always been the same. I see consistency in your life. And I know that the Cordillera is worth fighting for."

She paused and shook her head. "In some ways, it's been an honor to be able to make such a grandiose gesture." She turned towards Tess and saw in her expression a resolution that had evolved through centuries. Jesse was envious.

"Father Nilo told me that we all have a job to do. Ka Noel's was to fight for the revolution. Mine is to record what I see. And all my experiences—naïveté, anger, fear, and love are burned into every frame of my film."

"But you have proven that you are capable," Tess replied. "To be witness to the earth requires a strong conscience and a sense of justice. Isn't that enough to gain the respect of your people?"

Jesse thought about the narrow line she had crossed when her professional objectivity had collided head-on with the overwhelming pull of her emotions. Davidson, for one, would feel that she had overstepped her bounds.

"Months ago, Noel told me that there were no innocent people in this struggle. Why did I think I could walk away, untouched?" she asked her friend.

When Tess didn't answer, Jesse posed another question. "Tell me again how the Kalinga deal with justice."

"Silvero will be taken care of by tribal law. That is the custom."

"What about the men, women, and children who get killed in the process?"

"Some will die, but others will be born. And they will live in the land of their ancestors. The continuity of the Kalinga people will be our justice."

"So the secret's to live in the land of your ancestors, in a place that has neither a beginning nor an end. And if you know where you belong in this cycle of existence, then you know something about who you are. What about me? What should I do, Tess? I've got wounds that I'm cherishing at the same time that they're hurting. It's like I'm running through a maze that's filled with brambles, and in my mad rush to embrace life, I've skidded away from my family, my friends, and my lovers." Her head was spinning. It wasn't going to be easy to leave Tanduhan, to return to the western world of fleeting moments and disposable culture.

"Do you think you can forget us when you return to America?" asked Tess, "Here, the children will tell *salidummays* about Ka Flame who danced all night to the gongs. They will tell how your *anting-anting* wove a spell around the military. They will sing about your tears that fell like rain to the ground and mixed with our bones. Their chants will be woven into the web of our history."

Jesse smiled at her friend gratefully. For years she had been battling the demons raging inside, indulging her need to be alone yet wanting to share her life. She could picture the resignation in the commander's eyes. "He knew he was going to die."

"Noel was willing to give his life," Tess answered as she pulled out the wooden *bulul* from her backpack. Like a *hilot*, she knew how to counter the pain that was tightening its grasp through Jesse's chest. "Hold this," she ordered.

Jesse gripped the *bulul*. When she squeezed it to her heart, she could hear the Chico River race through the canyon. The rushing water harmonized with the sound of a flute. She looked up and a faint outline, like a thinly developed print, appeared in the bright white sky.

Tranquility had erased the pain and his lips, when they brushed her mouth, turned upwards into a smile. He spread her hair so the wild strands of copper could soar on the wings of the wind-god.

In that perfect moment, Jesse understood the truth of her vision: through exploring, observing, and listening, through her passion and following the wandering call of her heart, and through caring for others, she had been given a miraculous gift.

Tess reached down, picked up a handful of dirt, and placed it in Jesse's hand. "This place and the spirits that live in the terraces, the waterfalls, the trees, and the rivers will always be part of you," she promised.

Jesse unfastened the chain around her neck. "A remembrance," she said as she gave the Amitabha, her protective talisman and escort into the pure land, to Tess.

****

A week later, Jesse was showing Jonathan her edited photos. She had been enthusiastically describing what she'd seen of the war in the Cordillera when Hugh Bonner knocked on Davidson's door and announced he was leaving for Cambodia.

Bonner couldn't resist gloating and added, "Rumor has it, Beckerman, that most of your Philippine film got destroyed in a flood. Did I hear the news correctly?"

As her face turned a deepening scarlet, Jesse stood up and slammed the door behind him.

"Damn that man and his ego." She reached in her pocket to touch the fading Polaroid.

"Whoa, slow down. I've got something here for you," Davidson said, handing her the fax he'd just received. "It must be your lucky day. A six-page assignment for *CALIFORNIA Magazine*." He put his arm around her shoulder and read the memo out loud. "Guaranteed week in San Francisco. Photograph 'Yuppies' in the Haight area. Focus on trendy restaurants, boutiques, and upwardly mobile people who have replaced the hippies."

Jesse seemed preoccupied in picking a loose thread off her shirt cuff. Scarred into her memory were the callused hands that had reached out to touch her in the Philippine countryside; people who had given her their testimony, believing she possessed magical powers to relieve the fear, the pain, the grief, and the hunger.

"What is it? You don't want the job?" he asked.

"It's only that... what about these photos from the Cordillera? It would make a damn fine essay." When he didn't respond, she continued more forcibly. "Jonathan. There are rumors of another coup in the Philippines. I should go back in a few weeks. I've heard stories about contamination from toxic wastes around Clark Air Base and that radioactive wastes were dumped into Subic Bay. I've developed important sources. I can leave immediately for Washington and get some photos and quotes about whether the government's intending to clean up around the bases." When he still didn't reply she snapped, "I didn't want to tell you before I checked it out, but I heard from a reliable source about biological weapons that were supposedly stored there as well. What if some of them are missing, Jonathan? What if those stolen containers were transported to another location and the containers began to leak into the water or break open? Think about the ramifications if people start to get sick. C'mon. You know this is a big story."

Bonner knocked on the door, and said loudly, "You ready to get to work, boss? Or are you still working with the kiddie squad?"

"Okay, Jesse," he replied while easing her out his door as he handed her the slides. "You've got some good ideas. Let's talk about them later."

What she knew was that she had to put Noel's spirit to rest. She had to walk the terraces again, find the cross marking where he'd been killed, and sit by his grave. She had to tell him about the missing weapons and follow through on the story. No way Jonathan's going to blow me off, she thought, and headed for the nearest phone.

"I need a reality check," she explained to Alex when he answered. "I know it's dangerous, but I want to go back to the Philippines? What do you think, Alex?"

"Darling, I can't believe you're asking me this," he said. "You cried yourself to sleep last night. From what you've told me, you have the makings of an incredible exposé."

Her voice dropped to a whisper. "What about the Buddha? Did you believe what I told you about that as well? Do you think I'm a fool for not publishing that story?"

"Sweetums. "You're the one who's always telling me to do what is right. At any cost. I've attended far too many memorials and I couldn't do a fucking thing for my friends. How am I supposed to fight? You're the lucky one. Listen, girl," he said before hanging up, "you took your vows. Now it's your choice whether to show people the unimaginable."

Jesse stood at the desk with her Philippine slides and wondered about her destiny. Whether the screams from the ground would continue to haunt her. If she would always be a wanderer, looking towards the sky-world for voices and visions or searching under rocks for the roots of her own tribe.

"Later is too long to wait," she told Davidson barging back into his office. She spread her slides on his lightbox. "Here's my story. Call it 'Witness to the Earth.'"

****

By the grave near the ancient narra tree, Iss-oc was smoking her pipe while Vicky breastfed her baby and Gan-ao picked lice out of her daughter's hair. In front of her house, Agunay poured the morning's leftover gruel into the pig trough. Cecilia, walking back from the river with a stack of washed pots on her head, squatted down to talk to Tess, who was pounding straw-colored stalks of rice with a pestle that was longer than she was tall.

Over and over, Tess rhythmically caught the hand-carved stick as it bounced off the wooden bowl. She stopped once to touch the charm on her neck and look up at the quiet sky, then spit into her hands and continued her pounding.

Her village was safe. For now.

# Glossary of Tagalog & Kalinga Words and Phrases

*Aba*: exclamation of surprise or admiration

*Adobo*: national dish of the Philippines

*Ah, leche*!: Ah shit!

*Alam ko*: I know; *Hindi ko alam*: I don't know

*alam mo*: you know

*Ama*: Father

*ang ganda*: beautiful

*ang sarap mo*: totally delicious

*anitos*: ancient spirits, sculptured objects

*anting-antings*: protective charms

*Apo*: God (Kalinga)

*aran*: ghost, enchanted being

*atswete:* seeds to give a red and orange color to sauces

*Ay naku*: oh no

*Bakit?:* Why?

*Bakit doon?:* Why there?

*bakla:* homosexual

*balut:* unhatched duck embryo in its shell

*bangungot*: bad dream that causes death

*barangay:* village

*barong Tagalog*: the traditional Filipino white dress shirt

*basi*: Igorot sugarcane wine

**bayad**: here's my fare

**berdugos**: the executioner

**boleros**: liars

**borbortak**: plant full of the natural iodine

**bulul**: a carved wooden figure used to guard the rice crop by the Ifugao peoples of northern Luzon.

**dama de noche**: the white perfumed flowers that bloom only in the evening

**di ba**: right or isn't it

**ganda mo pa naman**: you're still nice

**gayuma**: love potion

**Ginayuma na naman**: they bewitched her with a love potion

**Ginebra**: 80 proof sugar cane alchohol

**guapo**: handsome

**hacienderos**: plantation owners

**halika na**: let's go

**hija**: daughter

**hilot**: healer

**Hindi ko alam**: I don't know

**hukbalahaps**: the Filipino guerrillas

**i-daw**: revered bird that forecasts omens

**Igorot**: people from the mountain

**Ina**: Mother

**Kaboniyan**: Igorot God

**Ka, kasama**: friend, comrade in the rebel army

**kamoteng kahoy**: cassava

**kare-kare**: a Filipino food

**Kawawa**: pathetic, pitiful, sad

*kiangan*: vegetable field

*Kidor*: god of thunder

*Kilat*: god of lightening

*Kumain na tayo*: Let's eat

*Kumusta ka*?: How are you?

*kuraraw*: cry of female ghost heard after midnight

*kuwentong kutsero lahat*: it's all gossip

*Lengua estofada, calderetang bibi*: Ox tongue braised in tomato sauce and duck stew

*Lola*: Grandmother

*mabuti*: I'm feeling fine

*malong*: fabric tied as skirt or dress

*Mahal kita*: Sweetheart, I love you

*mamagkit*: beautiful

*manamos*: washing

*mandadawak*: shaman (Kalinga)

*masarap*: delicious

*Masydong tahimik dito*: it is so peaceful here

*mataba*: fat

*Mayroon akong sulat para sa iyo*: I have a message for you

*merienda*: afternoon snack

*mestiza, mestizo*: mixed race person

*Miss na miss na kita*: I miss you so much

*nakakagulat*: surprisin, strange

*naku*: no

*Naalala mo*: do you remember

*nandoon*: over there

**nipa hut**: a type of stilt house indigenous to the cultures of the Philippines

**palikero**: playboy

**palanos**: an engagement party

**pancit**: noodles

**pan de sal**: bread rolls

**pangat**: tribal chief

**para**: stop

**Para hindi ka makalimot**: So that you will not forget us

**pare**: best friend or buddy

**piko**: traditional Philippine game hopscotch

**probinsiyanos**: poor boys from the provinces

**punte siete**: point seven

**puta**: prostitute, whore

**Putang ina mo umuwikana**: go home son of a bitch

**Saan ka pupunta**: Where are you going?

**sagsagni**: coutship dance

**salidummay**: a chanted oral history

**Saan ba nagmana 'yan**: where did she get her good looks

**Saan ka pupunta**: where are you going

**sari-sari**: local convenience store

**sampaguitas:** Philippines national flower, a species of jasmine

**sayang**: general term for too bad, love, an expression of regret, hello dear, not good, what a waste

**Sige na**: go ahead

**tabo**: dipper

**takbo**: run

**talaga**: really

**tapis**: hand woven wrap-around skirt

**teks**: children's card game

**Tita**: aunt

**Tito**: uncle

**tsismis**: gossip

**tumbang preso**: traditional Philippine game hit the can

**Tumingin ka sa akin**: Look at me

**ushnisha**: the topknot on Buddha's head

**Utang na loob**: Debt of gratitude

**Wala akong pakialam**: I don't care

**Wala pa dito**: He's not yet here

**Walang kaso**: everything is fine

**Walang problema**: no problem

TRIX ROSEN

www.ingramcontent.com/pod-product-compliance
Lightning Source LLC
Chambersburg PA
CBHW071453170626
46811CB00007B/2564